ROUSING ACCLAIM FOR GENE SHELTON'S
TEXAS LEGENDS SERIES:

"Mr. Shelton skillfully blends historical figures
and actual events with made-up characters
and imaginary situations."
—*The Dallas Morning News*

· · · · ·

"Engaging . . . filled with
the details and flavor of the West."
—*Publishers Weekly*

· · · · ·

"A fast-moving story brightened by
cowboy humor . . . Shelton's familiarity with
ranching and cowboys lends authority to his story."
—*Amarillo News-Globe* (TX)

· · · · ·

"A classic Western tale . . . bring[s]
the 1860s of Texas alive."
—*Tyler Morning News* (TX)

DON'T MISS THESE
AUTHENTIC WESTERN SERIES
FROM THE BERKLEY PUBLISHING GROUP

Westerns by Giles Tippette
The new star of the classic Western novel, Tippette captures the American dream in the saga of the Williams clan.

Westerns by Richard Matheson
Winner of the Spur Award for Best Western Novel. Look for *The Memoirs of Wild Bill Hickok.*

Westerns by Jack Ballas
His fiction tells the gut truth of the old West in all its raw action and glorious, hardfisted notions of swift vengeance and six-gun justice.

TEXAS HORSETRADING CO. by Gene Shelton
The rollicking, horse-thieving adventures of two unlikely partners—a Yankee gentleman and a Rebel hellraiser.

THE BAYNES CLAN by John S. McCord
An unforgettable saga of Frontier America . . .
Darnell Baynes and his sons find that surviving on the frontier is a long, lonely battle.

SLOCUM by Jake Logan
Today's longest-running action Western. John Slocum rides a deadly trail of hot blood and cold steel.

McMASTERS by Lee Morgan
The blazing new series from the creators of *Longarm.* When McMasters shoots, he shoots to kill. To his enemies, he is the most dangerous man they have ever known.

LONGARM by Tabor Evans
The popular long-running series about U.S. Deputy Marshal Long—his life, his loves, his fight for justice.

HOW THE WEST WAS LOST

GENE SHELTON

BERKLEY BOOKS, NEW YORK

HOW THE WEST WAS LOST

A Berkley Book / published by arrangement with
the author

PRINTING HISTORY
Berkley edition / November 1996

The Putnam Berkley World Wide Web site address is
http://www.berkley.com/berkley

ISBN: 0-425-15544-7

BERKLEY®
Berkley Books are published by The Berkley Publishing Group,
200 Madison Avenue, New York, New York 10016.
BERKLEY and the "B" design
are trademarks belonging to Berkley Publishing Corporation.

PRINTED IN THE UNITED STATES OF AMERICA

10 9 8 7 6 5 4 3 2 1

1

THE BRINDLE LONGHORN cow hit the end of the catch rope, spun around at the sudden jolt, dug her feet in, and bawled as she fought the lariat.

"Got you this time, you mossbacked old mama," Buck Hawkins said to the cow. "No more Singletree grass for you."

Hawkins's heart pounded almost as hard as that of the winded buckskin he rode. His chest ached; he realized he had been holding his breath during the last hundred yards of the chase.

Air whistled through the flared nostrils of the big buckskin between Hawkins's knees. The horse's ears perked toward the longhorn at the end of the rope, alert, cautious. The horse knew what he was doing.

Hawkins felt a bit smug. It had been a good catch. A nice, flat loop that settled over the horns that spanned almost five feet, and a smooth jerk of slack that snubbed the rope up under the horns without scraping across the cow's eyes. Hawkins had seen too many cattle lose an eye because some rope-crazy fool let a loop snap tight across it. Hawkins hated that. Even an old mossback like this one deserved to be treated with respect. Good cowboys didn't mistreat stock. Buck Hawkins freely admitted there were a lot of things he couldn't do, but he was a top hand with a rope, and he took pride in that.

The brindle cow quit fighting. Her head came up. Sharp tips of upward and outward sweeping horns waved and rocked from side to side. She took a step forward. The buckskin backed up a step to keep the rope taut.

Hawkins leaned forward in the saddle to pat the gelding on his sweaty neck. "Good job, Cornbread—"

The cow snorted and charged. Hawkins squawked in surprise and almost lost his seat as the buckskin ducked aside. Hawkins laid the trip as a horn tip barely missed his right leg. He shifted his weight to the left stirrup and braced for the impact to come when the trip swept the longhorn's front legs from beneath her.

The jolt never came.

The brindle cow whirled about, switching ends like a top cutting horse, her horn tips only a few feet from Cornbread's rump. Hawkins yelped again and slapped spurs to the buckskin. The spurs weren't needed. The gelding was in a dead run within two jumps. Cornbread knew trouble when he saw it. Hawkins glanced over his shoulder. For half a dozen strides, it looked like the cow was gaining. A couple more feet and the buckskin would have a horn stuck in his broad backside.

The horse seemed to sense he was about to get a spare hole in his butt and abruptly ducked to the right. Hawkins reined Cornbread into a sharper turn as the longhorn thundered past on the left, head lowered in the final few feet of her charge. The buckskin was turned sideways when the cow hit the end of the rope. The jolt staggered the big horse, but he managed to keep his footing, then spun to face down the rope. The longhorn hadn't gone down. She shook her head, walled her eyes, and pawed the ground.

"Well, Cornbread," Hawkins gasped, out of breath, "catching this old sow might be a sight easier than turning her loose."

The cow charged again.

Hawkins was ready. He waited until the last moment, then laid the trip. The cow made a mistake. She kept her head down this time. Hawkins whipped the slack just as the cow's front feet neared the rope. He touched spur rowels to the big gelding. The rope snapped taut with an audible twang. The cow went down hard in a cloud of dust and grass. Cornbread leaned into the rope, belly low to the ground as he pulled, not giving the cow a chance to get to her feet. Hawkins stepped from the saddle, ripped the tiedown string from beneath his belt, and sprinted to the cow's side.

A flailing rear hoof sent his hat flying before he finally managed to get the tiedown loop over one hind foot. He winced as a hoof grazed his right hand before he could force the cow's off leg close enough to complete the tie. He threw an extra half hitch on the tie; he'd already had enough of a set-to with the old cow for one day. He didn't want to see her shake the tie and get back on her feet. Hawkins stepped back, his chest heaving, and sucked at his skinned knuckles. The longhorn bawled at the indignity of it all.

"Got to hand it to you, mama. You're one tough old bird," Hawkins said. "Can I have my rope back now?"

The cow bellowed again.

"Didn't think you'd let me have it back easy, mama." Hawkins raised his voice. "Back, Cornbread!"

The buckskin backed up a few steps, letting slack in the rope. Hawkins caught a painful whack from a horn

on a forearm and a string of cow slobbers across his face
before he managed to strip the loop from around the
base of the cow's skull. She tried to get to her feet, but
with her back legs tied she could only flop around and
bawl.

Hawkins picked up his hat, dusted it off, and strode to
the buckskin. He patted the lathered horse on the shoulder. "We'll give her some time to think it over, Cornbread," he said, "then see if we can talk the cranky old
slut into coming back to headquarters with us."

He leaned against the saddle, sneezed the dust from
his nostrils, and let his gaze drift over the wide, shallow
valley that led to the Canadian River a half mile to the
north. The Singletree range was in as good a shape as he
had ever seen it. The Texas Panhandle country never
ceased to amaze Hawkins. Two brutal, stock-killing win-
ters had actually helped turn the place into a stockman's
paradise. Cold, driving autumn rains and heavy snows
left behind moisture that soaked deep into the soil.

Rich sideoats grama grass sprang up in profusion after
winter's grip finally eased. The grass now stood thick
and green, almost knee high, further nourished by gentle
spring rains and heavier summer downpours. Spring-fed
streams of clear, cool water snaked toward the river from
the surrounding breaks. Cattle were slick and fat from
the abundance of water and grass, especially the new
Herefords brought in to upgrade the Singletree herd.
Hawkins thought the Herefords looked more like round,
red-and-white balls of hide than they did real cattle. Real
cows were like the one he'd just tied down: rangy, mean,
and tough.

This particular valley had a special appeal to Buck
Hawkins. He thought it had to be one of the prettiest
places the Creator ever built. At least to a cowboy.

He coiled his Plymouth manila catch rope and winced at the fresh rope burn across the base of his left thumb. The sting of scobbed knuckles on his right hand battled for his attention with the ache of the bruise forming on his forearm. Hawkins tried to clear the dust from his mouth, but couldn't work up enough spit. It had been a good four hours since his last drink of water.

Buck Hawkins was butt-sore, tired, dirty, thirsty, hungry, scratched, bruised, blistered, and scabbed. And more content than he had been in months.

He draped the catch rope over the saddle, not bothering to loosen the honda from around the horn. He had been a tie-fast man ever since he noticed that all the dally men he knew were missing a finger or two.

The buckskin turned his head, rubbed his ears against Hawkins's shoulder, and snorted. Snot blew over Buck's new cotton shirt. Hawkins didn't mind. It wasn't like he'd just been snotted by a sorry horse. The buckskin was one of the best he'd ever saddled, and that covered more than a few. Hawkins lifted a hand to scratch between Cornbread's ears, but stopped as the horse's head came up, foxy ears pointed past Buck's shoulder.

A rider slouched in the saddle a hundred yards away. Hawkins waited as the horseman kneed his bay toward him.

"Son," Dobie Garrett said as he reined in, "there for a spell I thought you'd done forgot everything I ever learnt you about ropin' wild stock. That there was quite a show."

Hawkins squinted at Garrett. "Just how long have you been sitting up there enjoying the show, as you call it, while I was practicing to get killed?"

A hint of a grin twitched Garrett's bushy, tobacco-stained handlebar mustache. "Maybe five, ten minutes."

"Thanks for coming to help." Hawkins didn't try to hide the sarcasm in his words.

Garrett shifted his stocky frame in the saddle, rolled a hefty chew from one cheek to the other, and spat. The bay gelding ducked its head, but too late; the glob hit the horse on the right ear. The bay snorted and shook its head, jangling the curb chain, and stomped a front hoof in aggravation.

"Looked like you and Cornbread had that pore ol' skinny cow under control," Garrett said, a twinkle in deep brown eyes that were barely darker than the weathered, wrinkled skin of his leathery face. "At least the hoss knowed what he was doin'." He nodded toward the still-struggling longhorn. "Finally caught that ol' heifer, eh?"

Hawkins snorted. "All by myself. Got any ideas on how we can turn her loose?"

"Sure 'nuff. While you been playin' around tryin' to catch one scrawny old cow, I tied two more down just over the ridge. We'll ease them two over thisaway and see if she'll buddy up. If she don't, I reckon we'll just have to hobble her and drag her along."

"How many does that make, Dobie?"

Garrett scratched a stubby finger into the wild shock of gray-streaked hair above an ear that was missing a half-moon chunk. The lobe had been bitten off during a barroom brawl somewhere years ago. "Let's see, now. You caught two. I got five wrapped up all told. Fair mornin's work, I'd say."

Hawkins nodded. He knew better than to question Dobie Garrett's tally. The man was a top hand. He'd roped and tied five head to Buck's two. That was about average for wild stock roping days. Hawkins could beat

Garrett anytime, roping in corral or arena, but pasture roping was different. It was Dobie's specialty.

"Any sign of the boss?"

Garrett half shrugged. It was a half a shrug because one of his shoulders barely moved; it had been knocked down years ago by a green bronc. "Wouldn't fret none on him. That old man's a better'n fair hand. Likely he's done caught more cattle by his lonesome today than both of us put together."

"You're probably right, Dobie." Hawkins flexed his shoulders and rubbed the small of his back. "I'm starting to feel the miles, and it's still three hours to home."

Garrett sniffed in mock disdain. "Buck, son, I don't know what's got your tongue lolled out already. It ain't even much past noon—"

"And the day started at four in the morning."

"—Good cowboy'd just be gettin' warmed up now," Garrett said, ignoring the interruption. "You must have gone and got soft durin' that little spell of loafin' down in Albany."

"*I* got soft? *Me* loafing? I seem to recall you were the one who did nothing but drink and chase women the whole time."

Garrett's grin bared teeth that, for some reason Hawkins couldn't figure, seemed immune to tobacco stains. "Yes, sir, we sure 'nuff had some fun down there," Dobie said. "Kinda miss havin' all them folks buy my drinks and all them pretty women cuddlin' up." He sighed wistfully. "Sort of enjoyed bein' a big man in town."

"A big-man-in-town reputation that we did not earn," Hawkins said, "and one that could just possibly get us both killed yet. If you haven't already pickled your liver beyond hope."

"Man's gotta take his fun where he finds it." Garrett spat again. The bay horse with the indelicate but descriptive name of Duckbutt dodged just in time; the spit wad sailed over his ears. "Anytime you get tired of admirin' your shadow, partner, mount up. We're wastin' daylight."

Hawkins sighed. "Another glamorous and exciting day in the life of a working cowboy. And we get to do it all over again, starting before first light tomorrow." He toed the stirrup and swung aboard the buckskin.

"Aw, quit bellyachin', Buck. You still got some money in the bank. Wouldn't have to hit a lick of work, you didn't want to. You wasn't happy doin' nothin', and you wouldn't be happy doin' nothin' else. Cowboyin's the best life they is for men like us."

"Men like us. Men who never learned a real trade," Hawkins said. But he had to admit Garrett was right. Cowboying didn't pay for squat, the hours were long, and the work dangerous. He couldn't think of anything he'd rather do. The feel of a good horse under saddle beneath a big sky, the smell of fresh green grass, the whistling sound of a mourning dove's wings, or the lonely wail of a coyote under a full moon were the sort of things that got into a man's blood. It made up for the sweat, dust, and bits of skin a cowboy left spread across the outfit.

The two rode side by side for a few minutes before Garrett cut a quick glance at Hawkins. "I still don't savvy how come you wanted to get shut of Albany so quick. Right nice town."

"We had a job to do here. And I had my reasons."

"Heard from that reason lately?"

Hawkins shook his head. "Not in nearly two months."

Garrett didn't press the point. Hawkins appreciated

that; one thing that made Dobie Garrett a good man to ride with was that he knew when it was okay to rag a partner and when not to jab a finger into a sore spot. Well, most of the time, anyway. They had ridden together for six years, give or take. Ride with a man that long, Hawkins mused, you get to know what he's thinking and what he's about to do. Even Dobie Garrett was predictable. At least part of the time.

Hawkins had to admit he and Garrett didn't exactly look like a team. Hawkins stood a hair over six-foot-one and carried 180 pounds of wiry muscle on a narrow-hipped, flat-bellied frame. In animal terms, Hawkins was the mountain cat of the pair.

Garrett was the badger.

Dobie even looked like a badger, Hawkins thought, with his short, thick arms, bandy legs, and bristly gray hair. Garrett stood about five-nine with his boots on and his tongue stuck out. But he wasn't short from side to side. He carried enough flesh to match, or maybe even top, Buck's lanky 180 pounds. Not all of Garrett's poundage was muscle. Dobie seemed to have developed a bit more of a paunch during the last few months, Hawkins thought.

Buck also admitted that he himself looked more like a greenhorn than a seasoned cowhand, with his new clothes, custom boots, and brand-new saddle.

By contrast, Garrett actually looked like a top hand. The bum shoulder, bad hip, worn-out boots with a hole cut in the vamps to ease a bunion, gray flannel shirt that had so many patches on it that it looked checkered, Levi's so worn that only dirt held them together, and shotgun chaps worn slick at the inner thighs and stained with horse slobbers and cow manure—all marked Dobie as a real cowboy. He rode an old double-rig stock saddle that looked to be held together with little more than rawhide lace and hope. The saddle seat leather was worn thin and shiny. Deep rope burns scarred the big Mexican-style horn.

Hawkins couldn't tell for sure if Garrett had turned gray before his time, or just had a lot of hard miles on him. He wasn't as old as he looked. And on a Saturday night after payday he sure didn't act as old as he looked. Dobie had a few years up on Buck's twenty-five; he was somewhere in his late thirties or early forties, but looked more like he was going on fifty. Or maybe even past that mark. Green broncs, wild cows, and an occasional drunken brawl tended to put years on a man.

Hawkins idly wondered if he'd look like Dobie in another ten years or so. If he lived that long. There were no guarantees on that. Especially since that business down Albany way . . .

The plaintive bawl of a tied-down cow pulled Hawkins's attention back to work. He and Garrett rode into a shallow bowl that had been a buffalo wallow before hunters killed the last of the shaggy brutes and cleared the country of Indians. Hawkins reined in.

"So you finally caught Old Gotch," Hawkins said. "We've been after her longer than that mossback I caught."

The tied-down longhorn raised her head, walled her one good eye at the horsemen, and snorted dust as she struggled against Garrett's tie.

Garrett turned his head and spat out his used-up chew. "Yep. Sorriest excuse of a cow I even seen. Old sow stuck a horn in my butt a couple years ago." He sighed wistfully. "Reckon we 'bout got the culls cleaned out. Maybe them Herefords is better beef cows, but I'm gonna miss these old longhorns. It was them that made this country."

"Things change, Dobie. Times change."

"Maybe. I ain't sure it's always for the best, neither."

That was, Hawkins mused, about as close to grumpy as Garrett ever got, at least after he'd had his morning coffee. Hawkins was the fretter of the pair; Dobie was the spur-straight-ahead, devil-take-the-hindmost type who didn't worry about tomorrow. At times, Buck envied Dobie's approach to life.

Garrett slipped the thong from his saddle horn and started to shake a loop into his catch rope. "Untie her, partner. I'll try to keep her from snortin' in your pocket till you get mounted up again."

"I'll untie her if you'll untie mine," Hawkins said.

Garrett glanced at Hawkins and shook his head. "I reckon not. You cowboy enough to keep Old Gotch off me? I'd as soon not get hooked today, I had my druthers."

Hawkins unlimbered his own rope. "I'll keep her attention. Besides, I like to see a good hand's technique on the ground."

"Don't take much technique to untie one and run like hell." Garrett reined Duckbutt alongside the cow's rump, dismounted, pulled the cow's tail up between her legs, and reached for the tiedown rope.

The cow flopped a couple of times. Before she had her feet under her, Dobie was back in the saddle. "Let's herd this old heifer toward them others I got tied down, partner," he said. "We'll get yours later. Better screw down in that saddle—we may have to play cowboy around here."

"I thought we already had," Hawkins said.

*   *   *

The Singletree headquarters didn't look like much compared to that of the Panhandle's high-dollar outfits, but to Buck Hawkins the place was more welcome than the fancy Dodge House up in Kansas.

The Singletree was an outwardly nondescript cluster of buildings. The main house was small but solidly built, the shotgun-style bunkhouse tight enough to keep out the rain and wind. The best-made building on the outfit was the barn, but that was the real sign of a good working ranch, Hawkins knew. Competent ranchers took better care of their stock than they did themselves. The corrals were solid and stout. A windmill beside the barn clanked and creaked as it pumped clear, cool water.

What made the Singletree special, Hawkins conceded, was one simple fact. It was home.

He swung the corral gate shut behind the last of the culls. The cattle hadn't given them much trouble, at least by longhorn standards, once they had gotten them lined out. It had only taken four hours to get them here and penned.

Hawkins leaned against the gate post, pulled off his hat, and wiped his bandanna over his sweaty forehead. He cast a longing look toward the stock tank that doubled as a cowboy bathtub in the warm weather months. Every fold in his skin felt gritty. The wrinkles in his shirt were white with sweat salt. A bath would go a long way toward soaking the ache from his muscles, but it would have to wait. He had to tend the buckskin first. Good horses were hard to find these days.

"Boss's comin'," Dobie Garrett said, slouched in the saddle as he stared toward the lowering sun. "Reckon we'd ought to give him a hand. Looks like he's got fifteen head with him."

Hawkins peered through the heat waves at the shimmering blur almost a mile away, wondered how Dobie could count cattle Buck couldn't even see well, and shook his head in near disbelief.

W. C. Milhouse might be a bit long in the tooth, but Dobie had pegged it when he said the Singletree owner was still the best cowboy in Texas. The old man could work both Hawkins and Garrett into the ground any day of the week.

Hawkins swung aboard the buckskin. Cornbread snorted and shook his head, disgusted to be going back to work when his stall and a bait of grain were just a few yards away.

The two men circled the herd at a respectful distance to avoid spooking the still-rank longhorns and mixed-breed scrubs. The cattle shuffled along, heads down, slobber stringing from their mouths. To an outsider, they would have looked beaten, exhausted, and docile. Real cowboys knew better. The beasts still had plenty of run and a double dose of ornery left in them.

"Howdy, boys," W. C. Milhouse said. "Any luck?"

Garrett reached for his plug, gnawed off a half-dollar-size chew, and tucked it into his cheek. "We got a few. Reckon this bunch about cleans us out of old stock."

"Watch that spotted cow." Milhouse nodded toward a leggy red with a splotch of white shaped like an Indian war shield on her side. "The old slut like to have caused me to spill the whole bunch a time or two."

Milhouse didn't have to tell them what to do. They had worked together long enough to know what was expected. Hawkins shook out a loop, just in case, and eased into the drag slot. Milhouse moved out to the left flank, Garrett to the right. The small herd slogged along toward the Singletree headquarters.

Hawkins kept a close watch on the cattle, but glanced

at Milhouse from time to time. A quiet fondness for the crusty old rancher sat comfortable in Hawkins's chest. W. C. Milhouse was more than just a boss. He was a friend, even a sort of father, to the men who rode with him.

Milhouse looked a lot better than he had back at the end of the brutal winter a couple years ago, called the Big Die-Off, when he had ridden away from his life's work, slumped and beaten on the seat of a spring wagon filled with personal belongings, after he had lost the Singletree to a crooked banker. Milhouse had looked small and old then. Now that he had his ranch back, with help from Hawkins and Garrett, he rode relaxed in the saddle.

Milhouse stood barely five-foot-six, but seemed bigger these days. He rode with his back straight, thick shoulders square. He showed no outward sign of the rheumatic hip pain he must have felt after so long a day in the saddle. The Singletree owner seemed more at peace than he had been in a long time. Buck supposed that when a man got back what he had lost, he enjoyed every day a little more than he had the one before. Milhouse's hazel eyes above the thick gray handlebar mustache twinkled in a newfound zest for life. If he felt his fifty-some years, it didn't show, Hawkins mused. Milhouse handled the stocky, tight-twisted dappled gray gelding of mixed mustang and Morgan blood with a gentle rein and an occasional soft word. The horse had barely broken a sweat.

Hawkins was happy to see W.C. back home. He belonged on the Singletree. He was as much a part of the ranch as the flatland prairie to the south, the rolling hills near the river breaks, and the thickets along the reddish water called the Canadian.

The spotted cow lifted her head, apparently planning a

break from the herd, but changed her mind. Milhouse had the dappled gray in perfect position to head her. When it came to cattle, Milhouse was always in the right place at the right time, it seemed. Hawkins wondered if W.C. could really read a cow's mind. It was as if he knew what the cow planned to do before she even thought of it.

As the herd neared the ranch headquarters, Garrett kneed his bay ahead to open the catch pen gate. The spotted cow hesitated, swung her head from side to side, then snorted and followed the lead cow into the pen. Garrett swung the gate closed and latched it without dismounting.

Milhouse reined in between Garrett and Hawkins.

"Good day's work, boys," Milhouse said, a hint of a twinkle in his eyes. "Still some hope that you two may make halfway decent hands someday."

"Wouldn't count on Buck for that, W.C.," Garrett said. "I tell him and tell him till I got tears in my eyes big as horse apples, and the boy just won't learn nothin'." He rolled the chew in his cheek and spat, catching the bay by surprise. The glob spattered against the horse's right ear. The bay snorted, shook his head, and stomped a front foot.

Milhouse studied the cattle in the corral for a moment. "See you finally gathered old Mossy."

"Buck caught her," Garrett said. "Reckon he got lucky. Got between her and the river thickets and managed to waller a rope on her somehow. Like to got hisself in a wreck."

Milhouse lifted an eyebrow at Hawkins. "I've been chasing that old cow for five, six years. Can't say I really expected to ever see her caught."

The brindle longhorn lifted her head, as if she knew

they were talking about her, waggled heavy horns, snorted, and pawed the corral dirt.

The Singletree owner studied the brindle for a time, then sighed. "I can't do it, boys," he finally said.

"Do what?"

"Ship her off to the slaughter pens, Dobie," Milhouse said. "That old sow's about all that's left of the old days, back before barbed wire, rich foreigners, and Yankee-bred bankers ruined a cowman's country. Her mama's mama was one of the first mother cows I ran on this place. Not a year went by I didn't get a good calf out of that line."

Hawkins stared silently at the old brindle. He knew how Milhouse felt. Dobie was right. The longhorn *had* built this country. Maybe times were changing, he thought. Maybe the lanky, cranky cow was a relic of trail drive and open range days, a creature whose time had passed. Maybe there was no place for her amid the up-graded Hereford and Durham stock that now waddled over the Singletree range.

None of that mattered.

A man like W. C. Milhouse needed a cow like that. A tie to the past. A reminder that it took tough men and tough animals to settle this country. And that he had been a part of it.

Milhouse sighed. "Getting soft in my old age, I guess. Maybe it's not good business, but some things are worth more than money. We'll cut her out and turn her loose tomorrow morning. She's more a part of this outfit than I am."

Garrett nodded solemnly. "Was kinda hopin' you'd say that, Boss." His tone was soft, as if he were in a church chapel somewhere instead of sitting on a sweaty bay horse with tobacco-stained ears outside a corral full of wild cattle. But then, Hawkins mused, this was a sort of church. A cowboy church.

Milhouse glanced at the stock tank at the end of the corral. Several of the gathered cattle already had their noses buried past the nostrils in the water. "They have plenty of water, boys. We'll fork out some hay, take care of the horses, and I'll stir us up some supper. I might even have a bottle of Old Headacher stuck back somewhere, if you're interested in a snort."

Garrett's leathery face brightened. "Never turn down a free drink or a willin' woman, I always say." He swung down from the bay and reached for the dappled gray's reins. "Buck and me'll take care of the stock, Boss."

"I'll take care of my own, and quit calling me 'Boss,'" Milhouse said, sort of half-grumpy. "We're partners in this outfit. I wouldn't even have it back except for you two."

"Now, Boss," Garrett said, "there ain't no call to go whippin' that dead hoss again. Buck and me come into some money, that's all. We didn't need it. You did. We wasn't buyin' into the Singletree. That there was a loan."

Milhouse scuffed a boot toe in the dirt. "I still don't feel right about it—taking money from you boys, I mean."

"Mr. Milhouse," Hawkins said, "Dobie's right. It was a loan. I'm just glad we still had it. The way Dobie goes through money, we'd have been broke again within a couple of weeks anyway."

"*I* go through money?" Garrett sniffed in disgust. "Least I didn't hand most of mine over to some railroad big shot."

"It's not like we'll never see it again," Hawkins said. "That Forth Worth and Denver stock I bought will see us through our old age, partner. Provided we last that long."

Milhouse ignored the exchange. "I don't know when I'll be able to pay it back—"

"Do you hear us frettin' about it, W.C.?" Garrett shrugged. "Couple more years, the Singletree'll start makin' money. Then you can pay us a few bucks now and then out of the profits."

"You never would say how much interest—"

"None," Hawkins interrupted, his tone firm. "You pre-paid any interest, Mr. Milhouse. You took in two hungry saddle bums and gave them jobs when you couldn't afford to do that and there were no ranch jobs to be had. We never missed a meal on the Singletree. So we'll just call that part of the deal even."

Milhouse shook his head in resignation. "Man might as well butt his head against a stump as try to argue with you two. Downright bullheaded. Never met a good cowboy who wasn't. Let's get the stock tended. It's been a spell since breakfast."

"Noticed that about five hours ago," Garrett said as he led the bay toward the barn. "One thing ain't changed about you, W.C. You still work a man's butt off on this outfit."

Milhouse was a better than fair hand with a skillet, Hawkins thought as he put away the last of the dishes and utensils.

But then, a man who had been widowed as long as the rancher had been either learned his way around a kitchen or starved to death. Buck had never known Callie Milhouse in person. She had been dead nearly six years before he and Garrett rode up to the Singletree, but Hawkins still felt her presence. The faded pink curtains she had made once again hung at the windows. The glass-fronted hutch that held her prized china—dishes

that hadn't been used since her death—was back where
it belonged, against the west wall. Most of all, though,
he felt Callie's presence when Milhouse spoke of her.
And sometimes when he didn't speak: those times when
W.C.'s eyes went soft as he gazed at the hutch or the cro-
cheted shawl tucked inside the glass front, beside the
dishes.

Callie Milhouse lay in a small, well-tended plot pro-
tected from grazing stock by a three-rail fence east of the
main house. Hawkins had never known a day to go by,
no matter how busy or how long, how hot or how cold,
how wet or how dry, that Milhouse hadn't visited her
grave. In a way, Buck envied W.C. Milhouse despite the
man's constant inner pain of loss. At least he had had the
woman he loved for a time . . .

Hawkins pushed the thoughts from his mind with an
effort. It had been a good day. He didn't want to spoil it
by mooning over something he couldn't have—at least
not yet.

The soft murmur of voices from the porch drifted in
through the open door. W.C. and Dobie were already
outside, enjoying the evening air on the small front
porch. Hawkins picked up the coffeepot, gave it a shake,
and guessed it was at least half-full. That would hold
them until bedtime. He didn't even consider cleaning the
coffeepot. Milhouse wouldn't let anybody wash it. Said
it spoiled the coffee. Besides, the pot was almost always
in use when anybody was home at the Singletree.

Hawkins carried the tub of rinse water out back,
dumped it, hung the tub on its wall peg, and strode to the
front door.

"Company coming," Milhouse said as Buck stepped
outside.

A lone rider was skylighted against the reddish gold

wash of sunset. None of the three Singletree men spoke as the horseman neared. Hawkins leaned against the door frame and watched as the lean rider reined in his leggy, expensive-looking sorrel a few feet from the porch. The man was tall, maybe an inch taller than Buck, the stubble shadow heavy on angular cheeks. Despite the fading light, Hawkins could see the hard expression in the man's almost black eyes. The rider's right hand rested on his leggings, near the grips of a revolver holstered low on his thigh. Buck fought back a quick surge of concern. The man looked like what Hawkins thought a shooter—a professional gunman—should look like.

"Evening," Milhouse said as he rose from his straight-backed chair.

"Evening. This the Singletree?"

"It is. Something we can do for you?"

The lids narrowed a bit over the black eyes. Hawkins got the impression he was watching a rattler coiled to strike.

"I'm looking for two men," the rider said. "Couple of fast guns named Hawkins and Garrett."

2

BUCK HAWKINS'S BELLY clamped hard around his supper biscuits.

His holstered Bisley Colt hung on a peg inside the door. He couldn't even remember whether the weapon was loaded or not. The swarthy man had them cold. None of the Singletree men were armed. They'd be dead before they could hiccup if the rider on the sorrel wanted them that way.

Hawkins cut a quick glance at Dobie Garrett. Dobie didn't seem the least bit worried.

"I'm Garrett," he said with an amiable nod. "Tall, skinny feller there's Hawkins."

The swarthy man's eyes narrowed. "You two don't look much like gunhawks." There was a tint of amusement in his words. "Not even packing iron."

The knot in Hawkins's gut tightened. He lifted a hand. "Wait a minute, mister. We're not gunhawks."

"That's not what the newspapers and the campfire talk says."

Garrett leaned forward in his chair and spat. "Man oughtn't believe everything he reads, and I've heard a few campfire windies in my time. Even spun a few myself." Dobie's eyes narrowed. "You one of Silas Barker's bunch? Lookin' to settle up, maybe?"

The swarthy man half smiled. "No. From what I hear, you two put the Barker gang out of business. That's why I'm here."

Hawkins cleared his throat. "Then you're not planning to pull a gun on us?"

"Why would you think that?"

"You're carrying that hand awfully close to the holster."

"Oh. Sorry." The horseman dropped his hand clear of his revolver. "Habit. Man never knows in this country. I came looking for you two, but not for any shooting. I consider myself a better than fair gunhand, but I'm smart enough not to draw on you, just in case those campfire yarns are true. I just want to talk a spell."

W.C. Milhouse tapped the dead ash from his pipe against a boot heel. "Now that we've decided nobody's going to start shooting, step down and come inside. Singletree coffee's always hot. And usually stout enough to make nails from, if it's done right."

The rider dismounted, looped the sorrel's reins around the hitchrail, and followed Milhouse inside. The oil lamp Hawkins had lit cast a soft yellow light over the room. Shadows danced against the walls. The knot in Hawkins's gut eased, but didn't go away, as he poured the coffee all around.

Milhouse studied the rider for a moment. "I find it a lot easier to talk when I know a man's name."

The swarthy man offered a hand. "Ed Joyner, owner of the J-Bar over in New Mexico. I'm here representing the Texas and New Mexico Cattleman's Association, headquartered in Necesario. You know the town?"

"Heard of it," Garrett said. He didn't add that they'd planned on relieving Necesario's people of some spare cash once, but the Barker gang got there first. That was just one of many big plans that fell apart on them during their brief ride along the owlhoot trail. "Out in the middle of nowhere near the Texas and New Mexico line, best I recall. Hear it's a tough town. Funny name."

Joyner nodded. "Necesario's a Spanish word. Means 'Needful,' which is what we are. Needful of some big-caliber help. That's why the association sent me. To see if you two might be interested in a job."

"We got jobs here," Dobie said.

"The one we're offering pays a lot more." Joyner sipped at his cup. "Good coffee, Mr. Milhouse."

"I can warm up a bit of leftover supper if you'd like. We have a spare bunk and an extra stall for your horse. You're welcome to stay the night," Milhouse said.

Joyner shook his head. "No, thanks. I appreciate the offer, but I've got a herd of high-dollar Durham bulls due in from back East any day now. My *segundo*'s a good straw boss, but I'm not sure he knows how to handle anything gentler than Mexican-bred stock and longhorns. I've got to get on back. I just came to ask if Garrett and Hawkins here would help us out."

Garrett's forehead creased. "Help out with what?"

"Nothing that a couple of good men couldn't put a stop to," Joyner said. "The association members have been losing more stock than usual here lately. We'd like to see that stop. Odds are that just the reputations of Dobie Garrett and Buck Hawkins would end the problem."

Hawkins's blood chilled. "Messing with rustlers can get a man killed."

"So can forking a green bronc and chasing wild cows." Joyner's matter-of-fact tone was that of a man who had done his share of saddling rank horses and chasing wild stock. "Anyway, the association's bet is that as soon as any rustlers hear you two are in the area, they'll light a shuck for other parts. They wouldn't cross you. Not after what you did to Silas Barker's gang." Joyner shook his head in admiration. "Whole country's talking about that. Sure wish I could have seen it."

Hawkins sighed. "It wasn't the sort of thing I'd rather do for a living. I'd rather take my chances ranching."

"You don't have to give me an answer right now," Joyner said. "Talk it over. It would be easy money—a lot of it."

"How much," Garrett said, "do you fellers think is a lot?"

"Two hundred fifty dollars a month. Each. Plus expenses. Including room and board in the town's best hotel. Plus a share of any fines collected for arresting drunks and crooked gamblers and the like in Necesario itself. A dollar a head bonus on any rustled stock you recover. And on the off chance any wanted men happen to show up in the area and you catch them or put them down, you get all the reward money. It could amount to several thousand dollars, depending."

"Money doesn't stop a bullet," Hawkins said. "I've been shot at a sufficient number of times already, thank you."

"I understand that," Joyner said. "But, even though the risk is low, the association will guarantee you a bonus of $2,000 each, even if the job doesn't take but a couple of months. If it takes longer, the bonus goes up when the work's done."

Garrett mouthed a silent whistle. "That sure is a heap of money. 'Specially for a job you make sound simple as a Sunday church social."

Joyner shrugged. "There'll be enough going on to keep you from getting bored. You'll be expected to ride scout on both sides of the state line, keeping an eye on association stock, checking drift cattle brands and the like."

"Sounds to me like you fellows need a federal marshal or two," Milhouse said. "Why hire guns if the government pays them to start with?"

"We've already asked the government." Joyner fished in his pocket for the makings. "Checked with John Piersall. He says there aren't enough federal marshals to go around. We have to hire our lawmen. Piersall recommended you two. Said he's known you from way back. Even if you hadn't broken the Barker bunch, Piersall's say would be enough for us." He rolled his cigarette, offered the sack around, and tucked it back in his pocket when he had no takers.

"How can the association legally hire law enforcement people?" Hawkins said. "Seems to me that's nothing more than vigilante work."

Joyner flicked a match across his thumbnail and lit his cigarette. "No problem. The association owns a few state and local officials on both sides of the state line. You and Garrett would have legal badges. Special marshals with jurisdiction in both states. So you won't have any problems about who holds the biggest legal stick." He nodded his thanks as Milhouse refilled his cup. The pot was almost empty.

"Mostly, your jobs will be keeping the peace in Necesario." Joyner's black eyes twinkled. "But not *too* much peace. Necesario has several thriving industries. Saloons, gambling, prostitution—"

Dobie's ears perked up. "Women?"

"All a famous gunman like you could ever handle, Garrett," Joyner said. "And you'll have on-the-house accounts at all saloons and whorehouses. No charge. The association picks up the tab for the whole thing. Another small bonus, so to speak."

Garrett's eyes took on a misty, blissful look. "Now, by God, we're gettin' somewhere."

Hawkins shot a startled glance at Garrett. "Wait a minute, Dobie. Get your mind off bottles and bloomers—"

"What else is worth frettin' over, partner?"

"Getting dead, for one thing."

"You fuss too much over little stuff, Buck." Garrett winked at Joyner. "My partner's the worryin' sort. Always lookin' for a thorn to set on."

"And riding with you, I've found a few," Hawkins muttered.

Joyner pushed back his chair, rose, and offered handshakes around. "You fellows talk it over before you decide, but let us know soon." He pulled a slip of paper from his shirt pocket and handed it to Garrett. "If you decide not to take the job, send a note to this address. If you're game to help us out, just ride on over to Necesario. Tell the barkeep at the Crazy Woman Cantina who you are. He'll put you in touch with the right association herd bulls. We'd like to have your decision within a couple of weeks, one way or the other." He nodded to Milhouse and reached for his hat. "Much obliged for the hospitality. I'd better be on my way now."

"Sure you won't stay over?"

Joyner glanced at the sky. "I enjoy traveling at night this time of year, Mr. Milhouse. It's a lot cooler. There'll be enough moon to ride by."

"Best keep an eye peeled," Garrett said. "There's more'n one feller out there wouldn't mind takin' that flashy sorrel off your hands."

Joyner's slight smile was barely visible in the deepening twilight. He tapped the holster at his hip. "I'll stay alert. I don't plan to part with Jericho just yet."

"Jericho?"

"My wife named him. I tied him up to the outhouse door the day I got him. He pitched a fit and went to kicking. So the outhouse walls came tumbling down. Hence the name, Jericho. My wife was some upset over that. She was in the outhouse at the time." Joyner swung into the saddle and touched fingertips to his hat brim. "Be seeing you, boys. I hope."

The three men stood on the Singletree porch and watched as Joyner rode toward the faint gold wash the sun left behind as it slid below the rolling grasslands.

"Seems like a right nice feller," Garrett said after a time.

"Nice enough if you don't cross him," Milhouse said. "I've heard of Joyner, seen his type. That man, boys, is a *real* gunhawk."

Hawkins said, "So why doesn't he stomp the association's snakes instead of trying to hire outside guns?"

"Politics, I'd say." Milhouse peered into the twilight. Joyner had already disappeared over the crest of a low hill. "From what I hear, all's not sweetness and light and brotherly love with the association. Some of the big herd bulls don't like each other all that much, and they sure don't like the few ranchers who didn't join up. Outsiders might—just might—have a better chance of getting the job done without starting a shooting war between the different factions."

"That's not what I would call especially encouraging news." Hawkins shook his head. "It's a shame Joyner had to make a long ride for nothing."

"How come nothin'?" Garrett asked.

"Because we're not going, Dobie," Hawkins said

firmly. "I have dodged enough lead already to last two complete and entire lifetimes. I am *not* going to let that wild hair of yours get me in any more trouble."

"Trouble? What trouble?"

Hawkins sighed. "Pick a category and it will fit. Our luck was never all that good to begin with, if you'll recall, and we may have used it all up in that scrap with Barker's bunch in the Quitaque Valley. We aren't going to Necesario."

Garrett dug a finger into an ear hole. "I don't know, son. That's a mess of greenbacks for an easy job—"

"Easy as that owlhoot trail of yours," Hawkins interrupted.

"Aw, that come out all right. Why, we—"

"Almost starved to death. And I nearly had my hide peeled by a mad Mexican woman you had the bright idea to rob—"

"Now, that there was a sight, W.C.," Garrett said with a chuckle. "Sure wish you could've seen it. That gal lit into Buck with a leather strop when he tried to stick up that little store. Took half a skillet of bacon grease just to fix them welts."

"And it got worse from there. *I* was the one who got shot in that grand holdup scheme of yours up in Colorado—"

"Little bitty hole in your butt, that's all. Didn't hardly break the skin."

"For which we got nothing but counterfeit money, which in turn almost got us thrown into prison. And robbing a stage that carried no money. And working all day digging up the wrong set of tracks in a would-be train holdup—"

"You ain't still on the prod over that, are you, partner? I didn't know them was sidin' rails. Would have swore it was the main line." Garrett sighed. "Did sort of smart some when that ol' Flyer with all that money on board just went chuggin' on past. Always did fancy bein' a train robber like that Jesse James feller."

"And then tangling with the Barker gang, nearly getting shot by a Texas Ranger and hanged by a lynch mob—"

"Lynch mob?" Garrett shifted his chew and spat. "Buck, you ain't already forgot that wasn't no hangin' party waitin' for us back in Albany?"

"Well, it sure looked like it to me. At first, anyway."

"That there was a welcomin' committee, just sayin' thanks for us savin' their money." Garrett chuckled. "Course, they didn't know *we* was gonna rob the Albany bank, but Silas Barker and his boys beat us to it. Quit fussin', Buck. It all worked out. We made a passel of money 'fore it was all over and come out heroes to boot. Got wrote up in all them papers, too. What'd they call us? 'Fearless, hard-eyed, fast guns and crack shots who'd charge hell with a water bucket in the name of justice and fair play,' best I recall."

"Two men scared spitless blasting away with shotguns because that's all we could hit anything with is more like it," Hawkins said in disgust. "Hard-eyed. Fast guns. Crack shots. The most ridiculous thing I ever heard. Dobie, I'm better with a handgun than you are, and a cow can drop, raise, and wean a calf before I can pull a six-gun out of a holster. We were just plain lucky to get out of that fight alive. I don't intend to get into another one."

Garrett ignored the argument. "Why, we didn't buy not one solitary drink ourselves down in Albany after we got the town's money back for 'em. And all them pretty women hangin' on us like possums in a persimmon tree.

Now, this Joyner feller says we'd have all the whiskey and women we want for nothin' over in Necesario. It'd be Albany all over again. Like the man said, let's talk this here badger out of the hole 'fore we make us a real decide."

"There is nothing to talk about, Dobie. I have made a real decide. We are *not* riding into another nest of bad men with big guns, and that's all there is to it."

The flare of a match cut through the deepening darkness as W.C. Milhouse fired his pipe. The rancher peered over the flame at Garrett and Hawkins. "No sense standing out here arguing in the dark." He paused to puff the pipe into life. "Especially when there's a bottle of good whiskey inside."

Garrett was through the front door before Milhouse could shake out the match.

Dobie had the water glasses on the table by the time Hawkins shut the ranch house door behind him. Milhouse rummaged in a cabinet and pulled out a bottle of Old Overholt. "Not the best," Milhouse said as he poured a generous dollop into three glasses, "but I've had worse."

Hawkins sipped at his. The 80-proof amber liquid slid down easy and flared into a warm spot in his gut. Garrett knocked back half of his glass in two swallows and sighed, contented.

"Not that it makes any difference, Mr. Milhouse," Hawkins said, "but what else do you know about this association?"

Milhouse shrugged. "Not much, except that they have more money than the Catholic Church. And that they're hard men. Soft men don't build big ranches in that part of the country. Most of the ranchers out there are cranky old coots, like me." Milhouse paused to sip at his drink. "I sort of hate to bring this up, boys—"

"Damn, Boss, you ain't gonna fire us again, are you?" Dobie interrupted.

Milhouse cocked an eyebrow at Garrett. "I never fired you two."

"Threatened to."

"Just because you spilled the whole herd a few times before you learned how to handle cows. That's been a while back." Milhouse swirled the liquor in his glass. "What I'm thinking is that this might be an opportunity for you two peckerwoods."

"An opportunity to get killed," Hawkins grumbled.

"Let the man talk, Buck." Garrett squinted at Milhouse. "You ridin' around a herd, Boss, or you fixin' to take the point?"

Milhouse's expression turned even more somber. "Remember three, four years ago when I asked you two what you wanted to be when you grew up?"

Hawkins sniffed. "Dobie said he didn't want to grow up. I didn't plan on him dragging me to an early grave at the time."

"And," Milhouse said to Hawkins, "I seem to recall you said you wanted to own your own place someday, Buck. This could be your chance to do just that."

"What?"

"The Quarter Circle's for sale."

Hawkins's eyebrows lifted. The Quarter Circle was more than twenty square miles of prime grass, good water, and fine livestock, adjoining the Singletree's west line. "When did this happen?"

Milhouse sighed. "Came up a couple of days ago. I was prowling the west side. Ran into Meier Schriner."

"How's that old German doin'?" Dobie said.

"Not well. The cancer's eating him up." Milhouse's eyes seemed to mist over. "Damn shame. Meier's a good man and the best neighbor a fellow could want."

Hawkins's spirits sank. It was, as Milhouse had said, a damn shame. Meier Schriner and the Quarter Circle *had* been good neighbors. The two outfits had often joined crews to work their respective ranches during spring and fall roundups, helped each other with stray cows and drift problems. The four-man Quarter Circle crew were top hands. A man never had to worry when he worked with them. They'd be in the right place at the right time.

Schriner had been in this country almost as long as W.C. had been. He was a good cattleman, kept his stock healthy, the place clean, and his nose out of everyone else's business. Hawkins wondered why it always seemed that the worst things happened to the best people.

Milhouse's sigh broke the pained silence. "Meier can't even ride a horse anymore. Cancer's got him buggy bound. Anyway, he doesn't have any living relatives, and he's not primed and cocked to sell it to one of the British outfits who're buying up this country. He doesn't like the English much."

Garrett snorted in disgust. "He ain't the only one. Damn furriners and rich Back East bankers is ruinin' this country. Like barn rats. What they can't eat, they crap on." Dobie paused to loose a stream of tobacco. The brass spittoon he and Buck had purloined from the Equity Saloon in Tascosa during a memorable brawl a few years back pinged. "Be a sure 'nuff cryin' shame if some dude in town shoes that don't even talk Texan or speak cow got ahold of that place."

"Meier has to sell, and soon. His health is failing fast," Milhouse said. "He wants to spend his last days in

Dallas. There's a doctor there who promised to keep him pumped full of painkiller to ease the way for him." Milhouse squared his slumped shoulders. "Anyhow, Meier offered us first chance at buying the Quarter Circle before he puts it on the open market. Said he'd die more peaceful if the place was in the right hands."

"What'd you tell 'im?"

"That I needed to study on it a few days, Dobie," Milhouse said. "I didn't tell him that I didn't have the money. That I wouldn't even have gotten my own place back if you boys hadn't floated me a substantial loan."

Hawkins lifted an eyebrow. "What's the asking price?"

"On the open market, the Quarter Circle would bring two, maybe three dollars an acre—"

Garrett interrupted. "I got a knot in my rope when it comes to cipherin', Boss. How much is that in actual money?"

"Twenty-five thousand plus at the lower number," Milhouse said.

"Damn. There ain't that much money in the world."

"Rein in a minute, Dobie," Milhouse said. "Meier said he'd sell to us for a buck an acre. That cuts the price to under $13,000. And we wouldn't have to pay it all at once. He just wants enough cash to see him through to the end. After that, he wants the rest paid, whenever we can, to a college back East that's trying to figure out what causes cancer and how to cure it. A trust, he called it."

Milhouse paused to top off their drinks. Dobie's glass was empty, as usual. Garrett might not be fast with a gun, but he was quick enough on the draw where whiskey was concerned.

Hawkins glanced up, startled. "Mr. Milhouse, it just

dawned on me that you've been saying 'us.' That Mr. Schriner would sell to 'us' at less than half the place is worth. What do you mean by that?"

"Just that, Buck. Us." The old man's expression softened. "You two worthless saddle bums are like the boys Callie and I never had. I can't think of two other sorry, no-account cowpunchers I'd rather have as neighbors. And you'd have that place of your own that you want when you grow up." Milhouse sipped at his drink. "For a while, we could run the two outfits together. Then we'd be big enough to compete with the foreign syndicates, keep them from taking this land, too." He glanced around his beloved ranch headquarters home. "And when I'm gone, boys, this place is yours."

Milhouse's statement caught Hawkins by surprise. A knot formed in his throat. He couldn't conceive of W.C. Milhouse not being there. He always had been. Buck swallowed against the lump. He didn't trust his voice not to quaver a bit if he said anything.

Garrett had no such problem. "Aw, hell, W.C., you been here since the Rocky Mountains was pimples on the plains. You'll be around when they's wore down flatter'n Kansas."

A wry half grin touched Milhouse's lips. "Dobie, I'm not *that* old. But we might as well face it. Nobody lives forever. The only guarantees in life are that green broncs will buck on February mornings and that a man eventually dies. I've already changed the will. The Singletree is yours, boys—lock, stock, and creaky windmill. Which reminds me, Dobie—you need to shinny up there in the morning and grease that thing. It's keeping me awake nights. Well?"

"Well what, Boss?"

"Between the three of us, can we scrape up enough

cash to buy into the Quarter Circle? I can put my third of the Singletree up as collateral for a bank loan—"

"No more banks!" Garrett snapped. "A damn banker done stole this place once. Ain't gonna do it again." He downed another shot of whiskey, swiped the back of his hand across his bristly handlebar mustache, and lifted an eyebrow at Hawkins. "How much money we got, partner?"

Hawkins frowned over the mental mathematics for a moment. The reward money on Barker and his bunch, plus a bonus from the grateful owners and depositors of the Mercantile Bank of Albany, had come to $12,900 and change. A three-way split of $4,300 each, and their expenses hadn't been that much. They had loaned W.C. Milhouse $3,000 to reclaim and restock the Singletree; Buck had put a thousand into railroad stocks.

"Between the two of us, we have about $4,000 on deposit in the Albany bank," Hawkins said.

Garrett shook his head in disbelief. "Damn, that's sure a mess of money for a couple no-account cowboys." Dobie turned to Milhouse. "Reckon that'd be enough to get hold of the Quarter Circle?"

Milhouse frowned. "It might be. I'd have to ask Meier. And there would be operating expenses before this year's calf crop is ready for market. Part of the deal Meier insists on is that whoever buys the ranch keeps his hands on the payroll."

"Always did like that old German," Garrett said. "Man takes care of his hired help. Ain't many fellers like him and you left anymore, W.C." Dobie downed the last of his whiskey. "Hell, I'm game. Buck?"

A tickle of excitement twitched in Hawkins's gut. The Quarter Circle was everything he'd always dreamed of. A place of his own was something no cowboy in these changing times could ever expect to get his hands on. All the Quarter Circle and Buck Hawkins needed to grab hold of that dream was a good woman. If she hadn't met someone else by now . . .

"Before you decide to saddle this bronc, boys, think on this: If you put every dollar you have into buying Meier's place, you'll be flat broke again."

Garrett snorted. "W.C., bein' broke's one thing me and Buck's good at. I been flatter'n last summer's cow patties all my life, anyhow. Got plumb used to livin' on cowboy wages." He turned to Hawkins. "What say, partner? You always been wantin' your own spread. That money ain't doin' us no good where it's at."

Hawkins still hesitated, despite the excitement that chilled his fingers. "Dobie, Mr. Milhouse is right. It takes regular cash money to keep a ranch running—"

"We got cash money waitin'. In Necesario."

"And a better than good chance of being shot in Necesario." Buck ran a hand over his chin and winced at the stubble scrape against his palm. "It's chancy."

"Life's chancy, partner." Garrett half smiled. "Hell, if it didn't work out, we could always go back to robbin' trains and stages."

"And starve for sure," Hawkins grumbled. "I'm not going back on that owlhoot trail of yours, Dobie. We were, without a doubt, the worst outlaws the West has ever seen."

"Made money at it, didn't we?"

"By accident. With help. And a lot of luck. Forget it." He paused for a sip of whiskey. "Suppose, just for argument's sake, we did buy the Quarter Circle. Who would run the place? And who would help you here, Mr. Milhouse?"

Milhouse leaned back in his chair. "No problem there.

Tom Luce is Meier's top hand. He'd make a good *segundo*. I could drop by time to time to make sure everything's all right until you boys get back. There's a couple of cowboys hunting work over in Mobeetie. They're not as good hands as you two, but most of the heavy work's done here. I could hire them on."

"See, partner? Nothin' to it."

Still, Hawkins hesitated.

Garrett played his trump card. "I seem to recall a little red-haired gal who I bet sure would admire to come home to a real good workin' ranch. What we got to lose?"

"Four thousand dollars. And our lives." Hawkins sighed. "What the hell. We'll never have an opportunity like this again, Dobie. We'll either get rich, go broke, or get killed," He lifted his gaze from the glass to W.C. Milhouse. "Talk to Mr. Schriner. If he'll take say, three thousand down, we can finance more with the job in Necesario and be able to pay the Quarter Circle hands in the meantime."

Garrett slapped his open palm onto the table. "Now you're talkin', son. By God, we're gonna have us some fun over in Needful."

"Just don't get yourselves shot in the process," Milhouse said. "I'd sure miss having you two underfoot and in the way in my old age. We'll ride over and talk to Meier in the morning."

3

BUCK HAWKINS REINED Cornbread to a stop on the low ridge overlooking the town below.

Necesario looked a bit like the landscape that seemed to dwarf the isolated settlement. The buildings were sun bleached, wind scoured, and weathered. Some were adobe structures, others made of faded gray lumber and in need of paint; a few seemed on the verge of collapse. Private homes, some prosperous-looking two-story buildings, others little more than shacks, lined narrow side streets.

The town was shaped something like a squashed square, as if the west wind had mashed the far side of town up against the eastern buildings. The main east-west street was wider than the others, the legacy of the town's former prominence as a popular watering hole and overnight stop on the Southern Santa Fe Trail.

Buttermilk, Hawkins's palomino gelding now serving his day as pack mount, moved alongside the dun and scratched his left ear against Cornbread's shoulder and Buck's shotgun chaps.

"Don't look like much, does it?" Dobie Garrett said as he squinted toward the grayish-dun cluster of buildings. "Man wouldn't think they was twenty dollars in the whole town, just lookin' at it."

Hawkins didn't reply for a moment, his attention on the crude, hand-lettered sign beside the road:

NECESARIO, TEXAS
100 MILES FROM CIVILIZATION
75 MILES FROM WATER
FIFTY MILES FROM GRASS
A FOOT AND A HALF FROM HELL

"Doesn't sound too promising, either, according to this sign," Hawkins said. "I don't know why we're doing this."

Garrett shifted his chew and spat. The glob hit behind the right ear of the unsuspecting bay horse Dobie rode, triggering a snort of disgust and a head shake from Duckbutt. "You're doin' it for Marylou Kowalski, Buck."

Hawkins sighed. "Yes, I am."

"Don't blame you none. That red-haired gal—"

"It's auburn."

"—is some catch, son. I never seen a woman with that many smarts, at least till she set her cap for you for some reason." Garrett's voice took on an almost reverent note. "And ride, cuss, drink, and shoot better'n any man I ever met. Yes, sir, that's one fine filly, Marylou. And the way them blue eyes sparkles when she gets mad—"

"They're green, Dobie."

"Anyhow, partner, that's how come you're here. Me, I'm here for the free women and whiskey."

"Why else?" Hawkins muttered.

"Most of all, partner, we're doin' it for the money. Ain't no other way we could afford to buy the Quarter Circle so's you and that little red-haired gal can raise calves, colts, and kids."

Hawkins sighed. "It's auburn. And if we live through it."

"Won't be no trouble we can't handle, us bein' hard-eyed, town-tamin', dead-shot gunhawks and all." Garrett grinned. "And I get to droolin' spit just thinkin' about all them free drinks and fine women waitin' up ahead."

"Can't you think of anything besides women and whiskey?"

"Sure can. They get some hellacious poker games goin' on in Necesario once a month. Real high-stakes stuff. And cowboy poker, too, come paydays. Anything from nickel ante on up, dependin' on what a man fancies."

Hawkins cocked an eyebrow at Garrett. "I didn't know you'd been here before."

"Ain't. But I know fellers who has been. Some mighty salty poker players drop by Necesario."

"Professionals?"

Garrett shrugged. "Might be one or two professional cardsharps, but the rest is mostly Baptist deacons, Presbyterians, politicians, and other fine, upstandin' civic leaders who don't want to be seen doin' their gamblin' and whorin' in Santa Fe or Tucumcari." Garrett shifted his weight in the saddle, his gaze still on the dusty settlement below. "I hear Big Nose Kate and Poker Alice set in some high stakes games here a spell back. Never played poker with no woman gambler."

Hawkins cut a sharp glance at Garrett. "Dobie, do me a big favor. Stay away from the gambling tables, or you'll lose every dime we make."

Garrett's face twisted in a wounded grimace. "Son, that ain't no way to talk to a partner. How come you think I'd lose?"

"Because I'm a better poker player than you are," Hawkins said pointedly, "and I'm terrible at it."

"I'm gettin' better. Won four bits off W.C. night before we left the Singletree, didn't I?"

"Four bits. Not exactly what I'd call a great financial coup." Hawkins sighed in resignation. "Okay, we'll make a deal. Twenty dollars a month for gambling money. When you lose that twenty, you quit."

Garrett closed one eye in a slow wink. "Buck, you ain't studied this here gamblin' thing out too good. Who's gonna take a chance on beatin' a man knowed for his fast gun and dead-eye shootin'?"

"Fast gun?" Hawkins nodded at the Colt Single Action Army .44–40 revolver tucked into Garrett's waistband. "You don't even own a holster—"

"Never seen no reason to get one."

"And as for dead-eye shooting, neither of us could sit in a two-holer and hit any one of the four walls, the ceiling, or the floor. Or the door. You haven't started believing those newspaper stories, have you?"

"Sure do like seein' my name in them papers," Garrett said.

"Hearing it, you mean. I have to read them to you. Over and over and over—"

"Aw, Buck, quit fussin'. It ain't like I can't read. Just don't do it as good and as quick as you do, that's all." Garrett fell silent for a moment, studying the settlement below. "Looks mighty busy. This ain't Saturday or payday, is it?"

"Wednesday, I think. And it's still a week until payday, at least for cowboys." But Garrett was right, Hawkins thought. Even from here he could see spring wagons and buckboards moving along the wide main street, horses standing at hitchrails before half a dozen buildings. A big Studebaker freight wagon stood in front of what appeared to be a two-story clapboard structure. Individual workers swarmed over the freighter, lugging stuff inside. It was an impressive show of prosperity for a drab town in the middle of nowhere.

Garrett said, "Come on, partner. Let's see what this here Needful place has got for a couple of thirsty, lonesome men." He kneed the bay into motion.

Dust swirled like ground snowdrift along Necesario's main street as the two horsemen threaded their way through the bustle of buggies, horsemen, and pedestrians. Garrett grinned, nodded a greeting, and tipped his hat to a couple of pretty young women walking along the rough-hewn plank boardwalk that ran most of the length of the street. One of the women, a tall, bosomy brunette with a nipped waist and wearing a low-cut gown, smiled and nodded back.

"Yes, sir, partner," Garrett said, content, "I reckon I'm gonna like this place just fine."

Hawkins didn't reply. He studied the buildings as they rode. Behind the weathered facades, two general stores that covered a half block each stood on opposite corners at the intersection of the wide east-west roadway and the smaller north-south main street. The northbound street was little more than a trail cutting through the heart of town. The roadbed was worn deep into the earth from heavy travel over many years.

A thick-walled adobe building with barred windows stood unmarked by sign on the south side of the street. Hawkins figured it had to be either a bank or a jail. Next door to the barred building, where the west-bound street made an abrupt angle toward the southwest, a blacksmith whanged away with his hammer, shaping a metal strap against an anvil. A one-story adobe across from the smithy's shop had a display of guns, saddles, and tack behind a window that also was barred.

"I count two saloons and a sportin' house already," Garrett said, a smile on his face and a glint in his eye.

Hawkins nodded silently. When it came to finding cantinas and whorehouses, Dobie Garrett was a better tracker than Al Seiber. Hawkins studied the men riding along or lounging out front of one business or another. Most of them had the look of ordinary cowboys, teamsters, merchants, or broad-shouldered laborers. A few of the men carried a different stamp—clean clothes, cold, surly eyes, and revolvers strapped around their waists and hips. The surly ones paid more attention to the two of them than the other men did. Hawkins didn't especially like their type of attention. It left a cold, crawly spot in his gut.

Garrett didn't seem to notice the hard glares. "Where'd that Joyner feller say we was supposed to go?"

"Crazy Woman Cantina."

"Long as it's got the word 'cantina' in it, don't care what other monikers they lay on it. I tell you, son, I'm spittin' dust. Ain't been this dry since the drought of '75 down in the Nueces Strip. It was so dry mesquite trees was chasin' coyotes, hopin' one of 'em would hoist a leg. So dry that—"

"I'm sure it's a fascinating story," Hawkins interrupted, "but finish it another time, Dobie. We have to find that cantina."

Garrett reined in, glanced around, and pointed a stubby finger. "Up that little side street yonder."

"I thought you said you'd never been to Necesario."

"Ain't." Dobie spat; the bay ducked in time. The brownish glob hit the street and rolled into a dust-covered ball. "But I can sure 'nuff smell out a waterin' hole."

Garrett's sniffer was right, as usual. The cantina stood on one side of a narrow street, little more than a littered alley. No sign marked the chipped adobe walls. There was no boardwalk out front, as there had been along the more prosperous main street. Two saddled horses stood hipshot out front, dozing at a hitchrail worn slick and shiny from years of use.

Hawkins reined in and studied the one-story adobe for a moment. The walls were pitted with what appeared to be bullet marks. Cracks radiated from a round hole in the lone, smoke-stained window near the front door.

"Reckon this here's it," Garrett said. "Wonder where the Crazy Woman part come from."

"I don't know," Hawkins said as he dimounted, "but the crazy part makes sense if this is our headquarters. We have to be out of our minds to take on a job like this." He paused to loop the palomino's lead rope to the rear D-ring of his double-rig stock saddle, then wrapped the dun's reins around the rail.

Garrett beat Buck through the door by two strides.

The interior of the Crazy Woman Cantina was dim, murky with tobacco smoke, and smelled of man-sweat, stale beer, and spilled whiskey. Garrett paused for a deep breath. "Now, this here's a real man's saloon, Buck. I never smelt nothin' so sweet in my whole days." He headed straight for the bar.

Hawkins hesitated a moment, let his eyes adjust to the dim interior, and glanced around the single room. The Crazy Woman wasn't exactly packed with customers. Two Mexican vaqueros in dusty range garb nursed beers at the far end of the bar. A tall, lean man with a revolver strapped around his hips sipped at a whiskey at a corner table. The drinkers barely glanced at the new arrivals.

Buck stepped up to the bar. The row of bottles in front of a stained backbar mirror were name brands. Whiskey, tequila, gin, mescal, even expensive brandies, stood like good soldiers in a neat line. If the Crazy Woman was any indication, Hawkins thought, the people of Necesario preferred quality liquor, not the usual skull-buster rotgut of frontier towns.

"What'll it be, gents?" The bartender wore the brand of an ex-cowboy who had been used up and put out to safer pastures, past his prime. Bushy gray eyebrows and a bristly mustache framed a skewed nose and pale gray eyes in a face lined by wind and sun. A tough man, Hawkins thought, despite his age and a few too many encounters with rank horses and wild cattle. Buck suspected that a six-gun or maybe a sawed-off double shotgun lay on a shelf within easy reach.

"Couple beers and two shots of whiskey." Garrett rubbed his palms together in anticipation. "Don't know what my partner here wants."

"Beer's fine for me." Hawkins cocked an eyebrow at Garrett. "Go easy on the panther spit, Dobie. At least until we find out what we're getting into here."

"Now, son, don't go actin' like no mother hen already," Garrett said. "It ain't like I don't know how to handle liquor."

"That," Hawkins said with a sigh, "is open to debate." He dropped a five-dollar gold piece on the bar, hefted the mug, and sipped the brew the bartender placed before him. It was cool and surprisingly light for frontier beer. Dobie didn't waste time savoring the taste. He drained most of his first mug without pausing for breath, then reached for a shot glass.

"A man named Joyner said we should check in here when we got to town," Hawkins said as the bartender reached for the gold piece.

The barkeep's bushy brows went up. "You the two gunhawks I keep hearing about? The ones shot up the Barker gang?"

"Reckon that's us," Garrett said. He knocked back the whiskey shot and extended a hand. "Dobie Garrett. This here's my partner, Buck Hawkins."

Hawkins caught a quick glance of the lean man at the table in the backbar mirror. The man suddenly stiffened in his chair and stared at the two visitors.

"Ned Dawson." The barkeep's grip was firm, his grin genuine. "No offense, gents, but from what I heard, I expected you two to be nine feet tall with horns and tails and wearing rattlesnakes for bandannas."

"Just goes to show you can't put no stock in campfire yarns, Ned," Garrett said. "Always this quiet around here?"

Dawson shrugged. "Gets a little wild sometimes. Most boys who come in here know to behave themselves in the Crazy Woman. Others learn manners pretty quick. It sort of frosts my drawers when somebody tries to bust up my place." He put Buck's coin back on the bar. "On the house, gents. Your money's no good in Necesario."

Garrett's lined face creased in a wide grin. "Lordy, lordy, but I do believe I love this here town already."

The tall man at the table stood, his drink unfinished, and strode for the door. The abrupt departure sent a warning tingle along Hawkins's spine.

"Pleased to meet you two," Dawson said. "Been reading about you in the papers. We get a few gunhands in Necesario from time to time, but nobody with a rep like you boys have. Sure would like to hear about that shoot-out with the Barker bunch one of these days."

"Didn't amount to much," Garrett said with a shrug. "Them Barker boys couldn't shoot for squat. How's about a refill on this beer mug?"

"Sure thing. Hawkins?"

Buck shook off the offer. "The fellow who just left. Who was he?"

"Don't know the name," Dawson said. "Drifter of sorts, I expect. Comes through town every so often. Not a very sociable fellow. Doesn't say much."

"He didn't look like a cowboy."

Dawson grinned. "Not likely. He's always got a pocket full of cash money."

Garrett chuckled. "He ain't no puncher, then."

Hawkins couldn't shake his uneasy feeling about the lean man. He tried to put it down to just being tired and jumpy from a long ride across miles of nothing much but sandhills, cactus, yucca plants, and prairie grass.

The bartender stepped to the keg to pull a fresh beer for Garrett, and said over his shoulder, "You fellows signed on with the association yet?"

"Just rode in. Joyner said you'd know who we're supposed to talk at."

"That's be Fess McLocklin. He helped found the association back in the old days, when it was still a tad wild out here. Been president of the outfit several years now." Dawson put the fresh beer in front of Garrett. "This time of day, you'd find him over in the association office, most likely. Next to the Palace, down on Santa Fe Street. Know where it is?"

Garrett promptly downed about a third of the mug and nodded. "Know where the Palace is. Rode past it on the way in. Fancy place. Not nice and homey like this 'un."

Hawkins had ridden with Garrett long enough to read the signs. He decided he'd better get Dobie out of the Crazy Woman before he tripped over a liquor rope. Showing up drunk wouldn't make a very good impression on a prospective employer. And they needed the jobs. Getting hold of the Quarter Circle had reduced them to nearly empty pockets.

"Fess McLocklin's a good man," the bartender said. "Back in the old days, he'd stomp his own snakes. Rheumatics and liver trouble got him down now. Shame. Fess was a hell of a cattleman in his day. Him and me hunted buffalo and fought Comanches, blizzards, and drought many a year." Dawson's eyes narrowed. "A bit of advice, gents. Don't cross Fess. He may be old and crotchety, like me and a bunch of other old-timers around here, but he isn't a man to mess with. If you take his money, give him a fair day's work."

"We intend to do just that, Mr. Dawson," Hawkins said. He downed the last swallow of his beer and winced. It had gotten lukewarm. "Come on, Dobie. Let's go see Mr. McLocklin."

"Come back anytime, gents."

"Much obliged for the invite, Ned," Garrett said. "By the by, you got any women here?"

"Not in my place. This is a drinking establishment, not a whorehouse." Dawson snorted in disgust. "Women complicate a man's life no end, so I don't run a stable. Don't need the bother. I had a woman once. For about twenty years. She finally run off. On my best horse." He sighed. "Damn, but I sure do miss that pony."

Hawkins almost missed the office of the Texas and New Mexico Cattleman's Association.

As seemed to be the practice in Necesario, the place

was unmarked by sign, a single narrow building jammed between the two-story Palace Saloon and a row of small shops.

Hawkins had his hands full keeping Dobie Garrett out of the Palace; Dobie was still steady on his feet and able to make a complete sentence, but Buck knew from painful experience there wasn't much slack left before Garrett hit the end of the whiskey rope.

The association office was small, barely six by six paces, its furnishings as sparse and lean as the old man behind the scarred oak rolltop desk. A wooden bench and two unpadded chairs made up the only seating other than the stuffed armchair behind the desk. Ledgers and books lined half of one wall behind the desk. Hawkins noted that the bookshelves were hung low, within easy reach of a man seated at the rolltop. A thin Mexican cigar smoldered in a dish-shaped stone that probably had been a corn grinder for Indians before it was appropriated for an ashtray.

The man behind the desk glanced up as Hawkins and Garrett stepped through the door. He was rail-thin, stooped in the shoulders, with only a fringe of white hair above his ears. The dark eyes in the weathered face were anything but frail.

Buck had expected the head of the cattleman's association to be a beefy, big man wearing a suit and vest, maybe even a string tie, and a pound and a half of gold watch chain. The thin man behind the desk wore a simple cotton shirt, unbuttoned at the neck and frayed at the cuffs. A sturdy hickory walking stick with a handle carved from what looked to be elk horn leaned against the desk.

Hawkins removed his hat in respect. "Mr. McLocklin?"

"I'm him." The voice, like the eyes, carried a strength that had abandoned withered muscles and brittle bones.

"I'm Buck Hawkins. This is Dobie Garrett."

McLocklin nodded. "I've been expecting you two. Saw you ride past about an hour ago." He leaned over the desk and extended a hand; the fingers and knuckles were twisted into bony lumps. "Pardon me if I don't get up. This bum hip's been giving me fits lately."

The old man's handshake was more firm than Hawkins expected, but Buck took care not to squeeze too hard. He noticed that Dobie also was more careful than normal in returning the greeting.

"Pull up a couple of chairs, gentlemen, and we'll talk some turkey." McLocklin waited until Hawkins and Garrett moved the wooden chairs closer to the desk and sat. He flipped open a rosewood box, the only visible luxury in the room. "Cigar?"

Garrett accepted one with a nod of thanks. Hawkins passed; he had never developed a taste for tobacco. McLocklin plucked a sulphur lucifer from a holder, scratched it into life, and lit Garrett's smoke. He studied the two men over the flame for a moment before flicking out the match.

"Thought I recognized you gentlemen from the descriptions in the papers." Eyes so dark brown as to be almost black twinkled in inner amusement. "What was it the Santa Fe paper said? Oh, yes. Two outwardly nondescript cowboy types who look nothing at all like the West's most competent, feared yet fearless gunmen, with blinding speed on the draw and deadly accuracy."

"At least they got the nondescript cowboys part right," Hawkins said. "I don't know where they got the idea we were such great shakes with guns."

McLocklin puffed on his cigar, the faintest hint of a

smile on lips that curled up on the right side at the end of a long, ragged scar. "No need to be coy, Mr. Hawkins. However, I find it refreshing to find a gunhawk who isn't a braggart. Talkers talk. Doers get the job done. We need doers in this part of the country. I, and the rest of the association members, are pleased and more than a bit relieved that you chose to accept our offer." He tapped the ash from his cigar into the stone receptacle. "I assume Joyner told you the details?"

"The main point, yes, sir," Hawkins said. "A rustling problem, I understand."

"There is that, yes. The association has been losing more and more stock of late. Much of it has been missing from the Keylock outfit—my place."

The comment took Hawkins a bit by surprise. He had heard of the Keylock all his life. It had covered a half million acres or so back in free-range days. Fess McLocklin didn't look like the sort of man who could carve a ranch that size out of a wild land.

"I owned a Keylock-bred horse once, sir," Hawkins said.

"Good mount?"

"He taught me a lot about cowboying."

A slight smile tugged at McLocklin's lips. "We always did pride ourselves on good horses at the Keylock." The smile faded. "We've lost thirty Keylock horses to rustlers within the last six months, and God knows how many cows. And that, gentlemen, is one of the reasons you're here. Not just for my benefit, but for all association members."

Hawkins nodded. "Yes, sir, we understand."

McLocklin glanced up at a tap on the door. "Come in. It's not locked."

A young man with a pale, almost full moon-shaped

face stepped into the office. He wore a white linen suit, low-cut town shoes, and a dark blue cravat with diamond stickpin, and a gold watch chain that looked to weigh a pound spanned his brocade vest. He seemed a bit out of breath, as though he had been in a hurry. Beads of sweat dotted his forehead beneath a black bowler hat.

"Come in, son, come in," McLocklin said. "Gentlemen, my nephew, Marty Beecham. Marty, meet Buck Hawkins and Dobie Garrett."

Beecham's handshake was a bit on the weak side, Hawkins thought, but the man's smile seemed genuine. "A pleasure to meet two living legends of the West, gentlemen," Beecham said. Hawkins winced inwardly; he was beginning to wonder if anyone in the world had *not* heard of the two so-called living legends. "Am I intruding, Uncle Fess?"

"Not at all, Marty. There's another chair in the back room."

"I can only stay a moment," Beecham said. "I was about to change and ride out to the ranch. We could take the buggy, if you feel up to the trip."

McLocklin sighed. "Son, there's nothing I'd like better. I miss the old home place. Thanks for the offer, but I'm afraid even my buggy riding days are over." The dark eyes took on a fresh speck of fire. "But, by God, you and that damned quack doctor are going to play hell getting me into one of those wheelchair contraptions, so don't go thinking I'm completely worn out just yet."

"Wouldn't think of it, Uncle Fess. Anything you'd like me to tell the boys?"

"Tell them to keep making money, son. That's all."

McLocklin smiled as Beecham left. "Marty's my only surviving heir. My late sister's eldest—and only—son.

The last stud in the McLocklin bloodline, so to speak. The Keylock will be his when I'm gone."

"Reckon he can handle it?" Garrett said. "Don't look like a rancher to me."

"Marty's been away at college, Mr. Garrett. Don't let his looks fool you. He isn't as soft as he appears." McLocklin snubbed out his cigar and reached for another. "Let's get back to business, gentlemen. I worked too damn hard for too many years and fought too many battles to let some shiftless thieves who are too lazy to tackle honest work drive me into the poorhouse. Several of the other old-time ranchers around here, stove-up, cranky old bastards like me, are in the same boat. And it's sinking fast. So we're counting on you two to bail us out. A few good funerals would go a long way toward doing that."

A cold finger traced its way up Hawkins's spine. "Mr. McLocklin, no matter what you may have heard or read about us, Dobie and I aren't hired killers—"

"Doesn't matter," McLocklin interrupted, "as long as the sonsabitches who are stealing us blind think you are, that's all that counts." The old rancher leaned back in his chair, winced at a quick flash of pain, and grumbled a quiet curse. "Damned hip. If I wasn't so stove up, I'd host a few lynch parties myself. Joyner fill you in on the financial arrangements?"

"Yes, sir." Hawkins repeated Joyner's words as best he could recall them. When he finished, McLocklin nodded.

"That's the deal. We didn't expect you fellows to come cheap. We do expect our money's worth. I've made arrangements for your room, board, bar bills, and, shall we say, other amenities that you may feel a need for. You have rooms waiting at the Santa Fe Hotel two blocks east. Arrangements have been made for the care of your horses at the livery stable on the northeast side. Anything else you require, get it and sign for it, and the association picks up the bills. With the exception of any gambling losses, of course. Any questions?"

Hawkins had a hat full of questions, but decided they could wait. "No, sir. Well, one. When do we start to work?"

"In about four minutes, Hawkins. I have the papers here authorizing you as special range detectives and Necesario town marshals, already signed by judges in two states. All we need is your signatures. Of course, you'll have a day or two free to familiarize yourself with the town before the real work begins. Then I'll send for Joyner to show you around the different ranges and get you the lay of the land."

McLocklin pulled a sheaf of papers from a desk drawer, then paused. "Are you gentlemen absolutely sure you want to do this?"

Hawkins glanced at Garrett, caught Dobie's slight nod, swallowed against the cold knot in his gut, and said, "Yes, sir."

"Why? A sense of justice and fair play, perhaps?"

"No, sir," Hawkins said honestly. "We need the money."

"Good. That's what I wanted to hear. Cash carries more weight than philosophy, I've found." He pushed the papers across the desk, dipped a pen in an inkwell, and handed it to Hawkins. "Sign on the bottom line. We've already written into the contract that should any-thing happen to you, any money due will go to W.C. Milhouse as executor of your estates."

McLocklin picked up the pen, signed his name, and handed the instrument to Garrett. Dobie tucked his tongue out the corner of his mouth and scrawled his signature a letter at a time.

McLocklin retrieved the documents, puffed on the signatures to dry the ink, and reached back into his desk. He brought out two brass badges, one new, one worn and tarnished. The badges were similar to those worn by Texas Rangers, a star inside a circle.

"Who wants the new one?" McLocklin said.

"I'll take her," Garrett said. "Always wanted a shiny badge."

McLocklin passed the badges to the waiting men. "As duly elected county judge, I will now officially administer the oath of office."

Hawkins eyed the tarnished badge in his hand suspiciously. It had a bright smear and a dent at one edge, and what might have been a faint trace of dried blood in the outer rim of the engraving.

"Mr. McLocklin? What happened to the man who wore this badge before?"

"We buried him a couple months ago."

"I don't suppose he died from the plague?"

"In a way," McLocklin said, his tone matter-of-fact. "A plague of buckshot."

"Rustlers?"

"No. His wife shot him." McLocklin paused. "Before we get to the swearing in part, there's something I'd like you to know. The stable boy, Trace Willis. I'd appreciate your being patient and pleasant with him. He's a fine young man and very good with horses, but he has a problem. He has the body of a grown man but the mind of a twelve-year-old."

"Town idiot?" Garrett said. Hawkins fought back the urge to ram an elbow into Dobie's ribs. Hard.

"In a way, Mr. Garrett." McLocklin's tone had a sudden hard edge to it. "His father hit Trace in the head with a club when he was only twelve. Trace will never be any older mentally than he is now. He is also something of the town favorite. If you find anyone mistreating him, jail them and fine hell out of them."

Garrett nodded. "Be our pleasure. What happened to his old man?"

"We lynched him, Mr. Garrett. I furnished the rope. Now, raise your right hands and repeat after me."

4

BUCK HAWKINS STORED the last of his gear, propped his
.44–40 Winchester rifle in a corner, and glanced around
his second-floor room in the Santa Fe Hotel.

He had to admit he was a bit relieved that he and Garrett had separate, if adjoining, rooms. Hawkins knew
from sharing a room in Albany that Dobie tended to
stagger in—noisily—at all hours of the night. And Garrett snored like a whipsaw going through a knot in a mahogany log. At least, Buck thought, he might get a
measure of rest in the Santa Fe.

If he could get used to the luxury.

The room was a bit rich for a common cowboy's
blood. The room wasn't large, but the furnishings were
fancy enough to make him feel a bit out of place, as if he
needed to take off his boots before walking on the car-
peted floor. Hawkins had seldom walked on real carpets.
Or even throw rugs. Dirt floors or rough pine planking
felt more familiar beneath his boot soles.

The beds were soft, the chifforobes, cabinets, and tables solid despite the occasional cigar and cigarette burn,
and the window overlooking Santa Fe Street actually
had curtains. The room and board deal included maid
and laundry service twice a week; a man didn't even

have to pick up his dirty socks off the floor if he wasn't
of a mind to.

The Santa Fe even had a wash room in back of the
stairs on the ground floor, complete with a big galva-
nized tub and an even bigger black servant who fetched
and heated bathwater. The thought of a hot bath made
Hawkins feel the dust and grubbiness of the long ride.
He ran a palm across his chin and winced at the scratchy
sound. He never had been able to shake the feeling that
whiskers sapped a man's strength. He wasn't sure
whether it was considered proper for special marshals to
bathe before or after supper.

The question made his belly growl. He realized he
hadn't eaten since daybreak. Maybe after supper, he
thought, he'd get a bath and shave—and try to get Dobie
to do the same. It would be a struggle. It wasn't as if
Garrett had a particular aversion to soap and water.
Dobie just didn't think it was natural for a man to bathe
more than once a month unless there was some skirt
chousing involved. On the other hand, it looked like
there were plenty of petticoats to chase in Necesario, so
maybe Dobie Garrett was about to enter a "clean phase"
of his life.

The Santa Fe did everything in a grand manner,
Hawkins thought. He'd never seen a bigger outhouse
than the one just across the alley. It was a four-holer. Beside the big privvy with the *Gents* sign lettered on it
stood a similar one labeled *Ladies*. Buck knew it would
take him a few days to get used to such plush surround-
ings.

He had been more than a bit surprised at the accommodations. The Santa Fe looked ridden down and used
up from the outside, but the interior would compete with
the best hotel Denver had to offer, down to the chande-

liers above the tables in the dining room. Hawkins didn't know how much the Santa Fe charged for a night's stay, but he figured it would be more than a cowboy made in a month.

Even their horses were living the good life in the solidly stocked livery on the edge of town. Rolled corn, oats, and crushed barley laced with molasses awaited feed time in wooden, lidded bins. An overhead loft ran the length of the stables, loaded with prairie hay. Hawkins hoped Cornbread and Buttermilk didn't get too fat and sassy on such rich fare. The dun and palomino had a tendency to revert to their bronc days if they started feeling their oats too much.

Garrett tapped on the door and stepped into Hawkins's room. Buck suspected Dobie had already polished his new badge. It gleamed like a freshly minted dollar.

"Swankiest bunkhouse I ever stayed in, partner," Garrett said. "Reckon us honest-to-gawd lawmen is due the best if we're gonna clean up this town."

Hawkins frowned. "If we live through it," Hawkins said with considerably less enthusiasm than Garrett.

"Relax, son. Ain't nothing to worry about."

"How can you be so sure about that? We were miserable flops as outlaws, Dobie. What makes you think we'll be such hot biscuits as marshals?"

Garrett chuckled. "We done rode that horse once, Buck. Like I said before, Pappy told me that if a man ain't worth spit at one thing, he's bound to be good at the plumb opposite. As sorry as we was as outlaws, we're bound to be good badge toters."

"Why do I find so little comfort in those words?"

"Quit huntin' boogers, amigo," Garrett said with confidence. "When them bad guys find out us two cold-eyed, fearless fast guns is in town, why, they'll light a shuck for Mexico sure as a hound's got fleas." He puffed out his chest, admiring his reflection in the gilt-framed mirror.

After a moment Dobie said, "Now, partner, let's go check out this here Palace place and howl our wolves. I'm workin' up a awful thirst and I ain't had me a woman since Albany." He paused to punch Hawkins playfully in the shoulder. "And best of all, it's slap-dab *free*! Ever' drink and ever' woman, paid for by a bunch of ranchers who got more money than they got cows. Man couldn't ask for more."

"Speak for yourself, Dobie," Hawkins said. "I'm going to supper, then get a bath. I'll pass on the saloon-hopping and women—"

"Son," Dobie interrupted with a scowl, "I'm gettin' somewhat fretty about you. It ain't healthy, a man keepin' them urges all bottled up like a cork in a whiskey bottle. Might plumb explode one of these here days. Woman'd do you some good."

Hawkins sighed. "Not just any woman, Dobie."

"Buck, pinin' over that little red-haired gal—"

"Auburn."

"—ain't no way for a young man to waste his time, not with all the fillies in this town. It ain't natural, that's what it ain't."

"Maybe not," Hawkins conceded, "but it's the way I am. I can wait for Marylou."

Garret pursed his lips. "Reckon she's worth waitin' for at that. Wonder where she's at now."

"I don't know. And I'd rather not talk about it right now." Hawkins headed for the door. "Dobie, do me a favor?"

"Sure 'nuff."

"Stay sober. This place might not be too healthy for a drunken marshal."

"Don't you worry 'bout me, partner," Garrett said. "Ain't gonna be no trouble. No trouble at all."

"I have heard that before," Hawkins said warily, "and it doesn't sound a bit more reassuring this time around."

Hawkins leaned against a weathered veranda corner post of the hotel and worried a piece of supper meat from between his molars with a toothpick.

The Santa Fe Hotel served a fine steak and even better deep-dish apple pie. Even after a sundown foot tour of Necesario's main streets, Hawkins still felt the need to let out the notch on his belt. If he stayed in Needful too long, he figured, he'd be pushing two hundred pounds.

For now, it felt good.

He listened, contented, to the muted babble from inside the Palace. The town's most noted saloon, gaming hall, and whorehouse was packed with customers, but so far all seemed peaceful. Garrett, naturally, was already inside, determined to howl his wolf. At least, Hawkins thought, if Dobie howled the wolf loud enough and long enough tonight, he'd have it out of his system for tomorrow.

Hawkins nodded pleasantly to a young cowboy headed up the veranda steps. The puncher returned the nod, but Buck noticed the quick narrowing of eyes as the young man spotted the badge on his shirt. It wasn't the first hard look the lawman symbol had brought. Buck thought about unpinning it and tucking the thing into his pocket—even dull badges made good targets—but decided he might as well get used to the idea. And let the people of Necesario get used to it, also.

The walking tour hadn't taken long, despite Garrett's

grousing about losing valuable drinking and woman time to learn the town. Buck wasn't sure how much attention Dobie had paid, but at least Hawkins now had the layout of the settlement committed to memory.

The largest of the barred structures was, in fact, the bank. It didn't look prosperous from the outside. The bank had closed for the day, so he would have to wait until tomorrow to check out the interior and introduce himself to the owner and employees.

Both the general merchandise stores were well stocked and still open. The storekeepers had welcomed them with open arms and dollar signs in their eyes; anyone with an open account backed by the Texas and New Mexico Cattleman's Association was a preferred customer for anything from a new saddle to a penny candy stick.

Hawkins had picked up a box of .44–40 ammunition on the association, and treated himself to a new shirt and razor from his own dwindling cash supply. He didn't yet feel right just signing for any and everything he wanted or needed. He'd tried to get Garrett to spring for a holster; it didn't seem proper, a duly appointed officer of the law carrying his six-gun stuck in his waistband like a dirt farmer.

Garrett bought "the necessaries": a bottle of Old Overholt and a week's supply of chewing tobacco. On the association account.

They had more trouble finding the marshal's office and jail than they had locating the saloons and red light establishments. The little two-room adobe jammed between a harness shop and bakery was barely ten feet wide and maybe thirty deep. The office took up the front half. It held a spur-scarred, stained desk painted a faded but still bilious green, two creaky chairs, a hard wooden bench, and a small wood-burning stove with a scorched coffeepot resting on the single lid, and a sagging cot along one wall.

An empty gun rack with enough notches to accommodate six long guns stood next to the door, the security chain unlocked and a bit rusted. At least they would have a place to store Hawkins's rifle and Garrett's shotgun instead of having to lug them around when there was no need.

The jail, separated from the marshal's office by thick adobe walls and a heavy oak door, was even more crude and inhospitable than the office. Iron bars split the small space into two cells, each barely five feet wide by eight feet deep. The bars and cell door locks showed signs of neglect and rust. Each cell was equipped with a hard metal bunk, a chamber pot, and nothing else. A single, narrow window at the top of each cell provided the only ventilation. The sparse furnishings were covered by a layer of dust. The signs of neglect and non-use had somehow been comforting to Buck. Until he stopped to talk with the leathersmith next door.

The dour old man, with hands as leathery as the hides he worked, pointed out that the jail wasn't all that necessary, anyway, because a creek a mile outside of town had a fine hanging tree.

Hawkins sincerely hoped they wouldn't need either.

Full dark had come to Necesario, but the lantern light that spilled from windows left a sort of soft, golden glow along the main street. The wind had died to a light breeze at sunset. Most of the dust had settled. The harsh, hot sun had given way to pleasantly cool evening air.

It would have been peaceful except for the growing clamor from inside the Palace. Hawkins wondered if the

town ever slept at night; it seemed to have gotten louder
by the minute since sundown.

There wasn't much else he could do at the moment, so
Buck tossed the toothpick aside, strode through the open
front door of the Palace, and immediately wondered how
he was going to push his way through the mass of humanity. There wasn't a spare table or spot at the bar. Tobacco smoke hung over the huge room like clouds on a
mountaintop. It made Hawkins's eyes tear up. Or maybe
it was the scent of man and horse sweat punctuated by
the occasional whiff of toilet-water overdose from the
girls who worked the tables.

Hawkins didn't see Garrett anywhere. He tapped a
cowboy on the shoulder. "Excuse me, please?"

The young man turned, a sneer on his lips. His eyes
widened and the snarl vanished. "Sorry, Mr. Hawkins,"
he said.

Buck paused. "Have we met?"

"No, sir. But I sure know who you are." He stuck out
a hand. "Stony Callahan. Pleasure to make your acquain-
tance in person." Callahan pumped Buck's hand enthusi-
astically. "It ain't every day a man gets to meet a real
stud-hoss—I mean, a real lawman gunhawk like you. I
mean, the man who shot up the Barker bunch—buy you
a drink?"

Hawkins retrieved his hand with a wry grin. "Pleased
to meet you, too, Stony, but I'll pass on the drink. I'm
looking for my partner." Buck became aware of the
growing silence; it seemed that every man in earshot had
turned to stare at him.

"Hey, Buck! Over here!" Garrett's voice boomed
through the dwindling commotion.

The crowd parted in cautious respect as Hawkins
strode toward Garrett's table. Dobie was in the middle of

a crowd, with one hand wrapped around a quart of Old
Overholt and the other arm around the waist of the tall,
shapely brunette they had seen earlier in the street. Her
eyes looked older than the body they went with,
Hawkins thought.

"This here's my partner, Buck Hawkins," Garrett said.
"He's faster'n I am with a handgun, boys. Best not mess
with ol' Buck."

Hawkins winced. Garrett's voice, his words already a
bit slurred, carried well over the entire crowd. Buck
glanced around, half expecting someone to pull a revolver. Many of the faces bore scowls or expressions of
open disbelief; others were wide-eyed in wonder.

Buck forced a weak grin. "That may be partly true,
gentlemen," he said, "but that's only because Dobie's
slower on the draw than February molasses in Maine."

The remark drew a few soft chuckles.

"In a pig's butt," someone said in a loud voice. "I seen
both these boys at work. Pure damn scorpions with
handguns. Shoot the light out of a candle at two hunnert
yards with a rifle, too."

Hawkins leveled a steady gaze on the loudmouth. The
man appeared to be a wagon driver. He was about an axe
handle wide across the shoulders and was hauling a full
load of liquor. But he was grinning. "Belly up, Buck,"
the big man said, "I'm buyin'."

"No, thanks. I appreciate the offer, friend, but I just
came by for a word with Mr. Garrett." One of the men
seated at the table bounced up and offered his seat to
Hawkins. "Thanks, but keep your chair," Buck said. "I'll
be on my way shortly."

"Big money card game goin' on in the back, partner,"
Dobie said. "Want to sit in a spell? I'd go take them
boys' money"—he squeezed the brunette's waist—"but

Lucy and me got us a date. And as much as I like poker, I reckon it can wait another time. Lucy's got a partner, too. Little blond thing here name of Sally, you're interested."

Hawkins glanced at the girl, shook his head, and thought he saw disappointment flicker in the woman's blue eyes. "Sorry, Sally, but not tonight. I just wanted to let Dobie know I'm packing it in." To Garrett he said, "I'll be in my room if I'm needed."

Garrett's grin was crooked. "Reckon there ain't nothin' here I can't handle, then. See you in the mornin', partner."

Hawkins nodded and started for the door. The mass of bodies parted to let him pass.

"Lucy," Garrett said with a woeful shake of the head as Hawkins disappeared through the door, "I worry about that boy sometimes. He's got this here thing for that gal rode with us when we hit them Barker boys. Now, I ain't sayin' I ain't had horses that wasn't one-man mounts, but I swear I never seen a one-woman man. Least not a young, healthy feller like Buck. Ain't natural."

Garrett knocked back another swallow of whiskey and grinned at the brunette. "Ready, honey?"

"Sure, Dobie," she said, "just give me about ten minutes to freshen up first. My room's number nine. To the left at the top of the stairs." Lucy pressed a firm hip against Garrett's shoulder and flashed a deliciously lecherous grin. "I'll be waiting for you, sugar. Let's see if you're quick on the draw with *all* your guns."

Garrett watched her stride away and hip-sway her way upstairs. He licked his lips. It had been a long time. "Lord help me, but I love this here town," he said.

He helped himself to another drink, figured that accounted for Lucy's ten minutes, and made his way a bit unsteadily up the stairs. He paused on the landing to scratch his head as he studied the row of doorways that branched left and right.

Dobie never had been too swift on ciphering, but he had always thought six came after five, not nine. But there it was. A figure nine, hanging kind of slantwise, right between five and seven. And it was the first door on the right, not the left.

"I could have swore she said left," Dobie muttered in indecision. But it didn't matter. Sometimes when he got a bit liquored up, he couldn't tell left from right unless he stepped outside to throw a rock. He couldn't throw for spit with his left hand.

He strode to the door, started to knock, then decided to heck with it; Lucy wanted to see fast guns, by durn, he'd show her one.

He reached for his belt buckle. His fingers touched the wooden grips of the Colt in his waistband. Garrett pulled the weapon from beneath his belt, tried to figure out how he could unfasten his belt buckle and unbutton his pants without dropping the six-gun, then gave up studying on the problem. He could just pitch the Colt onto a dresser or something.

He toed the door open.

"What the hell?"

The startled squawk came from a young, sandy-haired man sprawled on his back in the middle of a narrow bed, a chunky blond girl snuggled against his right side.

"What the hell?" Dobie said. Must have got the wrong room, he thought.

The sandy-haired man started to reach across the blond's ample chest. A short-barreled revolver with bird's-head grips lay on the table beside the bed.

"Easy, mister," Dobie said, "no reason anybody to get hurt."

The man froze, his hand within a foot of the revolver, his gray eyes wide, gaze riveted on Garrett's right hand. Dobie realized with a bit of a start that he held the .44–40.

"Who the hell are you?" the man in the bed all but yelled.

"Sorry to bust up your fun, friend. Name's Dobie Garrett, and I was lookin'—"

"Garrett!" The man on the bed suddenly raised both hands high. "Don't shoot, Garrett! I give up! I ain't gonna pull iron on you!"

"What the hell?" Garrett said again.

"I said I'd go peaceful." The man's tone was pleading. "Just don't drop the hammer on me, Garrett. I won't give you no trouble. I know when I'm caught cold. I'll take my chances with a jury, but I ain't tradin' lead with no gunhawk legend."

Garrett's face lined in a puzzled frown. He didn't have the foggiest idea what was going on. "Legend?" he muttered.

"Please, Garrett. Just let me get dressed. At least my pants."

"What for?"

"On account of it'd plumb humiliate me, that's what for. Bad enough the Nueces Kid gettin' caught in a whore's bed—"

"Nueces Kid?"

"Just don't make me march through that mob downstairs in my nothin's, Garrett. Please?"

Dobie shrugged. "Suit yourself." Whatever was going on, he figured, the young man on the bed was scared half to death. His eyes were big as half dollars. Recognition jarred away some of Garrett's whiskey fog. The name bounced up from memory. The Nueces Kid. One of the West's most wanted shooters. A dozen kills, at least. He'd walked in on a cold-blooded killer instead of a willing whore. With his six-gun drawn.

Sweat dotted Garrett's forehead. The Kid always had a hideout gun somewhere, he'd heard. And the man was deadly as a mad rattler when he got his hand on iron. Dobie let his eyes narrow in what he hoped was a menacing gunman's glare.

"All right, Kid. You can put your long drawers on. But don't touch them britches, or I'll drop the hammer on you sure." He glanced at the chesty blond. Her eyes were big, too, but not as big as some other parts of her. She yanked the rumpled sheet up to cover the interesting parts. "Sorry to bother you, ma'am," Garrett said.

"Am I under arrest, too?" Her voice was thin and squeaky, like a stepped-on mouse.

"Reckon not, ma'am. You ain't broke no law that I know of." Garrett forced himself to turn his full attention back to the man. The Nueces Kid had hauled his skinny frame upright. He reached for the long cotton drawers at the side of the bed; Garrett noticed the quick glance the Kid cast at the twill trousers.

"Uh-uh," Dobie cautioned, "don't touch the pants. Might have a frog in one of them pockets, and I ain't hankerin' to pick up no warts. Just leave 'em lay."

The Nueces Kid, Garrett thought, looked nothing like a man killer as he hauled his drawers up over skinny legs. He couldn't have been more than twenty years old, tops. Not hardly to the shaving stage yet. He was close to six foot tall, but wouldn't weigh a hundred forty soaking wet.

"How'd you get in here, son?" Garrett said. "I been downstairs a spell. Don't recall seein' you."

The Kid nodded toward the rear wall. "Came up the back stairs. Who told you I was here?"

"Just good law work, Kid," Garrett lied. He motioned toward the door. "Okay, you got your skinny hiney covered. Let's go."

The thin, pale face reddened. "Do we have to go through that crowd downstairs?" He winced at Garrett's nod. "Sure is gonna be embarrassin'." He fastened the last button and squared his bony shoulders. A faint flicker of defiance lit the gun-metal-colored eyes. "I got friends."

"Don't matter. I got a gun."

"Then I reckon you're holdin' the aces for now." The skinny shoulders drooped. "Never thought it'd come to this. Damn pore way to get caught by the law."

"Could've been worse, Kid," Garrett said. "At least you got the kinks pulled out of your rope first." He stepped aside and waved the Colt muzzle toward the door. "Let's go."

The babble of voices faded to a hush as Dobie prodded the Kid in the back with the muzzle of the six-gun to start him down the stairs.

"My God," somebody said in awe, "he's got the Nueces Kid!"

The startled surprise gave way to a few mutters. The sea of faces parted, giving the two men a wide berth as they passed through the crowd.

"Somebody tell Lucy I can't make it, and I'm sure 'nuff sorry about that," Garrett said. "Looks like I'm gonna be spendin' the night in the lockup watchin' this jasper."

"No need to waste your time," a big man in overalls said. "We could just get a rope—"

"Hush that talk up, feller," Garrett snapped. "Ain't nobody lynchin' *my* prisoner. I'll put a hole square in any man's head that tries it. Savvy?"

They did.

The walk to the jail seemed to Garrett to take forever. He could imagine how it felt to the Nueces Kid. The young gunman muttered a curse and hopped along on one foot until he could pull a goathead from the tender underside of a big toe.

Garrett didn't start to relax until he had fumbled the rusty lock clasp into place. He realized that he had started sobering up rapidly the last few minutes. He tucked the Colt back into his waistband and leaned against the wall across from the cell.

"They say you've killed a dozen men, Kid," Garrett said. "That right?"

"Countin' Mexicans?" He pronounced it "messkins," Dobie noted. At least the Kid talked right and proper Texan English. The young man shrugged. "Maybe. Never bothered to count." He lowered his narrow behind onto the hard metal-framed bunk and looked around. "Sure ain't much of a hotel you run here, Garrett," he said. "You know you ain't got a prayer of keepin' me in here, don't you? I busted out of better jails than this before."

"Maybe you have, maybe you ain't," Garrett said, "but you ain't bustin' out of this one. Try it, and I'll put so much lead in you it'll take a six-horse hitch just to drag the coffin. How come?"

"How come what?"

"How come you kill all them folks?"

The Kid shrugged. "They made me mad."

"Reckon that's as good a reason as any," Garrett said. "By the way, Kid, I got to know. So's my partner can do the paperwork—"

"Partner?" The kid interrupted. "Is Buck Hawkins in town, too?"

Garrett nodded. "Matter of fact, he is. We're a team, me and him."

"Well, I'll be damned. At least I got caught by the best. What was you gonna ask?"

"Your name. Your real moniker."

"Percival Aloysius Stephenfester the Third."

Garrett pursed his lips in a silent whistle. "No wonder you went wrong, boy. What'd you ever do to piss your ma off so much she'd hang a handle like that on you?"

The Nueces Kid shrugged. "Named me after a great uncle. Union colonel."

"War hero?"

"Nope. He got lost on his way to Gettysburg. Wound up in Canada. Didn't know till sixty-eight that the war was done. I gotta pee."

Dobie nodded toward the chamber pot. "Use that. You ain't gettin' outta that cell, son. Not till me and Buck decide what to do with you come mornin'." Garrett started to turn away, then paused. "How come you was in Necesario tonight?"

"Come to see my fiancée."

"And wound up in a whorehouse with a big-tittied blonde?"

"That was her. My fiancée."

"Oh," Garrett said. "No offense intended."

"None took."

"Mind tellin' me why she's workin' in a whorehouse?"

The Kid shrugged again. "She makes more money'n I do. Outlawin' don't pay for squat these days."

"Ain't it the truth," Garrett said with a sympathetic sigh. "Like to starved to death on the owlhoot trail myself a spell back. What you two gonna do? If you don't get hung, that is."

"We'd figgered on movin' out West. California, maybe. Startin' over where nobody don't know us."

Garrett nodded. "Well, good luck to you, Kid. Hope you all make out all right. Just one thing, though, less you get some fancy idea. I'll be spendin' the night on that cot out there, and I'm a light sleeper. Like a cat. Spook me and I come up shootin'. Savvy?"

"Savvy. Good night."

"Night, son." Garrett paused at the heavy door separating the cells from the marshal's office. "By the way— we'll get you some britches come mornin'." He cocked his head at a faint rap on the front door. "Now, what the hell?"

A young man stood at the front door, the brim of his hat twisted in sweaty hands.

"Stony Callahan, Mr. Garrett," the young man said. "We met over in the Palace?"

"Oh, yeah." Garrett glanced over the youth's shoulder, half expecting a torchlight mob to be forming on the street outside. The street seemed quiet. "What's up, son?"

"I just wondered if I could maybe get a good, close-up look at the Nueces Kid. Maybe get him to sign his name on something for me? And you, too, since you were the one who captured him."

Garrett shook his head. "Later, son. Right now, I'm plumb dog tired, and when I get tired I get out of sorts."

Callahan hung his head. "Yes, sir. Should I tell Mr. Hawkins where you are and what happened?"

"Naw, leave Buck be. He needs his rest, and I got a

handle on things here." Garrett almost closed the door, then stopped. "Tell you what, Stony—I'll pay you, say, ten bucks if you'll fetch some coffee and breakfast over here come first light."

Callahan bobbed his head. "Yes, sir. It'd be my pleasure, Mr. Garrett. First light."

Garrett closed the door and sauntered to the sagging cot. It could be a long night, he thought.

Buck Hawkins woke at the crack of dawn, and felt a bit sheepish about sleeping so late. Cowboy habits died hard. Back on the ranch he could have already had half a day's work done.

He yawned, stretched, scrubbed the sleep out of his eyes, and dressed. He tapped on the door connecting his room to Garrett's. There was no response. Not even Dobie's raucous snores. Whoever the tall brunette was, she must have been good to keep Garrett out all night, Hawkins thought.

He started at the loud, urgent bang on the door. He paused long enough to grab his revolver from its holster. "Who is it?"

"Stony Callahan, Mr. Hawkins! You got to come quick! There's trouble—"

Hawkins swung the door open. "What trouble?"

"The Nueces Kid—he broke out of jail just a minute ago—I went to take breakfast and—"

"Slow down, Stony. I don't have the foggiest notion what you're talking about."

"Last night at the Palace, Mr. Garrett arrested the Kid. This morning the Kid pulled a gun—"

"Dobie! Is he hurt?"

"No, sir. Just locked up in his cell. You got to come

quick! The Kid's saddling up now! He'll be gone in a few minutes!"

Hawkins grabbed the .44–40 Winchester from beside the door and sprinted down the stairs, Callahan a stride behind. Buck stepped into the pale gray of early dawn just as the thud of horse's hooves bore down on them.

"That's him!" Callahan shouted, a finger jabbed at a lean horseman racing past. "That's the Kid! He's getting away!"

Hawkins flinched as a yellow-orange flash bloomed less than thirty feet away. The *thwack* of lead slug against adobe sounded atop the pop of a small-caliber handgun.

"Stop!" Buck yelled.

Another slug sent splinters flying from the veranda pillar only inches from Buck's head. He dropped to one knee, worked the action to lever a round into the Winchester's chamber, shouldered the weapon as the fleeing horseman veered sharply around the bend in the street. Hawkins cursed and started to lower the rifle.

The weapon's brass butt stock thumped against Hawkins's ribs. Over the crack of the muzzle blast he heard the *spang* as his slug ricocheted from the blacksmith's anvil, then a *whack*, a strangled yelp from beyond the bend of the street, and then silence above the ringing in his ears.

"My God," Stony Callahan yelped at Hawkins's side, "I think you hit him!" The young man was in a dead run toward the angle of the street before Hawkins could stop him. Buck sprinted after him, yelled a warning—and almost bumped into Callahan as he rounded the corner of the last building at the bend.

A lean young man crouched on hands and knees at the

edge of the street, an arm pressed against his side. A sorrel horse bucked away toward the edge of town, saddle stirrups flapping.

"Jesus!" Callahan stood wide-eyed, staring at the man in the street. "You nailed him sure, Mr. Hawkins! I thought I heard the slug hit something!"

Hawkins racked a fresh round into the Winchester, his brain still not adding up all the pieces. He strode toward the man on all fours, stopped a dozen feet away, and stared in disbelief. Blood frothed on the young man's side and bubbled on his lips.

"Damnedest—shot I ever—" The Nueces Kid coughed once and toppled onto his side into the dust.

Hawkins approached the thin man warily, toed the little top-break .22 rimfire aside, and stood staring down at the body.

"Jesus, Mary and Joseph!" Callahan's face was ash-white, his eyes wide. "Right through the ribs! You nailed him through the lungs, Mr. Hawkins!"

Buck swallowed hard. He didn't have any spit in his mouth. "I—what?"

"He's deader'n a froze badger, Mr. Hawkins—"

Callahan's voice was drowned in a chorus of curious yells and the thump of approaching footsteps. Within seconds, half a dozen men had gathered around the body.

"I tell you, mister," Callahan said to a grizzled old-timer, "I never saw a shot like that in my life! He—Mr. Hawkins—shot *around the corner* and nailed the Nueces Kid square!"

Hawkins's fingers trembled against the Winchester receiver. "I didn't—it was—acci—"

"Aw, come on, Stony," one of the growing crowd said in disgust. "It ain't possible to shoot around no corner!"

"Is, too!" Callahan sounded indignant. "I seen it! We were standing over there—" he pointed toward the veranda of the Santa Fe—"and the Kid was shooting at us, and Mr. Hawkins fired one shot, and it hit the blacksmith's anvil and bounced around the corner, and hit the Kid!"

The mutters and headshakes of disbelief grew until the skeptics strode away, checked the blacksmith's anvil, studied the angles, and came back to the group gathered around the body.

"Stony was tellin' it straight, boys," the old man said. "Happened just that way." He extended a hand to Hawkins, a glint of respect in his eyes. "Hawkins, that was some of the damnedest shooting I ever saw. How'd you figure it? Shooting around a corner, I mean."

Hawkins stammered, "I—never—it was—"

"Instinct, that's what it was," Callahan interrrupted, his words tumbling together in excitement. "And Mr. Hawkins didn't even have the rifle on his shoulder. Just pointed it from the waist and pulled the trigger."

A hand thumped against Hawkins's shoulder. "By God, I reckon everything we've heard about you boys is true. Man, this is gonna be some yarn to tell my grandkids."

The older man turned away. "Ed, you and a couple of the boys haul the Kid over to the undertaker. He'll be getting ripe mighty quick when it starts heatin' up."

Hawkins stood, still stunned at the absurd twist in events, as three burly men carried the body away. The back of his throat felt bitter. He was glad he hadn't had breakfast yet. The way his gut was churning and roiling, he might not have been able to keep it down.

Callahan tugged at Buck's sleeve. "Mr. Hawkins, we

should get over to the jail. I expect Mr. Garrett would like to get out of that cell now."

They found Garrett slumped on the bunk, mouthing a string of oaths that would have made a teamster proud. "'Bout damn time somebody showed up," Dobie said. "Heard shootin'. What happened out there?"

"The Kid's dead," Callahan blurted. "Mr. Hawkins shot him."

Garrett's eyebrows went up. "Buck? He actually managed to *hit* somebody?"

"Sure did, Mr. Garrett, and you won't believe how it happened," Callahan said. Hawkins sighed in resignation and waited patiently as the young man went through the whole incident again in detail.

Garrett finally nodded. "Reckon I got a idea what really happened. Kind of a shame, though. I took a likin' to that kid. You boys gonna let me out now? Kind of embarrassin', a marshal locked up in his own jail."

Hawkins finally located the key. "What happened, Dobie?" he said as the cell door creaked open on rusty hinges.

"Kid got the drop on me. Somebody snuck him a little gun. Dropped it through that there window, most likely." Garrett sighed in relief as he stepped from the cell. "He stuck that little peashooter damn near up my nose."

"It's a wonder he didn't kill you," Hawkins said.

"Reckon he took a shine to me some, too. Even said his sorries for bustin' out of my jail and left my six-gun on the desk. Said it warn't right to take a man's favorite gun."

Garrett retrieved his Colt and stuck it in his waistband. "So what we do now, partner?"

"I'm not sure," Hawkins said. He still felt strange. Detached from his own body, sort of. Like a man who had been standing and watching the whole thing instead of being part of it. "I suppose there will be some paperwork to fill out—"

The front door swung open. "Fess McLocklin wants to see you boys," a man said. "Right away."

The boss of the Texas and New Mexico Cattleman's Association sat behind his desk, a thin smile on his weathered face as Hawkins and Garrett filed into the small office.

"I have to hand it to you, gentlemen," McLocklin said. "Not on the job a full day, and you bring down one of the most dangerous men in nine states. Good work." He lifted a brow at Hawkins. "Shot him around the corner, did you?"

"Well, it sort of worked out that way." Hawkins's shoulders slumped. "Actually, Mr. McLocklin, it was an accident. I saw him go around the corner, started to lower the rifle, and it went off."

McLocklin peered at the two men over steepled fingertips for a moment, then nodded. "Don't admit that in public, Hawkins. A yarn like that—a dead shot who can nail a man by shooting around a corner—will put the fear of God into the rougher elements in and around Necesario. Besides, when the newspapers get wind of it, you can deny it until the world turns purple and nobody will believe you. Let it ride the way the rumors will have it. You've just added another chapter to the hard-eyed, fast-shooting gunhawk legend. I could halfway believe it myself."

Hawkins's face flushed, but he made no comment.

McLocklin rummaged in his desk, brought out a stack of papers, and thumbed through them. "Here it is," he said as he unfolded a flyer. "Reward notice on the Nue-ces Kid. Looks like you boys have made yourselves a

thousand dollars already. I'll file the reports and paperwork. There'll be an inquest, as a matter of record; we're
not completely without law here in Necesario. Now, pull
up a chair and tell me what happened. I'll fancy it up
some in the retelling . . ."

5

BUCK HAWKINS GLANCED at Dobie Garrett and frowned in aggravation.

Even out here in the middle of nowhere, there was no peace and quiet.

Garrett saw to that.

Dobie had spent the last fifteen miles laboriously reading aloud the latest in a string of wildly exaggerated newspaper stories, stumbling over most of the words on the wind-fluttered paper in his hand. Hawkins could already recite it by rote. He had read it to Garrett at least a dozen times. Which, Buck thought, probably accounted for the speed with which Garrett raced through the reading. At about twenty words a mile.

Hawkins had decided on the range patrol for no other reason than to get the hell out of Necesario. Three days of drink buyers and backslappers and handshakers had sapped Buck's limited reserves of patience.

It hadn't bothered Dobie. Garrett thrived on attention. Buck had started worrying anew that Dobie was actually beginning to *believe* that the two of them were heroes.

The news of the capture and subsequent killing of the Nueces Kid had swept the country like a dried grass fire in a high wind. The *Santa Fe New Mexican* had started the whole thing with a big, black headline a good two inches high:

FEARED GUNMAN SURRENDERS MEEKLY TO FEARLESS GARRETT

A smaller, but still big, headline embellished the story:

Nueces Kid Slain Attempting Escape; Unbelievable Rifle Shot in Necesario

And in even smaller but still impressive type:

Crack Shot Buck Hawkins Fires AROUND CORNER to Kill Kid

When the headline writers finally ran out of big type and let the story run, the article was as flowery and inaccurate as the stuff above it.

The story didn't mention that Garrett had wandered into the wrong room of a whorehouse because the top tack that held a 6 upright had come loose and the number turned upside down and become a 9. It didn't mention that Garrett already had his revolver in his hand, trying to unbutton his britches, when he walked in on the Kid and the woman. It didn't mention that Garrett didn't know the Nueces Kid from a hole in the ground.

It did wax poetic about how steely-eyed, fearless Special Marshal Dobie Garrett had tracked the Kid to the Palace; how the dangerously deadly Kid, facing only a cold glare from the famed gunman, surrendered meekly rather than chance a fast draw shoot-out with the marshal.

The article didn't mention that Buck Hawkins, the keen-eyed, deadly rifle shot, accidentally fired the slug that whanged around half of Necesario before happening to catch up with the unfortunate Kid instead of nailing some innocent bystander. It didn't say a word about blind luck.

It embroidered in florid phrases the sharpshooting marshal's deliberate calculations and careful aim that sent a rifle bullet pinging from a blacksmith's anvil to solidly strike a man riding a fast horse in a dead run out of the line of sight of the man behind the Winchester—

"Buck?"

Hawkins sighed. "What now, Dobie?"

Garrett peered at the newspaper clipping rustling in the wind. "What's this here word? Rico-what?"

"Ricochet, Dobie. Like I've told you a dozen times already, it means to bounce off something."

"Oh, yeah. Now I recollect." Garrett folded the paper, tucked it back in his pocket, and grinned. "Sure do like seein' my name in the paper like that." He shifted his chew and spat; the bay ducked in time. The glob sailed well to the right of Duckbutt's tobacco-stained ears. "That there story says we're the fastest guns, best shots, and the finest lawmen ever pinned on a badge," Garrett said. "Even tells again how we single-handed shot up the Barker Gang—"

"Dobie," Hawkins interrupted, "I know what it says. Now, how about just dropping the whole topic? We're supposed to be out on scout, you know. Not riding along admiring our shadows and our undeserved reputations as slayers of dragons and defenders of the poor and downtrodden."

"Ain't that what we're good at?"

"It's what we're lucky at, dammit, that's all!"

Garrett lifted an eyebrow. "No need gettin' testy, partner. 'Sides, things is workin' out just fine. Where we at, anyway?"

Hawkins's gaze scanned the landscape. The gently

rolling, grassy plains around Necesario had given way to a rocky stretch of broken hills pierced by shallow canyons and arroyos dotted with Spanish dagger, cactus, shrub brush, and spotted bunchgrass. Buck figured their ride to the west had brought them well across the border into New Mexico.

"Four or five miles north of the J-Bar range, I'd say."

"Mighty empty country." Garrett snorted dust from his nostrils. "Ain't much for livestock, either. Way this bunchgrass is scattered out, a cow'd have to graze at a lope just to get her belly full in a day's time—"

Hawkins reined his palomino up short.

"What is it, partner?"

Buck stood in the stirrups, staring toward the northwest. "Dust cloud up over the next ridge. I could have sworn I heard a cow bawl a few seconds ago."

Garrett cocked his head, listened, and then nodded. "Sure 'nuff did. Heard it myself. Roundup, you reckon?"

"Could be." Hawkins settled back into his saddle seat. "Not enough dust for a big herd, though. Cowboys gathering strays, most likely. Guess we'd better go have a look. Could be they need some help."

Garrett spat out his used-up chew and reached for his plug. "Might's well. Kinda miss chousin' cows, much as I hate to admit it. Reckon they're as wild as them up on the Canadian?"

"It wouldn't surprise me." Hawkins kneed Buttermilk into an easy trot toward the dust cloud.

The two men reined in for a moment atop the ridge. In the floor of the shallow canyon below, two men struggled to keep a small herd bunched up. It wasn't an easy chore. The cattle, mostly thin and rangy with a Mexican-bred look, had a lot of wild in them. Turn one back, and another tried to break out of the herd.

"Yep," Garrett said, "them boys got their hands full, sure 'nuff. Let's lend 'em a hand."

Hawkins and Garrett kneed their mounts into a lope. They had come within a hundred yards of the herd before one of the cowboys spotted them and raised a yell; at the same time, a roan steer took advantage of the distraction to break back toward the south.

Hawkins spurred the palomino into a run and headed the roan steer. The animal had a J-Bar brand on its left hip. The roan ducked back into the herd. Hawkins reined in as Garrett swung around to the west and turned back a couple of wild-eyed cows.

The herd, sensing that they were outnumbered now, quieted.

Hawkins noticed for the first time that the two riders seemed to have forgotten the cattle. They exchanged quick glances, hands near the six-guns on their hips. Buck let his gaze drift over the herd. There were about sixty head in the bunch. The animals all seemed to wear the J-Bar brand.

"Afternoon, boys," Hawkins said with a nod of greeting. "This J-Bar stock seems to be a bit wild."

The younger of the two riders, a gangly boy barely in his teens, stared wide-eyed at Hawkins. The other horseman was older, thicker in the chest and shoulders. The older one kept his hand on the butt of his revolver, his eyes narrowed in suspicion. Hawkins didn't blame him. For all the J-Bar men knew, he and Garrett could be rustlers out for easy pickings. The man's knuckles were white from his grip on the revolver.

"No need to get edgy, mister," Hawkins said. "Be a shame to see someone get hurt. We'll help you ease this bunch back to J-Bar range."

"Who . . . are you?" the thin youngster said. His Adam's apple bobbed when he talked.

"I'm Buck Hawkins. Fellow on the bay over there is Dobie Garrett."

"Oh, Jesus . . ." The youngster's eyes went even wilder; his face seemed to pale beneath the layer of dust.

The older man yanked his hand away from his revolver. He lifted both hands to shoulder height. "Don't shoot, Hawkins," he said, his voice shaky. "I ain't gettin' in no drawin' contest with the likes of you. We won't give you no trouble."

Hawkins frowned, confused. "Shoot? Trouble? Mister, I don't have the foggiest idea what you're talking about. There won't be any trouble unless you start it."

The two cowboys exchanged nervous glances. "Look, Hawkins," the broad-shouldered one said, "we know who you two are. We sure didn't plan on meetin' up with no gunhawks out here. You want them cattle, just take 'em and leave us be."

"Take them?" Hawkins was more befuddled than before. "Why would we want to do that?"

"I . . . We . . . just thought . . ." The older rider's voice trailed away. "You don't know us?"

Hawkins shook his head. "Can't say that I do. You ride for the J-Bar, don't you?"

The young man's Adam's apple bobbed furiously. "Yes, sir. I reckon you could say that." His words came fast, one tumbling almost atop the other. He cast a quick glance at his saddle partner, as if to send an unspoken message. "And I reckon we'd appreciate some help. Soon's we drift this stock back to J-Bar land, we'll be on our way. Got a lot of ground to cover yet. Ain't that right, George?"

George nodded; the tension seemed to ease a bit from

the broad shoulders. "That's right, Hank. Lot of ground to cover." He grinned at Hawkins. The smile seemed forced, Buck thought. "Sorry, Hawkins. About nearly throwin' down on you a minute ago. Didn't know who you was."

Hawkins relaxed. "Glad we got that straightened out, boys. Now, if you two'll take the flank, Dobie and I'll push the drags. You know the way back to the J-Bar." He motioned to Garrett, who still sat the saddle forty yards away, on the west side of the herd. Garrett kneed the bay a couple of strides, cutting off a brindle cow's attempt to bolt, then waved back.

George and Hank moved out to the point, frequently turning in the saddle to look over their shoulders. They seemed to be talking quietly.

The herd gradually took shape, strung out a bit, and began to move. Garrett reined Duckbutt alongside Hawkins's palomino.

"What's got ants in them boys' britches, you reckon?" Dobie asked.

"I'd guess our reputation as hard-eyed man-shooters," Hawkins said, a touch of disgust in his tone. "Sure is hard to be friendly when everybody we meet thinks we're about to put bullet holes in them."

Garrett shifted his chew, spat, and nailed the bay squarely on the left ear. Duckbutt snorted, shook his head, and stamped his front foot. "Reckon havin' a rep has got a downside, at that," he said. "Way them boys acted, you'd've thought we was about to hang 'em or somethin'."

The cattle moved along at a steady walk and showed no sign of bolting. Hawkins wasn't surprised. Most times, cattle calmed down when they were headed for home range.

The canyon floor narrowed and deepened, dotted now and then by wind-twisted cottonwood trees, as the herd slogged along. They had covered a couple of miles before the canyon made a sharp bend to the west; for a moment, the lead animals and flank riders were out of sight. Hawkins heard a startled squawk and a faint cry of dismay from up ahead.

"Now, what the hell," Garrett muttered.

It wasn't long before they found out.

Hawkins pulled Buttermilk to an abrupt stop as they rounded the bend. Four horsemen, rifles drawn, sat in their saddles, two on each side of the canyon. The skinny youngster and his older companion slumped in the saddle, hands again raised.

One of the riflemen was Ed Joyner.

"What's going on here, Ed?" Garrett said as the J-Bar owner kneed his horse alongside.

"Good work, boys," Joyner said, his jaw set in anger. "We've been tracking these two since early morning."

"What two?"

"The Miller brothers. George and his little brother, Hank. The slickest rustlers who ever raided J-Bar herds."

Hawkins swallowed hard. "Rustlers?"

Joyner's dark eyes glittered. "I hadn't expected to take them without a fight, and those two are waspy with short guns. But then, I didn't know you two were on their trail." Joyner sheathed his rifle, flipped the tiedown thong from his lariat rope, and shook out a loop. "By God, these two've stolen their last cattle. There's a good hanging tree about a mile ahead."

Two of Joyner's men disarmed the Miller brothers. The rustlers sat with heads down, their hands bound to saddle horns by rawhide thongs.

Hawkins's gaze flicked back and forth from the forlorn Miller brothers to Joyner; he realized with a jolt what had happened. He and Garrett had ridden up on the rustled stock and assumed the riders were J-Bar hands. A chill fingered its way up his spine. They had faced two dangerous gunhands without the foggiest idea what was going on. Hawkins glanced at Garrett. Even Dobie's face seemed to have paled a touch.

Buck swallowed again. He wasn't sure he had enough spit to speak.

Joyner studied the cattle milling about on the canyon floor for a moment, then nodded in satisfaction. "Looks like you got every head of our stock back, too. The association's getting its money's worth out of you two. Short drop from a tall limb'll cut down on the stock losses around here."

The cold spot between Hawkins's shoulder blades grew. He had seen a man hanged by vigilantes once. It wasn't a pretty sight. His gaze was drawn to the younger Miller. Tears trickled openly down the boy's cheeks and a stain spread at his crotch. The kid had wet himself. Hawkins was about to do the same. His bladder was yelping mighty loud.

Garrett turned his head and spat. "I reckon not, Ed."

Joyner's gaze snapped to Garrett. "What did you say?"

"I said I reckon not. We can't let you hang these boys. Why, they ain't much more'n puppies."

Anger flared in the J-Bar owner's eyes. "They're rustlers, dammit! You caught them cold with J-Bar cattle—"

"And every man deserves his day in court," Hawkins said, and immediately wished he had kept his mouth shut. He was going to help Garrett talk them into an early grave for sure, he thought.

"Rustlers? Court? What the hell are you talking about, Hawkins?" The cold threat was clear in Joyner's hard tone.

"Mr. Joyner, we hired on with the association to stop the rustling around here," Hawkins said, wondering if his voice quavered the way his gut did. "We didn't take the job to stand by and see people lynched."

"And you're going to stop us?"

Garrett turned his head and spat. "If need be. You and your boys want to fuss on it, let's get her on."

Indecision flickered in Joyner's dark face. "You think the two of you can take four of us?"

"Maybe," Garrett said, his words calm. "Maybe not. But study on it a bit, Ed. We done caught your rustlers. You got your stock back. Never cottoned to bein' part of no lynch party. And even if you did throw down on us, and lived through it, Fess McLocklin wouldn't be just real tickled was your boys to put a couple slugs in the association's hired guns."

Hawkins's gut clamped tighter. If Joyner called Dobie's bluff, they were both dead men. "Dobie's right, Mr. Joyner," he said. "These boys didn't resist arrest. And if you take them from official custody at gunpoint and hang them"—he paused to work up enough spit to speak—"we'll have to take you in. For murder. Listen to reason, man. It's in your own best interest and the association's. If these boys are going to hang, let the law do it. Properly and after a fair trial."

For a moment, Hawkins was sure he was looking at sure death. Joyner was about a heartbeat away from killing all four of them, then and there.

"'Sides that," Garrett said, "we ain't had a chance to question these boys yet. Not official-like."

An eternity seemed to pass before Joyner's face softened into what might have been a wry grin. "Damned if you two haven't got more *cojones* than a prime Mexican stud." He shrugged. "All right, you win. Take them in."

Hawkins breathed a sincere sigh of relief. "I'm glad you see it our way, Mr. Joyner."

Joyner turned to the three riders. "Put the rifles up, boys. Lead those two rustlers over here. It's over. Let's get this stock back on J-Bar range. We have work to do." He reluctantly retied his rope to his saddle horn and stared at Garrett and Hawkins for a moment. "Hell," he finally said, "even if you wouldn't let us hang them, you still did a good job in catching them. Next time, though, if I were you, I'd disarm any dangerous men before trying to take them in. Stunt like that could get you killed."

"We'll keep that in mind, Mr. Joyner," Hawkins said.

Joyner started to rein his horse about, then paused. "When you question those boys, make it a point to ask if they're working for Clell Reynolds."

"Who's Reynolds? Mr. McLocklin didn't mention a Reynolds as one of the association members."

"He's not. Reynolds owns the Rocking R northwest of here." Joyner leaned over and spat. "He'd like nothing better than to run me out of business and take over the J-Bar. Some of the stock we've lost has been drifted onto Reynolds's outfit. If the Millers are on the Rocking R payroll, you better arrest Reynolds damn quick. Before I get to the troublemaking son."

Hawkins and Garrett exchanged confused glances. "We'll check into it, Mr. Joyner," Hawkins said.

"Do that." Joyner glowered at the captives, then

turned back to Hawkins. "Looks like you two are building yourselves up quite a nest egg in a short time."

"How come?" Garrett said.

"There's a three hundred dollar reward on the young
Miller. Five hundred on his brother. Between them,
they've killed four men. I'd keep a close eye on them on
the way back if I were you, gentlemen."

Hawkins took the lead rope of the elder Miller's horse
from a surly J-Bar rider. "We'll let you know when the
trial's set, Mr. Joyner. We'll need your testimony."

"Fair enough," Joyner said, almost amiably. "See you
boys back in town."

Hawkins and Garrett sat and watched as the J-Bar
boss and his crew pushed the cattle back toward their
home range. Then Buck turned to Dobie.

"I don't think you realize just how close we came to
getting killed here today. Twice," Hawkins said.

Garrett shrugged. "If you was somebody who knowed
about us, would you pull iron on the fastest guns in the
country?"

Hawkins sighed. "No. No, I guess I wouldn't." He
didn't bother to point out to Garrett that they'd stumbled
into another stretch of good luck like a blind sow finding
an acorn. "I'll lead, Dobie. You bring up the rear. Like
Joyner said, keep an eye on these two."

"Won't be no trouble. Will there, boys?" Garrett said
to the Millers.

The elder brother shook his head. "No, sir. Not a bit.
Never thought the day'd come that I'd be happy to see a
jail cell." He fell silent for a moment, then added, "Much
obliged, Marshal Garrett—Marshal Hawkins. You saved
our necks today for sure. It won't be forgot."

Garrett said solemnly, "Son, you ain't out of the

woods yet. You got to stand trial for cow stealin' and murder. You boys really kill all them men?"

"No, sir, we didn't, and that's the God's truth," the young Miller said, his voice still quavering. "We never dropped a hammer on nobody. Them killin's was done by association—"

"Shut up, Hank!" George Miller barked. "You say one word and we're dead men for sure!"

"What about the association?"

Hank's Adams apple bobbed, but he wouldn't speak. He just shook his head.

Hawkins said, "Hank, anything you can tell us, we'll appreciate. You're going to need all the help you can get. You might want to think it over on the way to Necesario. For now, we'd better make tracks before Joyner changes his mind."

How in the blue blazes did they know? Hawkins wondered as he led the prisoners down Necesario's main street.

The crowds were three deep in places. Hawkins picked up bits and phrases of conversation as they passed the throngs:

"By God, they done it—that's the Miller boys . . ."

"Didn't think nobody'd ever take them two alive . . ."

"Ought to have a necktie party for them Millers . . ."

Hawkins sensed a surliness beneath the outwardly excited murmur of the crowd. The knot in his gut tied itself tighter. He couldn't relax much even after the Miller brothers were behind the rusty bars of the Necesario jail and a pot of coffee boiled on the cast iron stove in the marshal's office.

Garrett had decided he needed something a little better than coffee to cut the trail dust. He had lit a shuck for

the Palace saloon a few seconds after the key turned in
the cell lock.

Hawkins realized just how twitchy he was when he
jumped half out of the chair at the unexpected tap on the
door. He drew a deep breath to calm his nerves and
opened the door a crack.

A young man stood outside, a gray bowler hat in
hand, the wind rippling fine, wavy blond hair. The
youth's pale face was red from sun and wind. Dust
dimmed the glossy shine on black storebought shoes and
had filtered into the creases of the man's clothing. Despite the heat, he wore a gray three-piece wool suit with
a red cravat neatly tucked into his vest.

"Yes?"

"Marshal Hawkins? Buck Hawkins?"

Hawkins nodded cautiously, his hand near the grips of
the Bisley Colt at his waist. "What can I do for you?"

"My name is Archie Wescott, with the publishing firm
of Haskell and Grant, New York. May I have a word
with you?"

Wescott looked harmless enough, Hawkins decided.
He didn't appear to be carrying a weapon. The young
man's pale blue eyes were as big as a hound pup's. Buck
swung the door open. "Come in, Mr. Wescott."

"Thank you, sir. My friends call me Archie."

The young man stopped dead in his tracks a stride inside the door. He stared at the two men slouched despon-
dently on the jail cell cots beyond the open door. "Is
that—are those men—the Miller brothers? The notorious
rustlers and killers?"

Hawkins nodded. "That's the Millers. I don't know
about the notorious part, or the killer part. They seem to
be just a couple of scared kids at the moment. You know
about them?"

"Yes, sir," Wescott said with a touch of awe. "I heard the whole story over at the stage station." Wescott's words tumbled out so fast that Hawkins had trouble following him. "About how you and Marshal Garrett surprised them with a herd of a hundred or more stolen cattle, and how they started to pull their guns and fight, but just gave up when they knew it was you and—"

Hawkins lifted a hand. "Whoa up a minute, Mr. Wescott—"

"Archie, please."

"Archie. It didn't happen exactly that way." He strode to the heavy oak door separating the office from the cell space, pulled it shut, and turned to Wescott. "Have a seat."

"If you don't mind sir, I'd like to stand for a few moments." Wescott rubbed his rump. "I just arrived in town an hour ago. The stagecoach seats aren't exactly well padded out here in the West."

Hawkins nodded toward the stove. The heat was already beginning to build in the small room. "Coffee will be ready in a minute."

"No, thank you, sir. I'm a tea drinker myself. I don't suppose you might have a nice mint pekoe?"

"Sorry. We don't get many requests for tea here in our little two-room hotel." Hawkins half smiled. "You might be able to get a cup at the Santa Fe Hotel down the street, or maybe at the Palace. They're pretty civilized for a town like this." Buck took his seat behind the desk and studied the young man for a moment. "Mind if I ask what brings you from New York out here to the middle of nowhere?"

"You do, Marshal Hawkins. You and Marshal Garrett."

Hawkins lifted an eyebrow. "Why?"

Wescott's blue eyes glimmered in excitement. "I've been sent here on special assignment. To write a book. About you and Dobie Garrett."

Hawkins's jaw dropped. "A what?"

"A book, Marshal Hawkins. A novel. Are you familiar with our *Heroes of the West* line of books?"

"Your what?"

"True-life chronicles of the escapades of the fearless, competent men struggling against all odds to bring law and order and justice to the wild frontier." Wescott's voice rose in pitch as his excitement grew. "You and Marshal Garrett are naturals for the series, sir. Genuine heroes."

"Heroes?"

"Most definitely. Protectors of the honest settlers of the raw land. An inspiration for all the readers of the world. Your story will be read in homes and schools throughout the United States and abroad—"

"*Our* stories?"

"Yes, sir. Chronicles of your exciting adventures in bringing law and order to the West, your prowess with weapons, your absolutely fearless nature regardless of the odds—"

"Archie," Hawkins interrupted, "are you sure you have the right people in mind? That doesn't sound like Dobie and me."

Wescott smiled and nodded. He pulled a pen and notepad from his coat pocket. "Modesty. A most refreshing trait in a fabled gunman, Marshal Hawkins."

"Fabled gunman?" Buck shook his head in disbelief. "No doubt about it, son. You definitely got off the stage in the wrong town."

The young man ignored Hawkins's protest. "We'll start the book with your dramatic and violent gunfight with the Barker gang—no, even before that. With your life story. Both of you. Profiles of the fastest guns and deadliest shots in the West, and how you came to be such."

Hawkins snorted in disbelief. "Son, somebody's been pulling your leg. Fast guns. Deadly shots." He shook his head. "Hate to disappoint you, Archie, but our life stories won't make two paragraphs, let alone a book. We're just two common, ordinary cowboys."

"That's not what the newspapers say."

"Forget it, son." Hawkins sighed. "Catch the next stage back to New York."

Wescott shuffled his feet nervously. "I—can't do that, sir. We've already had advance orders for the book. Dozens of orders. Maybe thousands by now." The young, sunburned face took on a bit of a hangdog look. "Please, Marshal Hawkins. I have a stake in this, too. This is my big chance. This book will establish me as one of the top writers in the publishing business."

Hawkins leaned back in his chair and peered at the young greenhorn for a few moments. The kid seemed likeable enough, he thought. Dumb as a stump where gunmen were concerned, maybe, but likeable. What the hell, he decided; it couldn't hurt, as long as Wescott didn't get in the way. Nobody would read the book anyway.

"Okay, Archie. But you'll have to get most of your information from Marshal Garrett. I'd as soon not discuss it myself."

Wescott smiled, flashing a full set of white teeth. "The reluctant gunman. That might make an excellent title for the book." He scribbled for a moment on his notepad. "Now, could you tell me something about your earlier

days, Marshal? I understand you were a working cowboy before—"

Hawkins lifted a hand. "Archie, excuse me a minute.
There's something I have to do."

"I'll go with you," Wescott said eagerly. "I'm supposed to stick with you all the time, learn more about
you, how you work, how you live, the details of a gunman's everyday life. Small things, but highly important
in the context of the novel."

Hawkins had to grin. "You won't find much glamour
and excitement this time. I'm going to the outhouse."

Wescott's face flushed beet-red. "Oh."

"I'll be back in a minute, Archie." Hawkins couldn't
resist ragging the greenhorn a little. "It doesn't take us
fast guns long to tend to business."

The young writer was still standing when Hawkins returned.

"Now, Marshal," Wescott said, "we were about to ex-
plore your early years. Tell me where you were born, all
about your folks, the kind of childhood you had."

Hawkins shook his head. "Archie, I have work to do.
Why don't you interview Dobie first? You'll find him at
the Palace Saloon, a couple of blocks west of here.
Dobie, I expect, will be more than happy to tell you anything you want to know." Most of which, he thought but
didn't add, would be a windy of the first order. "When
you find him, ask him to come over here and watch the
prisoners while you talk. My horse seemed to be favoring a front leg when we rode in. I'd like to check on
him."

Wescott scribbled again. "A true Westerner. A man
who sees to his horse's needs before his own. I like that,
Marshal Hawkins. And I can guarantee you that my
readers will, also." He tucked the notepad and pencil

back in his pocket. "I'll ask Mr. Garrett to relieve you here, Marshal. And thank you for your cooperation. I truly believe we are beginning a mutually profitable relationship. It is our firm's policy that the subjects of our books—or their descendants or survivors, if any—receive a share of the net profits of book sales."

Hawkins watched as the young writer left in search of Garrett, then sighed. The world just kept getting stranger and stranger, Buck thought. He rose, filled three chipped china mugs from the coffeepot, and carried the two extra cups to the Miller boys. The Necesario jail might not be the nation's finest accommodations, he mused, but at least it could be halfway sociable. And he wanted to talk to the Millers.

He hadn't been able to shake the uneasy feeling since the younger Miller had hinted that there might be more to the cattleman's association than met the eye.

6

BUCK HAWKINS TRIED to blink the sweat from his eyes as he ran his hands over and down the palomino's right foreleg.

He felt nothing out of the ordinary in the tendons and muscles. The gelding's shoes showed wear, but he had found no problem with the fit, no stones in the tender frog of the hoof.

Hawkins straightened, wiped the back of a hand across his forehead, and patted the palomino on the shoulder.

"Find anything, Mr. Buck?"

Genuine concern showed in the one good eye of the young man holding the palomino's halter. The youth's left eye was clouded and turned outward, pulled out of line by the sunken hollow where his cheekbone had been until his father had belted him with the club. Spittle drooled from the boy's slack lips onto the front of his soiled, threadbare shirt.

"I can't find a thing wrong, Trace," Hawkins said. "Maybe I just imagined Buttermilk was favoring that leg on the way back."

"Can I take a look?"

Hawkins nodded. The child in the man's body had little going his way except his love of animals and capacity for hard, dirty work. The body had continued to bulk up and flesh out until Trace carried a solid 190 pounds on a five-foot-ten frame. But his mind would never grow. He would never be more than twelve years old above the shoulders.

"Lead him around for me, Mr. Buck."

Hawkins led the palomino in a wide circle at a walk, then at a trot, as the stable swamper studied the horse's movements.

"You was right, Mr. Buck. He's limpin' some," Willis said as Buck brought Buttermilk back. Willis ran a gentle hand down Buttermilk's foreleg. His thick fingers, soiled with stall dirt, probed the palomino's fetlock.

"Here it is." Willis lifted Buttermilk's hoof. "Poor feller's got a thorn." The look in the boy's good brownish-hazel eye softened in sympathy. "Bet that hurts somethin' awful."

Hawkins stepped to Willis's side and studied the fetlock. The thorn was almost invisible, a slight swelling just above the hoofline. Buck glanced up at Willis.

"Good work, Trace. I'd never have noticed that." He flipped out his pocket knife. "Watch him. He may jump or try to paw when I start to dig that thorn out, and I don't want to see you get hurt."

"Don't you worry none about me, Mr. Buck. Buttermilk won't hurt nobody. He's a good horse. He likes me." He turned the injured foreleg over to Hawkins and took his place at the palomino's halter. "Don't hurt him more'n you got to, Mr. Buck."

"I won't, Trace. I promise."

Buttermilk never flinched.

A few seconds later, Buck had the offending thorn in his hand. A single drop of bright red blood marked the small wound above the hoofline. Hawkins sighed in relief. No pus had drained from the tiny cut; there was no sign of infection. He held out his hand to show Willis the thorn.

"It's a strange thing, Trace," Hawkins said, "that a tiny little sticker like this could cripple a thousand-pound horse."

Willis rubbed his undamaged cheek against Buttermilk's neck. "Horses is special. I reckon God knowed what he was doin' when he made horses. They're nice. Not like some folks."

"You've got that right, Trace," Hawkins said. He reached in his pocket and handed the young man a silver dollar.

"You don't owe me nothin', Mr. Buck. Mr. Halliday pays me good, a whole five dollars a week. I'm just happy Buttermilk won't be hurtin' now."

"Take the money, son. Buttermilk would give you a dollar for finding that thorn if horses had money."

Willis swiped a hand across the dampness at the corner of his mouth, then nodded. "Okay, Mr. Buck. I'll give him a special rubdown and a good feed, soon's I finish cleanin' out them last two stalls . . ." His voice trailed away.

Hawkins followed Willis's gaze. Lucy Ledbetter, the Palace's most popular prostitute, strode along the street past the stable, her face shaded by her yellow parasol. She caught the two men's gaze and waved a greeting with her free hand.

"Hi, Trace," she called brightly, "how are you? It's good to see you! You, too, Marshal Hawkins! I'd stop to talk, but I've some shopping to do before work." She waggled her fingers in a fluttery good-bye gesture.

Buck waved back and glanced at Willis. Pure adoration showed in Trace's good eye.

"She sure is pretty." Willis's voice had gone soft. "And Miss Lucy, she . . . she always says nice things to me. Not like some of the other folks in town. I get this funny feelin' ever' time she comes along."

"So do most men, Trace," Hawkins said.

"People say bad things about Miss Lucy." A touch of hurt, or perhaps anger, tinged Willis's words. "They say she . . . she does things . . . with men . . ." His voice trailed away.

Hawkins put a hand on Willis's shoulder. "What people say isn't important, son. People can be mean and spiteful about folks they don't understand. It's what's in a person's heart, man or woman, that really matters. I think Miss Lucy's a nice lady."

Willis's hazel-brown eye seemed to mist. "Sometimes I wish I was a man growed, so's I could talk better with Miss Lucy. I know I ain't like—like the others."

Hawkins's throat tightened up. He knew the misery some people dealt to the brain-damaged stable hand— the teasing, the mocking, some of it playful, some just downright vicious. He put a reassuring hand on the youth's solid shoulder.

"No two people are alike, Trace. And you're special. I've never known anyone who's a harder worker, or a better hand with horses, than you are. I'm glad to call you my friend."

Some of the hurt faded from the brownish eye. "Am I really your friend, Mr. Buck?"

"One of the best. And if you ever need help, you know you can come to me." Hawkins glanced at the lowering sun. "I hate to leave, Trace, but I have work to do. I'll see you later, okay?"

"Yes, sir. I got work to do, too." The young man patted the palomino on the neck. "I'll take good care of him for you, Mr. Buck."

"I know you will, son. Buttermilk's never been in better hands."

Hawkins watched as Trace Willis led the palomino toward the barn and the row of box stalls inside. He hadn't lied to the kid. Trace Willis *was* a friend. Buck still got mad every time he thought of what Trace's old man had done to a basically kind and gentle boy. If Trace's father was still alive, Hawkins thought, he could happily pound the bastard into a bloody mush.

He pushed the thought aside. A man couldn't put spilled milk back in the bucket.

He strode toward the Santa Fe, intent on a hot bath, a shave, and—with any luck at all—a night of peace and quiet. Garrett could watch the Miller boys and talk to the young writer at the same time. At least it would keep Dobie out of the saloons, and hopefully out of trouble, for one night.

Hawkins pushed through the door of the Santa Fe Hotel and started for the stairs. The balding, bespectacled clerk behind the registration counter called his name.

"Stage brought some mail for you, Marshal," the clerk said. "I sent the official stuff over to the office." He handed Hawkins a stack of envelopes. "This seemed to be personal, so I kept it here."

Hawkins took the envelopes with a muttered thanks, leaned against the counter, and thumbed through the stack. Some of the letters had been forwarded from Albany, a few from Mobeetie. It looked like the same old stuff, he thought: letters from all over the country, school kids and grown-ups alike wanting to be pals with the famous Western lawman: a couple of perfumed notes that

most likely were proposals—decent and otherwise—
from women who got all swoony over men with reputations as fast guns; and the usual gaggle of rantings
against violence. Buck had quit counting the number of
times he had run across the phrases "Thou shalt not kill"
and "Those who live by the sword . . ."

Nothing of much importance—

His heart skipped a beat as he uncovered the last envelope in the pile. He recognized the flowing, feminine
script at a glance. His fingers trembled. It was Marylou
Kowalski's handwriting. The envelope showed signs of
wear and travel. The original address, "Doubletree
Ranch, Mobeetie, Texas," had been scratched through.
W.C. Milhouse's cramped scrawl spelled out "Forward
to Necesario, Texas" near the bottom of the envelope.
The postmark was smudged. All Buck could make out
was that it had been mailed somewhere in Ohio.

Hawkins checked the urge to rip it open on the spot.
His heart pounded in anticipation as he keyed open the
door of his room. He tossed the bundle of assorted letters
aside, pulled his knife, and carefully slit open the top of
the travel-stained envelope.

"My Dearest," the letter began.

*It has been so long since I have heard from you that
my heart aches—*

So, Buck thought, none of his letters had caught up
with the Bar C Wild West Extravaganza in some time.
He wasn't surprised. Trying to track down a traveling
show through newspapers that were weeks or months
old took more detective work than he could handle.

*—and, I must admit to more than a touch of fear
that you have found a sweetheart more deserving
than myself.*

Not a chance, Hawkins mused with a wistful sigh.
After all, there was only one Marylou Kowalski. Only
one woman in the life of one Buck Hawkins. He quickly
scanned the rest of the letter. His heartbeat surged at the
news she was well and healthy, at her vow of undying
love and that she slept with his face and voice in her
dreams. He had to smile at the almost formal prose. In
real life, Marylou used more direct language, often
phrased in such a way as to give a teamster a lesson in
creative swearing.

His enthusiasm faded a bit as he read that she was
"having a wonderful time, seeing so many exciting new
places of which I have always dreamt," and that she still
found it a bit amusing

*that a mere slip of a girl could gain so much atten-
tion simply by riding and shooting; I cannot yet believe that the Colonel has given me top billing in his
show. The crowds have been marvelous and so
warm in their applause . . .*

There was, Buck thought with sinking spirits, nothing
that a simple cowboy and the dull routine of ranch life
could offer to match that kind of appeal. He feared that
despite the words on the page, he was losing her. If he
hadn't already.

His heart sank further as he read the final paragraphs:

*Colonel Cartwright says we will be going soon,
within the next few weeks, to Chicago, then to St.*

Louis, which will be our final stop before the travel-
ing company boards ship for a long tour of Europe,
perhaps as long as two years.

Hawkins had to swallow hard against the lump in his
throat. Two years. It sounded more like two hundred,
Buck thought.

The mails are so dreadfully slow, dearest, that I'm
not sure where we will be when you receive this—or
where you should address a letter, should you
choose to write me, as I pray you will soon, for it
has been three months now with no word from you.
I treasure the memory of our brief moments to-
gether, and carry them always in my heart.

Please *write.*

                                        All my love,
                                        Marylou

Hawkins placed the letter on the bed beside him and
studied the envelope with care. The date on the smudged
postmark was unreadable. Marylou had not dated the letter. Buck had no way of knowing if it was a week old or
three months old. He swore softly through his disappointment. He had written to her faithfully every week,
sending the letters to her last known address. And she
hadn't received one in months . . .

He folded her letter with care, returned it to the envelope, and pulled a nub of pencil and sheet of paper from
the bottom drawer of the chest near his bed.

He didn't know what to write.

He wanted to beg. To plead with her to come to him,
to forget the two years in Europe.

He couldn't do it. Two things could happen. Marylou could tell him to forget her. Or she would agree to his request, and he would always know he had cost her part of her dream.

Buck Hawkins stared at the blank page for a long time. The right words just wouldn't come.

The memories did. They rushed back with a vengeance. The small, slender young woman with auburn hair and green eyes. Eyes that at times reflected the mischief of a young kitten's, at other times flashed in anger. And eyes that could be so gentle they put an ache in a man's chest.

He knew he would never forget the first day they met, at the river crossing when he and Dobie had held up the wrong stage.

There was no money on the stage, of course. That particular holdup had become a symbol of their inept outlaw days. All work and no payday. The only thing of value on the stage was a young woman who stepped from the carriage, pulled a dinky little derringer on Hawkins, and demanded to be kidnapped. Marylou Kowalski was bored with her life and anxious for adventure on the owlhoot trail. Except that she never got the word quite right. She always called it the hoot owl trail.

Whatever she called it, Buck mused, Marylou had been the only one of the three with a larcenous bent. The only one who could draw up a workable plan. The only one who could shoot worth a flip. And the one who led the attack in the Quitaque Valley that meant the end of the Barker bandit gang and made them all famous.

Marylou Kowalski had a figure that would make a grown man whimper and more nerve than a Methodist preacher holding four aces. He had ridden with her for

weeks before it finally dawned on Buck Hawkins that he
was hopelessly in love with Marylou.

And ever since they had parted in Albany, he had
lived with the fear that he would lose her to the lure of
the city and the excitement of faraway places. He could
stand getting killed; he lived with that possibility every
time he saddled a horse, or uncoiled a rope. Or picked up
a gun. He wasn't sure he could stand losing Marylou—

An urgent knock at the door jolted Hawkins from his
musings. Stony Callahan stood in the hallway, his eyes
wide and face flushed.

"Marshal Hawkins, Mr. Dawson over at the Crazy
Woman needs to talk with you. Real quick."

"What's the problem, Stony?"

"Don't know. He just said tell you it was awful important."

Hawkins grabbed his hat. Almost as an afterthought,
he picked up his rifle on the way out.

Buck stepped into the Crazy Woman Cantina and
glanced around. The place seemed quiet. There were
barely enough customers to get up a decent card game.
Ned Dawson stood behind the bar. The lines in his
weathered face seemed deeper than usual.

"Trouble, Mr. Dawson?" Buck said.

"Maybe on the way, but it's not here just yet." Dawson nodded toward a small back room. "Stony, watch the
bar for me a minute while Hawkins and me parley." He
limped to the storeroom, Hawkins a step behind, and
perched on a crate to ease the arthritic hip. "Shut the
door."

Hawkins toed the door closed. "What is it, Mr. Dawson?"

"Couple of Rocking R hands were in a little while
ago. It wasn't their first saloon stop. They were packing

a pretty fair whiskey load when they came in." The old man pulled a tobacco sack from his pocket. "Overheard them talking. Didn't much like what I heard."

"Which was?"

Dawson's brow furrowed even deeper. A few flakes of tobacco dribbled into his lap as he rolled his smoke with twisted fingers. "Way I got the drift, Clell Reynolds isn't just real happy you put the Miller boys in the lockup. Sounded to me like there's going to be a lynch mob come calling tonight. The Millers won't see sunup if Reynolds gets his hands on them."

A chill crept up Hawkins's spine. "Why? For rustling a few cows that weren't even his?"

Dawson lit his cigarette and squinted through the smoke. "Can't say for sure. The Miller brothers are just two-bit cow thieves. But Reynolds doesn't do anything without a reason." He held out the tobacco sack, then tucked it back in his pocket when Hawkins shook his head.

Buck leaned against the door for a moment, brow furrowed. Nothing about this made sense, he thought. Unless—

"Mr. Dawson," Hawkins said, "we ran into Ed Joyner just after we caught the Millers. Joyner seems to think the brothers might be on the Rocking R payroll. Is that possible?"

Dawson's frown deepened even more. "One thing I've learned in life is that anything's possible. I wouldn't bet the ranch on it. That's not Clell Reynolds's style. He doesn't hire people to stomp his snakes." He struck a match, lit his smoke, and shook out the lucifer. "Ever meet Reynolds?"

"No. All I know about the man is that Fess McLocklin told me Reynolds never joined the association."

Dawson nodded. "Clell's always been sort of a maverick. And there's been bad blood between him and the other association men. Especially Ed Joyner. The feud between those two has gone on so long I don't think either one of them remembers what started it."

"So Joyner would have a reason to think Reynolds and the Miller brothers were linked up, somehow," Hawkins said. He rubbed his temple. He could feel a headache coming on.

Dawson dragged at this cigarette and let the smoke trickle from his nostrils. "Reynolds does have a reason to want the Millers dead. Two Rocking R hands have been bushwhacked in the last year. Reynolds has all but come out and said Joyner killed them. I'm not buying that. Joyner's a hard man and tough, just like Reynolds, but that's not his style, either." Dawson ran a hand through his wiry gray hair. "Those two are going to tangle one of these days. When they do, a lot of people are going to get dead."

Hawkins ran a hand over his chin, thinking. "The younger Miller, Hank. He started to say something about the association before his brother shut him up. I haven't gotten a word out of either one of them since, but I get the idea they know something about some killings. The Millers say they never shot anyone."

"You believe 'em?"

Hawkins sighed. "I'm not sure. I'm not sure of anything, Mr. Dawson, except that we caught them trailing J-Bar cows. Ed Joyner was going to lynch them on the spot. Now Reynolds wants them dead. None of it makes any sense. Maybe the Millers are just two-bit rustlers, like you said. Caught in the middle of a feud."

"Badge gets heavy, doesn't it?" Dawson puffed at his quirly and squinted through the smoke at Hawkins. "I'm

fixing to add a pound to it, Hawkins. It isn't Reynolds—
I'd stake my life on that—but somebody *is* paying the
Miller boys."

Hawkins's brows went up. "How do you know that?"

"On account of they come in here time to time, and
they always got money. Lots of it. Gold coin. Two-bit
rustlers don't get rich. Not stealing a few head of stock
at a time." Dawson dropped the cigarette and ground it
beneath a heel. "That tall fellow who left in such a hurry
when you and Garrett showed up. He paid for his drinks.
With a $20 gold piece. I checked it after you left. That
coin was minted at the same place, same year, the Miller
boys' gold was."

Hawkins leaned against the door, questions without
answers bouncing from one side of his brain to the other.
After a moment, he sighed. "Do you have any idea
what's going on, Mr. Dawson? If Reynolds didn't hire
them, and Joyner obviously didn't or he would have
killed them on the spot, who did?"

Dawson shook his head. "All I know, Marshal, is that
you got trouble coming. High-stakes trouble. Take an
old man's advice. Don't tangle with Reynolds. That little
man's poison. Five-foot-two of pure rawhide and rattler.
If he comes, he'll bring half a dozen or more men, most
of them as tough as he is. I don't care how salty you and
Garrett are, you wouldn't stand a chance against the
Rocking R crew. Especially Reynolds and Nace Keller.
Those two are *pistoleros*. Real gunhawks."

Hawkins felt the knot in his gut tighten. "What would
you do in my place?"

The old man shrugged. "Smart thing to do is step
aside and let Reynolds have them. Couple of cheap
rustlers aren't worth getting shot over."

"I can't do that, Mr. Dawson," Hawkins said.

"Didn't think you would." A faint twitch that might have been a grin wiggled Dawson's handlebar mustache. "I figured you for a man with sand."

"Mr. Dawson, the only sand I've got is what's drying my mouth out right now. But those men are my prisoners. I can't turn them over to a lynch mob. I didn't let Joyner have them, and I won't let Reynolds have them, either."

"Call me Ned. If I'm going to be one of your pallbearers, we might as well be on a first name basis."

Hawkins squared his shoulders. "Maybe there's a way out of this without anyone getting hurt."

"I sure hope you find it, Hawkins." Dawson winced as he rose from the crate. He offered a hand. "Good luck, son."

Dobie Garrett had worked up a full rolling boil with his tongue when Hawkins strode through the door of the marshal's office.

". . . I tell you, Archie, when the Kid looked up and seen who was standin' there, he went white as a sheet. Wouldn't even try to go for a gun—" Garrett glanced up. "What you doin' back already, partner? Archie and me was just gettin' to the good part about the Nueces Kid—"

"Let it go for now, Dobie. Something's come up." He nodded toward the door opening onto the cell block. "The Miller boys awake?"

"I reckon," Garrett said. "Took 'em a cup of coffee apiece not a quarter hour ago."

"Good." Hawkins glanced at the young writer and noticed that Wescott's sunburned nose was beginning to peel. "Mr. Wescott, would you excuse us for a minute? Go have yourself a cup of tea or something."

"Marshal, I'm supposed to stay . . ." Wescott's objection faded when he saw the look in Buck's eyes. "Yes, sir," he said meekly.

Hawkins waited until the door closed behind Wescott, then turned to Garrett. "We've got a problem, Dobie, and not much time to solve it. We're going to have to play some head games with the Miller boys. Follow my lead."

Garrett said, "You sure ain't my first pick as a dancin' partner, Buck, but I reckon I get your drift."

Hawkins wrapped a rag around the handle of the coffeepot, carried it into the cell block, and refilled the Miller brothers' cups. He deliberately left the door between the cells and office open a crack when he returned. The men inside, he figured, could hear every word spoken in the office now. He put the coffee cups back on the shelf and turned to Garrett.

"This is a good night for us to be somewhere else, Dobie," Hawkins said, making sure to speak loud enough that his voice would carry to the cell block. "Thought I'd take a little night ride myself. Any special place you want to spend the night?"

"Sure 'nuff. In Miss Lucy Ledbetter's room. She was kinda put out with me the other night for not showin' up. Till she heard about the Nueces Kid. We're back in the same saddle again now, though. How come we're takin' the night off?"

"Word is that Clell Reynolds and Nace Keller are getting a Rocking R crew together, a dozen or more men. They're coming after the Millers with a rope. I thought when they get here might be a good time for us to be occupied elsewhere."

Garrett glanced toward the partially opened door. "That there's the best idea you've had in a spell, partner, and that's a sure 'nuff fact. How come Reynolds wants 'em?"

"I don't know, Dobie. Maybe the Millers know, but they won't tell us. So as far as I'm concerned, Reynolds can have them." He decided to play his trump card. "Let's go, Dobie."

"Marshal!" The yelp from the cell block quavered. "Wait! You can't leave us like this!"

Hawkins sighed in relief. The fish had taken the bait. He waited a few seconds.

"Marshal Hawkins, for God's sake!" Metal chattered against metal, the shaking of a cell door against the lock. "Marshal, please!"

Hawkins strode to the cell block, Garrett a step behind. Hank Miller's knuckles were chalk-white from his death grip on the bars, his face as pale as his knuckles. George Miller stood beside his brother; he didn't look nearly as surly as he had earlier, Hawkins noticed. The notion of being a guest at a lynching party had a way of knocking the stubborn out of a man in a hurry, he thought.

Garrett slouched against the wall and spat, the tobacco juice pinging into a gallon bucket near the door. "Son, there ain't no way we can help you now. I reckon that skinny neck of yours is gonna be about two foot long 'fore daylight. Sure hate to lose a prisoner, but we don't get paid near enough to get kilt over a couple two-bit cow thieves."

Tears flowed down the young rustler's cheeks. His lower lip trembled. Hawkins knew he was right. Hank Miller was just a scared kid, not a man-killer.

"Hank," Buck said, "Dobie's right. The two of us couldn't stop a dozen gunmen. And we don't have a real reason to try. So I'm afraid you're going to hang, sure enough."

Hank moaned in despair and terror. He slid partway down the bars of the cell door and lowered his face into his hands.

"For God's sake, man," George said, "let us out of here. We'll leave the country—"

"We can't do that, George," Hawkins said with a grim shake of his head. "It would be a disgrace to the badges we swore an oath on—"

"Then at least give us our guns." The elder Miller's voice quavered. "I'd rather go down shooting than face a noose."

Garrett spat again. "Can't do that neither, George. It's agin the law for a peace officer to hand a gun to a prisoner. I reckon your goose is plumb cooked."

George Miller's knees almost buckled. "You mean you're going to just walk off? Leave us here to be strung up?"

"Reckon so," Garrett said with a shrug. "You boys dug your own hole in the ground."

Hawkins stroked his chin for a moment as if in deep thought. "Dobie," he finally said, "there might be a way to save these boys from a short drop off a tall limb." He shrugged. "But then, we don't really have a reason to do that. We offered to put in a good word for them with the court, even gave them a chance to talk to us." He sighed. "But since they won't cooperate, I suppose they've made their choice. It's out of our hands now. Let's go. I want to be a couple of miles from here when the Rocking R outfit rides in." He turned to walk away.

"Wait, Marshal! For God's sake, please!" George Miller was almost on his knees now, pleading. "We'll

talk! We'll tell you everything we know! Just get us out
of here!"

Hawkins turned to Garrett. "What do you think,
Dobie?"

Garrett shifted his chew. "Don't matter spit to me neither way, partner. Kind of a shame, though, a man gettin'
lynched when most likely, was he to cooperate with the
laws, he might get five, ten years, tops, on a little rustlin'
charge. But then there's them killin's—"

"We didn't kill anybody," George said. "Please. We'll
do anything you want. For God's sake, man! You can't
just turn us over to Reynolds!"

Hawkins stepped up close to the cell bars, his face
only inches away from George's fear-twisted face. "All
right, George. I'll make this offer once, and only once.
We'll get you out of here to someplace out of Reynolds's
reach. In exchange, you and your brother will tell us
what you know about what's going on here. And you
will agree to testify in court, if need be. Do we have a
deal?"

"Lord, yes! Just get us out of here!"

"Thought you might say that. Trace Willis should be
out back with the horses by now. Dobie, fetch the mana-
cles."

"The what?"

"Wrist irons. And you might hustle up with them.
We'll be losing daylight in three hours." Hawkins nodded toward the younger Miller, who half crouched,
whimpering, on the floor. "Get Hank on his feet."

Minutes later Hawkins led the manacled prisoners into
the alley behind the jail. Willis waited there with three
saddled horses.

"I brung your buckskin," Willis said. "Didn't think

you'd ought to be ridin' Buttermilk, what with his sore
foot and all."

"Thanks, Trace. You did well." Hawkins toed the stirrup and mounted as Garrett boosted the weak-kneed
Hank into the saddle. The younger Miller's racking sobs
had dropped to hiccup level. Hawkins took the lead rope
of the two captives' mounts.

"You ain't said where you're headed, Buck."

"San Jon. We'll catch the northbound stage there and
be in Santa Fe by tomorrow. These boys should be safe
there. I'll be back in two or three days. Think you can
stay sober enough to handle Necesario until I get back?"

"Reckon so," Garrett said, "but I'd feel some better
about it was I goin' along with you."

"One of us has to stay, Dobie. Don't give Reynolds
any trouble if they ride in tonight."

"Hadn't planned on it. Should I oughta tell Fess
McLocklin what's goin' on?"

"Not just yet," Hawkins said. "I'll talk to him when I
get back. Watch yourself, Dobie."

"You, too, Buck. I'm too old and cranky to be
breakin' in a new partner."

Garrett stood beside the alley and watched as
Hawkins led the prisoners away from town at a steady,
ground-eating trot.

"That Buck Hawkins is a right smart feller, ain't he,
Marshal?" Trace Willis said as the horsemen grew small
in the distance.

Garrett clapped the retarded boy playfully on the
shoulder. "He is that, Trace. Most times, anyway. How's
about we go get us a beer?"

"Uh-uh. Not me. Some fellers made me drink whiskey
once. Made my head feel real funny. It hurt bad the next
day." Willis sighed. "I sure didn't like that much. I gotta

go now. Still got some stalls to clean and make sure the horses got plenty of water and hay."

"Okay, son. See you around. By the way—might be best if you didn't say nothin' to nobody about where Buck's headed."

The one-eyed boy grinned. "Like a secret? Just 'tween us?"

"Just 'tween us."

Willis put a soiled finger over his lips. "Our secret. Won't tell a soul."

"Good man. Tell you what I'm gonna do, Trace. I'm gonna make you a sort of deputy. A sidekick to Buck and me, sorta. Think you'd like that?"

"Yes, sir!" Willis's eyes brightened. "I'd like that a bunch!"

"Now, son, I can't let you have a badge or gun. You'll be a secret deputy. You hear anything that you think Buck and me needs to know, you come tell us. That okay with you?"

"Yes, sir!"

"Raise your right hand. Do you swear you'll do good and work hard and mind the laws of the state of wherever you're at?"

"I swear it."

"Okay, Trace. You're swore. Now, run on about your business. I got to go find that writer feller. Didn't get to finish the yarn about me catchin' the Nueces Kid."

7

DOBIE GARRETT LEANED back in his customary chair at his regular table in the Palace, one arm around the trim waist of Miss Lucy Ledbetter and a drink in his free hand—both paid for by the Texas and New Mexico Cattleman's Association—and sighed, content. Life didn't get much better than this, he thought.

"Mr. Garrett?"

"Oh. Sorry, Archie." Garrett winked at the young New Yorker and patted Lucy on the rump. "I done rode down a side trail there for a minute. Where was we?"

Archie Wescott's face reddened. He tapped the edge of his pencil against his notebook. "You were telling me about the fight with the Indians in Buffalo Flat."

"Oh, yeah. I recall now." Garrett paused to down a slug of the Palace's finest Kentucky bourbon, licked his lips, and glanced around. Spectators stood three deep around the table, listening. "Well, there we was. Comanches all around us. Son, you ain't seen that many feathers on a chicken farm. Ol' Sittin' Bull's boys was game scrappers, I tell you."

"I thought Sitting Bull was a Sioux."

"By golly, you're right, Archie. Must've got my Injun fights mixed up. After thirty, forty of them fracases, a man sort of loses track. Them in Buffalo Flat was Quahadi, sure 'nuff. Part of ol' Quanah Parker's bunch." Garrett slid his hand from Lucy's haunch to her upper thigh. "Now, Quanah, he weren't there, or there wouldn't've been no trouble, on account of him and me's blood brothers. Shared a scalp or two, we have. Comanches don't like Utes much, and Quanah and me—"

"Please, Mr. Garrett," Wescott interrupted, "could we just deal with one episode at a time?"

Garrett downed the rest of his drink. Lucy refilled it. "Much obliged, honey," Dobie said. "Now, there was at least a hunnerd of them savages facin' just me and Buck, and we was down to maybe five, six cartridges apiece. Yes, sir, it was lookin' mighty grim there for a spell, I tell you . . ." His voice trailed off as Lucy leaned close and whispered something in his ear.

"In a minute, sugar," Garrett said with a grin. "Just let me finish this here drink. Sort of grease the old wagon axle for the trip, so to say."

"What happened?" Wescott prompted.

"Huh?"

"How did you escape the Indians?"

"Oh, that. Well, son, it weren't easy. But a man knows Injuns, he knows how to plumb pluck their medicine feathers. There was this here big chief, sittin' on this paint war pony way off on a hill, watchin' the scrap, them war bonnet feathers of his dang near touchin' the ground. Stepped it off later at nigh onto a thousand yards. Well, sir"—he paused for another swallow—"when you take down the big boss, them other Injuns plumb lose interest in takin' a man's scalp. So I pulled out this here old Sharp's buffalo gun. Had one shot left that I'd been savin' for somethin' special. I laid her acrost that hoss had been kilt out from under me, and—"

"Garrett! Dobie Garrett!"

Garrett looked up. The crowd around the table thinned out in a hurry. A small man, barely over five feet tall, narrow in the shoulders and bowed in the legs, stood a few feet from the table. A tall, lean man was at the short fellow's side, his hand on the butt of a big Smith and Wesson Russian .44 holstered at the hip. The tall man had cold, narrow eyes. Several other men fanned out behind the two in front.

Dobie set his glass down. "That's me, I reckon. What can I do you for?"

"Damn you, Garrett! Where are they?"

"Where's who and who's askin'?"

"I'm talking about those Miller boys, that's who. The ones you're supposed to have in jail."

Garrett studied the wiry little man for a moment. "Mister, you're gonna pop both eyeballs plumb out of your head if you don't settle down some. They ain't there."

"Dammit, I *know* they're not there! I've *been* there. I want to know what you've done with them, and I want to know *now*!"

Garrett noticed that the rest of the crowd had edged even farther away from the tables. "You still ain't answered my question, friend. Who's askin'?"

For a moment, Garrett thought the little man was going to bust a gut; his face was almost purple.

"I'm Clell Reynolds, and I want those Millers. You got about thirty seconds to tell me where they are, Garrett, or my man here'll put half a dozen holes in your sorry hide!"

Garrett glanced up at Lucy Ledbetter and sighed. "Sure is some unfriendly folks in these parts, honey." He let his hand drift down her leg, patted the lump beneath her thigh garter, and lifted an eyebrow. Lucy dipped her head in understanding. "You might ought to sort of step aside for a minute, Lucy," Dobie said. "This here's man talk. But don't you go too far."

The brunette moved away a couple of steps.

"You, too, Archie."

The young writer snatched up his notebook, his face the color of ashes, and stepped away from the table. His gaze, eyes wide, flicked from Garrett to Reynolds and back.

"Well, Garrett," Reynolds said, "what's it going to be?"

"Aw, hell, Reynolds. Pull up a chair and have a snort on me." Garrett stretched out a leg, toed out a chair, and filled an empty shot glass. Only a couple of fingers of whiskey remained in the bottle. Dobie sniffed the neck of the bottle and grinned. "Prime stuff. Set down and let's talk this out."

Reynolds made no move to sit. Rage danced in his pale blue eyes. "There's nothing to talk about, Garrett. Give me the Miller boys and you won't get hurt."

Garrett leaned back in his chair and for a moment studied the tall man at Reynolds's side. The silence in the Palace was almost deafening. The lean man looked to be only a split second away from whipping out that big, ugly handgun. "This man your best shooter, Reynolds?" Dobie said.

"He's the best. Anywhere."

"Maybe he is, maybe he ain't." Dobie sighed. "What's your handle, feller?"

The lean man glared at Garrett, his weight on the balls of his feet. "Name's Nace Keller." The voice was low and rumbly.

Garrett nodded. "Glad to make howdys with you,

Nace. Was I in the mood for gunfightin', that there name'd fit nice on a headstone. But I ain't in the mood."

"You don't have a choice, Garrett," Reynolds snapped. "All I have to do is say the word."

"Wouldn't do that, Clell," Dobie said casually. "Might not be good for your health. Gettin' dead can wreck a man's whole day."

Reynolds sputtered. "You think you can take Nace—and me?"

"Reckon I could handle ol' Nace here, was I to decide to," Garrett said. "Wouldn't have to fret over you, Clell. While I'm shootin' your man, Miss Lucy'd put a slug in your head. Take a quick squint off to your left there."

Reynolds half turned—and found himself looking down the barrels of a derringer in Lucy's dainty hand. Surprise clouded the anger in his eyes.

"See, Clell, we got us a standoff here. Lucy can flat handle that little gun. You sic your pet wolf on me, I'll kill him while Lucy's killin' you." Garrett clucked his tongue. "Seen what one of them little .32 rimfires'll do to a man's left eye, Clell. Punches it clean back into his skull."

For a tense moment, Garrett thought Reynolds was going to try it anyway. Dobie pushed back his chair and stood. "While you're studyin' on it, Clell, I'm gonna have me a drink." He lifted the almost empty bottle from the table and downed a quick swallow. "Well, what's it gonna be, Clell?"

"My boys would shoot you both to pieces."

"Maybe me, if they got lucky. Don't reckon they'd throw down on Lucy, on account of all them boys knows what happens to man hurts a woman out here. Even if they was that dumb, you wouldn't get to see it, Clell.

Not out of that left eye, anyhow. Might think on that a minute."

Dobie stepped around the table and strode to within arm's length of Nace Keller. The lean gunman's knuckles were white from his grip on the revolver. Keller shifted his gaze from Garrett to Reynolds for an instant.

Garrett swung the bottle from waist level. The heavy glass cracked into Keller's forehead and shattered in a spray of shards and liquor droplets. Keller went down like a poleaxed steer.

Reynolds started. "What the hell—"

"I said I wasn't up to no gunfightin' tonight, Clell. Lucy, shoot this little bastard before he plumb gets me riled up."

The color drained from Reynolds's face. He lifted a hand. "Wait a minute!"

"'Bout time you showed some sense, friend. You and the boys drop them gunbelts. Slow and easy. Lucy, if anybody tries to get cute, pop one in ol' Clell's head."

Reynolds's thin shoulders slumped. "Do as he says, boys."

Garrett heard the thump of gunbelts against the hardwood floor as he bent and plucked the big Russian .44 from Keller's holster. The gunman twitched and moaned.

"Hard-headed cuss," Garrett said in admiration. "Thought I'd hit him harder'n that."

"Damn you to hell, Garrett!" Reynolds's words were choked with humiliation and anger. "You can't hide behind a woman's skirts forever. I'll find you—"

"Won't be hard," Garrett said. "On account of you and your boys is all gonna be in my jail."

Reynolds's face went purple again. "What?"

Garrett shook his head. "Didn't know you was hard of hearin', Clell. I said you're under arrest."

"What the hell are you talking about?" Reynolds sputtered. "What for?"

Garrett sniffed at Nace Keller. "This one smells like a still. Drunk and disorderly. Rest of you, disturbin' the peace—"

"Disturbing the peace?" Reynolds yelped.

"You sure 'nuff disturbed mine, Clell," Garrett said. "I reckon I can come up with some other charges, too. Course, I don't read real fast. Might take me two, three days to wade through all them law books over in the jail."

"You can't do this!"

"I got a badge. And this here big, ugly six-gun. I reckon that's all I need." Dobie stared into Reynolds's eyes for a moment. "Reckon what I'll do is, before I turn you loose, I'll pour a slug of salts down your pipe, Clell. Clean you out some. Might improve your disposition." He waved the muzzle of Keller's handgun. "Line up, boys. It ain't a long walk to the jail. Gonna be mighty crowded in there for a spell." He glanced at the men nearby. "Couple you fellers lend a hand here and drag this big, bad gunfighter along to the lockup. Some of you others take these boys' horses down to the livery."

The Rocking R crew lined up single file, faces downcast, embarrassed. Garrett waited until two hefty teamsters had dragged the half-conscious Nace Keller to his feet, then turned to Lucy.

"Much obliged, honey," he said. "Lockin' these boys up won't take long. I'll be right back."

Lucy Ledbetter flashed a lecherous grin. "I'll be waiting, Dobie."

                    *   *   *

Buck Hawkins tugged his hat down against the freshening wind and peered at the thunderclouds building in the west.

The towering clouds swirled and twisted. Lightning painted quick flashes of brightness through the grayish-white mass. And it would be on him soon.

He had seen summer storms build above the New Mexico mountains many times before. When they boiled and turned back into themselves like this, a man could lay odds it would be a bear of a storm when it flung itself down the mountains and onto the rolling plains below. At least, he thought, there was one good sign in this one. There was no greenish cast to the clouds or the sky beneath them. That meant hail was unlikely. Being caught in the open in a big hailstorm was not Hawkins's idea of a fun time. He had seen hailstones big enough to drop a full-grown steer dead in its tracks.

The buckskin between Hawkins's knees twitched its ears and snorted. Hawkins leaned forward and patted Cornbread on the muscular neck in reassurance. A half mile or so up ahead, a shallow arroyo would provide some protection from lightning strikes, if not from the rains that would hit like a solid wall of water. The storm would pass as quickly as it came, Hawkins figured, as he straightened in the saddle and studied the roiling clouds.

Hawkins could already feel an occasional gust of cool air on the shifting breeze. It helped ease the heaviness in his bones and the scratchy sensation beneath his eyelids. At least Cornbread was still fresh and rested from three days and two nights in a San Jon stable. Hawkins hadn't had that luxury. He had never been able to sleep on a stagecoach. Especially with two drummers on board who never stopped yammering about business and politics all the way back from Santa Fe. Those were two topics in which Buck had absolutely no interest.

And he still didn't have the missing pieces of the puzzle. Hank Miller had wanted to talk. George wouldn't let him. They would talk, George said, only to the governor. And only then after they were safe behind the walls of a federal pen. Otherwise, their lives wouldn't be worth a wooden nickel.

Hawkins had had to fight back the urge to whip the both of them with his pistol until they talked. Or stop the stage and hang them from the nearest tree. George Miller had gone back on his word. Buck tried to console himself that at least two men hadn't been lynched, and that eventually the whole story, whatever it was, would come out. The notion wasn't much help.

Cornbread came to an abrupt stop and stood with head extended, ears perked toward the north. The buckskin's nostrils fluttered in a soft, rolling snort. Hawkins's gut tightened. It was the horse's way of telling him something was out there.

Hawkins lifted himself in the stirrups and studied the rolling, rocky terrain dotted by low greasewood brush clumps, clots of cactus, and stunted, wind-warped cedars. He saw nothing except a wisp of sand from a nearby rise. Probably just a coyote on the prowl, he thought. But he loosened the Winchester in its scabbard, just in case.

"It's all right, Cornbread," he said, more to reassure himself than to settle the buckskin. "Come on, now. We want to make that creek up ahead before the storm hits."

Cornbread shook his head, jangling the curb chain, then lifted into a fast walk at the touch of Hawkins's heels. Another quarter mile, Buck figured, and they would be in the questionable cover of the arroyo.

A sudden, hard gust of wind all but staggered the big buckskin. Wind-blown mist whipped across Hawkins's cheek. He reached behind the saddle, untied his slicker, and struggled into the stiff canvas as he nudged Cornbread into a fast trot. The light went flat and gray as the storm clouds rolled over the sun. The first fat drops of rain spattered against Hawkins's slicker and ticked against his hat. Another two hundred yards—

He saw the muzzle flash a split second before he heard the buzz of lead just over his shoulder; the sharp crack of a rifle jarred his ears a heartbeat later. He ducked low on the buckskin's neck, reined Cornbread sharply aside, and dug heels into the horse's ribs. The buckskin was in a dead run within three strides. Hawkins yanked at the stock of the Winchester, and mouthed a silent curse of desperation as the hammer snagged in a fold of his slicker. A slug spattered into the sand six feet ahead of the buckskin; a second whined past Cornbread's hip a few strides later. A third whistled high overhead as Cornbread topped the lip of the arroyo and skidded down the shallow but steep slope.

Hawkins glanced around. The only cover available was a jumble of driftwood at a bend of the creek twenty yards upstream. He racked a round into the rifle chamber as he reined the buckskin toward the deadfall. The scattered drops of rain came harder and faster as he bailed off the horse, wrapped the reins around his forearm, and crouched behind the driftwood. He spotted a flicker of movement at the bank of the creek, slapped the rifle to his shoulder, and fired. Dirt flew thirty feet short of the target. He ripped off three more rounds as fast as he could work the lever; moments later he heard the muted thud of horses' hooves, moving fast. He caught a quick glimpse of a lone horseman, a slicker or duster whipping in the wind, as the rider topped the creek bank better than a hundred yards away. Hawkins thought he saw a rifle in the rider's hand. He tried to bring the Winchester sights into line, but the man disappeared over the bank before he could fire.

The storm hit with the force of sledge on anvil, an almost solid wall of water dumped from the sky. Hawkins huddled against the driftwood and squinted in vain through the sheets of rain. He could see no more than thirty feet. The hairs on his forearms prickled a second before a flash of white light ripped through the near darkness; at almost the same instant an ear-numbing thunderclap drowned out the drum of raindrops and the thump of Hawkins's heart against his ribs. A small cedar almost above his head exploded, blown apart by the lightning bolt. The sharp odor of the afterstrike almost took Hawkins's breath away. The startled buckskin yanked back against the reins, hooves churning.

"Easy, Cornbread!" Hawkins yelled against the pound of rain and near constant crack and roll of thunder. The horse quit fighting the reins and shoved his head almost under Hawkins's armpit. "It's all right, son," Buck said. He heard the quaver in his own words. At the same time, he offered up a silent prayer of thanks that the buckskin was so well trained.

For what was probably little more than a quarter hour but seemed an eternity, horse and man endured the drenching downpour before the storm began to ease. The wall of water faded to steady rain, then to scattered spatterings. The landscape brightened as the storm clouds sped away. Hawkins lifted his head above the drift deadfall and studied the arroyo. There was no sign of movement in the area the shots had come from.

Still, he waited.

The storm had rumbled several miles to the southeast before Hawkins dared stand. The arroyo seemed to be empty.

He remounted, struggling with the rifle and slicker, and kneed Cornbread into a slow, cautious walk up the creek bed. His muscles tensed, anticipating the wallop of a slug, his heart thudding in his chest.

No shot came.

Hawkins reached the spot where the bushwhacker had been. The rain had washed away any tracks the man had left. Buck's gaze flicked around the arroyo. The shallow walls seemed to close in on him; he struggled to keep the strangling sensation in check, fought back the urge to put the buckskin up the nearest bank. If the rifleman came back, Hawkins knew he was a dead man.

A wink of light against brass caught his attention at the edge of the creek. He looked around again, saw nothing, and swung down. The first cartridge case lay half-buried in the mud. A second gleamed from beside a small rock at the base of the creek bank. Hawkins picked up the shiny, rain-washed case and studied the markings. It was a big case, the headstamp marked ".50–95–X." Not many men in this neck of the woods carried a rifle of that large a caliber. The .50–95 Express was a big-game load, more suited to elk or grizzly than man shooting.

Hawkins tucked the two brass casings into a shirt pocket. He studied the muddy soil, not really expecting to find anything after the downpour.

He almost missed it.

The glint of sunlight from a thimbleful of water caught his eye. The bit of water was trapped in an indentation in a prickly pear pad four feet from where he had found the cartridge cases. Hawkins squatted to study the spiny leaf. The indentation was in the shape of a hoof-print. The horse had apparently stepped away from the pad quickly; the leaf wasn't crushed. But the print the shod horse left behind was sharp and clear. And unusual. A small triangular piece was missing from the right front quarter of the shoe—

Hawkins's heart leapt at a distant, whooshing rustle. He knew the sound. A flash flood. And he and Corn-bread were standing at the lowest point of a narrow neck in the arroyo. The first trickle of brownish-red water swept past a stride away, a small stick tumbling atop the leading edge of the muck.

Hawkins all but vaulted into the saddle. "Come on, Cornbread," he said as he reined the horse about and dug his heels in, "we've got to get out of here."

His heart skipped a beat as a front hoof slipped and the buckskin stumbled, almost went down. Then the horse had his feet back under him. Twenty yards down-stream a narrow trail led out of the arroyo. Hawkins leaned over Cornbread's neck as the horse lunged up the slope, hooves digging for purchase on the slick mud. They topped out a few seconds before a four-foot wall of rolling red water roared down the arroyo. Driftwood and living trees torn out by the roots tumbled on the turbu-lent water.

Hawkins reined the buckskin to a stop. He let the winded horse blow for a moment as his gaze raked the surrounding land. Nothing moved. The sun was almost blinding after the dull gray wash of the storm. Hawkins finally let out a sigh of relief, but his heart still thumped heavily against his ribs. He realized with a start that the storm had probably saved his life. If he hadn't been moving at a fast trot—he shuddered at the thought. A

man with a .50–95 lined up on a slow-moving target
wasn't apt to miss at under a hundred yards.

The chill in his gut spread through his shoulders and
trembled his fingers before the raw fear began to give
way to a small ember of anger. He started to sheath the
Winchester, but changed his mind. If some bushwhacker
tried to nail him again, he'd be ready this time. Not that
it would do that much good, he grumped to himself, the
way Buck Hawkins handled a rifle.

He shrugged out of his slicker, rolled the canvas, tied
it behind the saddle, and touched heels to the buckskin.
"Let's go, Cornbread. We've still got a long ride
home . . ."

Hawkins found Garrett in the last place he had expected
to find him.

In the marshal's office.

"Damn, partner," Garrett said as Hawkins stepped inside, "you look like you been rode hard and put up wet."

"I feel like it." Hawkins stowed his rifle in the rack
beside the door and slumped onto the cot by the wall.
"Anything happen while I was gone?"

Garrett shrugged. "Nothin' much. Had to put a few
folks in the lockup till they cooled off some. Cut 'em
loose this mornin'. How'd it go with you?"

"Except for the fact that I haven't slept six hours in
the last three days and the fact that somebody took a few
shots at me on the way back, pretty good."

"Reckon they missed."

"Remarkable deductive powers, Marshal Garrett,"
Hawkins said, his tone a bit more caustic than he'd intended. "I found this where the shots were fired from."
He pulled one of the big brass cartridge cases from his
pocket and tossed it to Garrett. Dobie caught it in midair

and studied the casing for a moment, then pursed his lips in a silent whistle.

"Fifty-ninety-five. Buck, the Army's got cannons that ain't that big. Slug from that thing would sure 'nuff tear a wooly bear of a hole in a feller."

"Tell me about it," Hawkins said. "You know anybody around here who carries a rifle like that?"

"Nope. Reckon we could mosey around town and see has anybody bought cartridges this caliber lately."

"I'm too tired to mosey anywhere right now," Hawkins said as he removed his hat and stretched out on the cot. As exhausted as he was, he couldn't sleep; his mind kept hopping in circles like a jackrabbit in a patch of loco weed. "Dobie, I think we've got troubles."

"Ain't never had nothin' but," Garrett said. "What's eatin' you?"

"This rustling business. And the shootings. The Miller brothers wouldn't talk on the way to Santa Fe. But I'd bet a month's wages those two weren't just stealing a few cows on their own—" Hawkins started as the door banged open.

"Here it is, Marshal Garrett," Archie Wescott yelped as he scurried into the room, a newspaper in his thin, sunburned hand. "Your story. Copies of the *New Mexican* just came in."

"What story?" Hawkins said.

"About how Marshal Garrett backed down the fastest gun in the West and locked up a whole crew from the Rocking R." The young newsman's words tumbled out in an excited rush. "And I got another byline—my name's on it. As author."

Hawkins sat up. "Backed down who? What happened, Dobie?"

Wescott handed a newspaper to Buck. "It's all there,

Marshal Hawkins. Just like it happened. A firsthand account." The reporter's chest had swelled until he looked like he was about to pop a vest button.

Hawkins glanced at the headline on the two-column story beneath the big type that screamed something about a silver strike in southwestern New Mexico.

NECESARIO MARSHAL SUBDUES
FABLED GUNMAN, FACES DOWN
MOB OF DOZEN ARMED MEN

The secondary headline—Wescott had told him they were known as "drop heads" in the newspaper game— read, in smaller type:

Incident Averted, No Shots
Fired in Saloon Showdown

"Come on, Buck," Garrett pleaded. Eagerness and excitement tinged his words. "Read her aloud."

Hawkins silently scanned the first few paragraphs of the column-length story, then glanced up at Garrett in surprise. "I thought you said nothing happened. You didn't tell me you went up against Clell Reynolds and Nace Keller."

"Didn't amount to squat, partner. Go ahead, read it out loud. I sure do admire seein' my name in them newspapers."

Hawkins wiped a hand across his eyes, trying to clear away what seemed to be a film over his vision, and read:

Necesario, Texas—Special Marshal Dobie Garrett, world-renowned Indian fighter and lawman, armed only with the sheer force of personality and reputation, single-handedly averted a potentially deadly showdown here Tuesday last, subduing and jailing a

mob of unruly cowboys bent on mischief and possibly murder in a confrontation in the crowded Palace
Saloon and Gaming Hall, and in the process disarmed and humiliated a man known as Nace Keller,
one of West's most notorious and feared gunmen.

Hawkins lowered the paper and stared in disbelief at
Garrett. "*You* went up against Nace Keller? Dobie, I
thought I asked you to stay sober."

Garrett answered the charge with a wide grin. "I was
sober, Buck. Well, mostly sober, anyway. There weren't
much to it. I just whapped that feller in the head with a
whiskey bottle. Shame, too. There was at least one more
drink left in it. Who's this Nace Keller, anyhow?"

"One of the fastest guns in the country," Wescott bur-
bled, his eyes wide. "The story is that he's killed twenty
men, maybe more. In stand-up gunfights. The classic
Western duel in the street."

Hawkins shook his head. "Dobie, you sure have a
knack for stepping in it. Keller isn't going to take that
lying down."

"Come to think on it, he did say somethin' about
seein' me again," Garrett said. "Didn't pay much never
mind. Figured it was just talk. Anyhow, I ain't scared of
him."

"Any thinking man would be," Hawkins said, "so I
suppose that explains it."

Garrett turned to Wescott. "You mention Miss Lucy in
that story?"

"I certainly did. It's right there under that small headline—we call them 'break heads'—about halfway down
the story."

"Lucy?"

"She lent a hand, Buck. What's it say about her?"

Hawkins scanned the page until he found the smaller headline. "It says that Miss Lucy Ledbetter, a local businesswoman—Businesswoman?"

Garrett grinned and flashed a quick wink at Wescott. "Damn good at that business, too." The writer's face flushed. "Go on, Buck."

Hawkins read the rest of the article silently, then lifted an eyebrow at Garrett. "She actually pulled a derringer on Clell Reynolds?"

"Got a lot of sand, that gal," Dobie said in admiration. "Mighty fine woman, Miss Lucy. She's gonna be plumb tickled to see her name in that there paper."

"Why?"

"Why?" Garrett frowned, puzzled. "Don't everybody like to see their names in the paper?"

"That's not what I meant. Why did you arrest the whole crew?"

Garrett shrugged. "They made me mad. Me and Miss Lucy had plans for the evenin'." He started to rise from his chair. "Speakin' of which, her and me got a tad behind on our business lately. Now that you're back, partner, I reckon we can catch up some. I'll take a copy of that paper over—"

"Sit down, Dobie," Hawkins snapped. "Mr. Wescott, I'll have to ask you to leave us alone for a moment."

"But—why? My editor wrote me that I was supposed to stick to you two like glue. Ride with you, make rounds with you, get the whole story—"

Hawkins pinned a hard glare on the young reporter. "I don't have the time or energy to argue about it at the moment, Mr. Wescott. Now, clear out, or I'll put you in a jail cell."

Wescott's expression was that of a whipped hound pup. It got to Hawkins a bit. The kid hadn't really hurt anybody, if you didn't count the wildly exaggerated stories he cranked out.

Hawkins sighed heavily. "I'm sorry I snapped at you, Archie." He deliberately softened his tone. "Right now, I'm tired, cranky, confused, and just generally out of sorts. We'll talk about this later. Okay?"

Wescott nodded and trudged from the office.

Hawkins waited until the door closed behind the New Yorker. "Dobie, something has dawned on me in the last few hours."

"What's that, partner?"

"That the two of us better learn how to shoot."

8

"BUCK," DOBIE GARRETT said in a half whisper, "you think that old coot can *really* shoot?"

Hawkins studied the buggy a few yards ahead and nodded. "That old coot, as you call him, was killing buffalo and fighting Indians long before our time, Dobie. If anyone can teach us to handle firearms, Ned Dawson can."

The two rode in silence for a moment. They trailed the buggy by twenty yards to avoid the rooster tails of dust kicked up by the wheels. The wind was still little more than a breeze in the early morning. It wouldn't pick up until the sun was midway up the eastern sky. Then it would blow until sundown, and die down again at dark. Hawkins didn't know why it happened that way. It just did.

"We been doin' okay so far," Garrett said.

"We've been riding the coattails of blind luck, Dobie. Sooner or later that luck's going to turn. When that happens, we'd better be able to take care of ourselves. Carrying a gun and not knowing how to use it can get a man seriously dead."

Garrett rolled his chew and spat; the bay horse, still fresh and alert, ducked. The glob sailed over the gelding's ears. Garrett swiped a hand across his stubbled chin and sighed. "Reckon you might be right, at that." He glanced back toward Necesario, more than a mile behind. "Archie warn't too happy, us ridin' off and leavin' him behind."

"He'll get over it." Hawkins's lips twitched in a wry grin. "We don't want Archie to find out that his fearless, fast-gun, dead-shot, town-taming, rustler-catching, outlaw-nabbing heroes can't hit an outhouse at four paces with a rifle or handgun. And that we ride spooked most of the time."

"Reckon not. Smart thinkin', though, tellin' him top gunhawks like us don't let nobody watch 'em practice. What was it he said that done?"

"Added to the mystique of the fast gun."

"Don't know about no miss-teek," Garrett said, "but I reckon we're fair hands at the missin' part already when it comes to shootin'. Archie said he was gonna spend the time workin' on that there book about us. Sure be interestin' to see what he writes. How much further we gonna go?"

"Looks like we're there." The buggy stopped on the east side of a shallow draw a couple of hundred yards wide. A higher bluff on the west side would stop any but the wildest slug. At least they wouldn't have to worry too much about killing somebody's cows, Hawkins thought as they reined in beside Dawson's buggy.

"This'll do, boys," Dawson said. He tossed the hitch anvil down and stepped from the buggy, his movements stiff and a bit creaky from the rheumatism. He tied the buggy reins to the ring fitted into the heavy iron chunk and patted the rangy, swaybacked sorrel mare on a bony hip. "Hitch your ponies to the tailboard and fetch your hardware."

As Hawkins and Garrett dismounted, Dawson reached

beneath the buggy seat and pulled out a full-length doe-skin rifle cover decorated with porcupine quills and intricate beadwork. He draped the rifle sheath over a shoulder. Fringe rippled in the light breeze and sunlight glinted from silver spots that dotted the soft, supple leather.

"Nice rig," Garrett said with a nod toward the sheath.

Dawson fingered the doeskin. The expression in his eyes went soft. "Gift. My wife, rest her soul, made it for me."

"Didn't know you was ever married, Ned."

"Ten years. To the prettiest Blackfoot girl you ever saw."

Hawkins said, "What happened to her?"

"She died." Dawson didn't elaborate. Hawkins decided it might be best not to press the point.

"Haul those target boards out of the back of the buggy," Dawson said. "You'll have to set them up where I tell you. I'm not up to walking much. Hip's giving me miseries this morning."

Hawkins had broken a sweat by the time they had the targets in position. The targets were roughly square, five feet by five feet, made of old door panels nailed to two-by-two frames and propped up by sections of wrist-size cedar posts. One target was positioned at twelve feet, another at twenty paces, and the third at a hundred strides.

The Crazy Woman Cantina owner studied the targets and grunted in satisfaction. "That'll do for starters," Dawson said. "Now, fetch that little wood chest from the buggy floorboard."

Garrett grunted aloud as he lifted the two-foot-long chest. "What's in this thing, Ned?"

"Shooting stuff." Dawson eyed the two men for a moment. "Where's your holster, Dobie?"

Garrett tapped the butt of the Peacemaker tucked in his waistband. "Ain't got one."

"Better get one."

"How come?"

"Take a close look at where the muzzle of that hand-gun's pointed," Dawson said. "If that thing happened to go off right there, you wouldn't be able to do Miss Lucy much good."

Garrett blanched and pulled the weapon. With care.

"Hand that six-gun here a minute."

Dawson tipped up the muzzle, ejected the cartridges, and examined the weapon, scowling. "When was the last time you cleaned this revolver, Dobie?"

Garrett shrugged. "Don't recall ever cleanin' it."

Dawson sighed. "Looks like I have a real chore ahead of me with this class of pupils. Garrett, the way this thing's fouled, it would be a pure wonder it ever shot at all. First thing you learn is to keep your weapons clean. Like you would a saddle or any other tool. A gun is a complicated weapon. Black powder fouls moving parts something fierce. Open that chest."

Dawson examined Hawkins's rifle and Bisley Colt while instructing Garrett in the art of thorough cleaning of a Single Action Army revolver with solvents, oil, cleaning rods, swabs, bristled wire bore scrubbers, and assorted rags from the shooting chest.

The old man handed Buck's guns back. "Not bad. Still fouled some, but it looks like you've made a half-assed try at cleaning them. We'll do it proper before you start. And again when you're finished. A gun that doesn't work is more dangerous than a woman who doesn't talk, boys. Keep that in mind."

The better part of an hour passed before the weapons

met with the old man's approval. He lifted an eyebrow at Garrett. "Where's your rifle?"

"Don't have one. Can't shoot a rifle good as I can a six-gun."

Dawson shrugged. "Suit yourself. But keep in mind that handguns are for close work. Any hit over a hundred yards with a six-gun's just pure luck unless you happen to be Bill Cody, and I suspect you boys fall a bit short of Bill's ability." Dawson nodded toward the waiting targets. "We'll start with the short guns at the closest one."

"It sure ain't very far off," Garrett said, skeptical.

"It's twice the distance at which most handgun fights happen. You'd be surprised, my grubby friend, at how difficult it is to hit a man-sized target at five feet. Especially if the target happens to be shooting back." Dawson tipped his head toward Garrett. "Let's see what you can do, Dobie."

Garrett grinned, spat, tucked the Peacemaker back into his belt, and turned to face the target, knees slightly flexed.

"What in the blue-eyed hell are you doing, Garrett?" Dawson grumbled.

Dobie looked puzzled. "Fixin' to do one of them fast draws, that's what," he said.

Dawson sighed heavily. "The one thing a fast draw will get you is crippled. Try to yank that six-gun out fast, and most likely you'll blow your kneecap or foot off. The key to living through a gunfight is to have your weapon in your hand before the other guy does. Best of all is to have it in your hand while his back's turned to you. Savvy?"

"You mean back-shoot a man?"

"Depends on how much you enjoy life, whiskey, and women," Dawson said. "Forget this 'code of the West' crap you've read about in those dime novels, Dobie. you have two options in a gunfight. Play fair and get killed, or do it right and let them bury the other man. If that means back-shooting, then blaze away. Any gunhawk who doesn't will live a painfully short life."

Garrett's face flushed, but he nodded. "Reckon that makes sense."

"Glad we agree on it. Now, ease that six-gun out. Take your time, line the sights on the middle of that near target, and squeeze the trigger. Don't yank—squeeze. One shot."

Garrett lifted the six-gun, squinted down the barrel, and fired.

"Well, I'll be damned," Dawson said.

Garrett grinned. "Surprised, Teacher?"

"Sort of. I never saw anybody completely miss a five-foot-square target from this range. If that had been a man with a gun, we'd be measuring you for a pine box right now, Dobie." Dawson shook his head in disgust. "Give it a try, Buck."

Hawkins eased the Bisley from his holster, drew a bead, and squeezed the trigger. The thump of slug against wood followed the muzzle blast by a split-second.

"High right, barely on the target," Dawson said, his tone heavy. "This is going to take longer than I thought." He held out his hand. "Give me the Bisley." He cocked the weapon, raised it, and fired, all in one motion. Splinters flew; a small, round hole sprouted six inches to the right of center. "Sight's off, Hawkins." He drew a heavy skinning knife from his belt sheath, tapped the hasp against the front sight, and fired again. The hole was dead center. "Try it now."

Hawkins's next shot went a foot high and right of center. Dawson reached over and pushed Buck's hand down a fraction on the Bisley grips. "Butt of a Bisley's got a different curve to it than a Peacemaker. Sets different in the hand. Try it now."

Buck's slug again went right. So did the next.

"Reload and try again. This time, shut your left eye," Dawson said.

Hawkins raised the weapon, closed his left eye, then lowered his hand. "I can't see anything clearly," he said, perplexed. "The sights won't focus."

"Can't say I'm surprised," Dawson said. "Figured your left eye was dominant."

Garrett said, "What?"

"Most men have one eye that's stronger than the other. A 'shooting eye,' we call it. Try the left hand, Buck."

Hawkins shifted the Bisley to his left hand; it felt awkward, but his next shot hit within three inches of center target. The next two were even closer.

"Not bad, Buck. I think we have your problem solved. Reload."

"Reckon that's what's wrong with my shootin'?" Garrett asked hopefully.

Dawson lifted a cynical eyebrow at Garrett. "What's wrong with your shooting, Dobie, seems fairly simple. My guess is you can't shoot for squat with either eye. Try it left-handed if you want."

Dobie did. Then he switched back to his right hand. Four rounds, and not one hit the target. Garrett frowned at the handgun. "Gotta be somethin' wrong with this six-shooter."

Dawson spun on a heel and started toward the buggy.

"What's the matter, Ned?" Garrett asked.

"Just checking to see if Dobie had somehow managed to kill one of the horses. Safest place to be when he's shooting is dead square in front of him." Dawson took Garrett's weapon, reloaded, and promptly put six slugs into the target. A playing card would have covered all half dozen holes. He shook his head. "Nothing wrong with the Peacemaker. This is going to take even longer than I thought. Good thing the association's paying for your ammunition."

A hundred rounds later, Hawkins was beginning to get the left-hand feel of the Bisley; he was punching holes in a hand-span cluster near the center of the target. Garrett had yet to draw a splinter.

"Dobie," Dawson said, "maybe you better get that holster for another reason. To carry a club in." He sighed. "Let's see if you boys are any better with a long gun." He reached for the doeskin rifle sheath, untied the strings that held the flap over the butt, and slid the cover from his rifle.

"What's that thing?" Garrett said.

"Custom job. Caliber .45–100 Ballard. Built on a Remington rolling block single-shot action." Dawson popped the tang sight up behind the receiver and flicked the sighting bar down to its lowest notch. From his shirt pocket he pulled a cartridge that looked to be nearly four inches long and chambered the round. He shouldered the big rifle and squeezed the trigger. The thunderous muzzle blast fluttered Hawkins's hat brim; the target a hundred paces away seemed to bounce at the impact of the heavy lead slug.

"Should have been an inch high over center," Dawson said through the dense gray-white cloud of powder smoke. "Got her sighted for one-fifty at this notch. Might be off a bit, though. Haven't dropped the hammer on it in over a year."

Hawkins squinted at the distant target. He could see

the dark, round hole—exactly one inch above dead center.

"You called it, Ned," Hawkins said in awe through the ringing in his ears. "Exactly where you said it would hit."

"Just checking the range." Dawson worked the action, retrieved the heavy brass case, and dropped it in his pocket. "Have to reload special for this baby." He fondled the receiver of the custom rifle for a moment, then slipped the weapon back into its sheath.

"Just how far'll that cannon shoot?" Garrett asked.

Dawson shrugged. "Longest hit I've ever had was right at eight-fifty."

"Yards? Hell, that's a half mile."

"Nearly. I don't recommend taking shots at that range, even with a weapon like this, unless it's absolutely necessary."

Hawkins fished the .50–95 brass from his pocket. "Speaking of big-bore guns, Ned, do you know anybody who carries a rifle of this caliber?"

Dawson studied the cartridge for a moment, then shook his head. "Nobody that I know of. Read about the .50–95 in a new Winchester catalog. Haven't seen any in this part of the world yet. Any of my business why you ask?"

"Somebody took a few shots at me on the way back from San Jon," Hawkins said. "I found a couple of those cases at the spot the shots were fired from."

Dawson's frown deepened. "Get a look at the shooter?"

"Just a glimpse. It was just before the storm hit. I couldn't even tell what color horse he rode."

The old man jiggled the big shell case in his palm for a moment. "If I hear about anybody packing a cannon

like that, I'll let you know. In the meantime, I suppose
we've got a serious enough reason for you to learn to
shoot." He handed the cartridge back to Hawkins.
"Okay, let's see how you boys can do with Buck's Winchester. Use the twenty-yard target."

The Winchester .44–40 had a mild recoil, but Hawkins's shoulder was beginning to bruise from the cumu-
lative pounding before Dawson called an end to the
day's lesson. Hawkins was reasonably well satisfied,
even if he was still spraying lead a bit much at the
hundred-yard range. He could tell it was going to take
time to learn left-hand shooting.

Dobie had managed to nick one corner of the target.
Most of his lead was buried in the soil of the far bluff.

"That's it for today," Dawson said. "Clean the
weapons tonight, like I showed you. We'll come back tomorrow and try it again. And keep on coming back until
you two get where you can hit something. In the meantime, I strongly recommend that both of you stay out of
any gunfights."

Three days and a half a general store's stock of .44–40
ammunition later, Dawson called it quits.

"We could work at this until we're knee-deep in spent
brass, boys, and neither of you would get much better
than you are now." He nodded to Hawkins. "You're
passing fair with the handgun and rifle now, Buck. Not
good, especially, but fair enough you could at least scare
somebody. With enough practice you might even get to
be a decent shooter. Dobie's a lost cause, though."

"Aw, Ned, it ain't that bad," Garrett protested. "I'm
gettin' better."

"Well, you did get three out of twenty shots somewhere on the target, at that," Dawson conceded. "But

better isn't good enough, Dobie. Second place in a gun-fight won't win you anything but a headstone. I've got something that will help you."

Dawson limped to the buggy, reached under the seat, and hauled out a strange-looking weapon in an even stranger-looking holster. He tossed the rig to Garrett. "Try this."

Garrett looked quizzically at the weapon. "What the hell is this?"

"Knew right off that you'd never learn to handle a regular six-gun or rifle for squat, Dobie, so I had that made for you. It's a double shotgun, twelve-bore, barrels cut off to fourteen inches, stock nubbed off behind the pistol grip. At close range you ought to be able to at least raise some dust with it." Dawson tossed a couple of shot shells to Garrett. "Double-ought buck loads. Give her a try on the close target, Dobie. I'd better warn you, though. It's going to kick some."

Garrett slid the ugly weapon from the long leather holster, chambered a round in each barrel, and cocked the heavy scroll hammers. He pointed it toward the target and pulled the front trigger. Both barrels went off. Splinters flew eight feet high, dirt and sand billowed from beyond the target, and the sawed-off shotgun almost sailed from Dobie's hand. When the thick smoke cleared, a jagged hole bloomed in the center of the wooden target.

"That's better," Dawson said with a nod of approval. "At least you would have lived through it if that had been a shoot-out. Provided you got the first shot off. Strap the rig on and see how it fits." He rummaged under the buggy seat and tossed a new gunbelt to Hawkins. "Had this made for you, Buck. Left hip carry." Dawson turned to Dobie. "How's the fit?"

Garrett had the bulky weapon strapped around his waist. The muzzles of the sawed-off shotgun reached almost to his right knee. "Feels good," he said. "Kinda heavy, but sort of reassurin'." He thumbed shot shells into the half dozen loops on the gun side of the thick harness-leather belt.

"Try a fast draw with that, Dobie, and you'll lose more than a kneecap."

"What's this here holder for, Ned?" Garrett had three fingers stuck into an angled loop on the left side of the belt.

"That's for your close-up weapon," Dawson said. He reached into the buggy again and tossed a thick, two-foot-long stick to Garrett. Dobie caught it in midair. "Had that made especially for you, too. It's good, stout hickory."

Garrett slapped the stick against the palm of his free hand, winced, and shook his stinging fingers.

"Lay that up beside a man's head, he won't feel much like making trouble," Dawson said. "Be careful you don't hurt yourself with it. It's loaded. I had the wheelwright sink a half-inch bolt in the business end."

Dawson waited until Hawkins had settled the new rig on his left hip, then inclined his head toward Necesario. "School's out, boys," he said. "Afraid you're on your own now."

"Much obliged, Ned. How much we owe you?"

"Don't worry about it, Dobie. I had all this stuff billed to the association." Dawson glanced at the sun almost overhead. "Best head on back now. It'll be time to open the Crazy Woman in a couple of hours."

"Been meanin' to ask you about that, Ned," Dobie said as they prepared to leave. "How come the place got that Crazy Woman name?"

"Did you notice the bullet holes in the outside wall?"

"Sure did. Quite a mess of 'em."

"Happened about ten years ago, just after I opened the place." Dawson grunted with effort as he heaved himself into the buggy. "Old Man Callishaw's wife never had been exactly right in the head. She got crossways with her hubby one day. Come after him with a buffalo gun. Old Sharp's Fifty. Shot the place up."

Hawkins swung into the saddle. "Did she kill him?"

Dawson shrugged. "Not that day. She shot about like Dobie does. Killed him later, though. Took a double-bit axe to him one night while he was passed out drunk. Hacked him up something fierce. Ruined a good axe, too." The old-timer slipped a wink in Hawkins's direction. "Might keep that in mind, Dobie. If I were you, I'd stay on Miss Lucy Ledbetter's good side."

Garrett chuckled. "Shoot, Ned, *any* side of Miss Lucy's the good side. Speakin' of which, Buck, you need me tonight?"

"I suppose not. We don't have anyone in jail."

"Reckon I'll say some howdys to Lucy, then. That gal's makin' a right good livin' off me. Sure glad the association's payin' the bill. Couldn't afford it, my own self."

Hawkins and Garrett let Dawson's buggy take the lead. They rode in silence for a half mile before Dobie turned to Buck.

"You ought to come over to the Palace with me tonight, partner. Might help your disposition some. They got a nice yellow-haired gal there, new to the filly stable. And I know you're partial to yellow horses and yellow-haired women."

Hawkins shook his head. "Just the horses, Dobie. Not the women. Not anymore."

Garrett sighed heavily. "Son, I sure get to frettin' about you somethin' fierce at times. It just ain't natural for a young feller like you not to go get his wick dipped once in a while. It ain't like that little red-haired gal'd know about it."

"Auburn, Dobie. Marylou's hair is auburn." Hawkins sighed. "Maybe she wouldn't know, but I would."

"Long as she don't what's it matter?"

"It matters. Just take my word for it."

The bay horse ducked too late as Garrett spat. The glob hit Duckbutt on the left ear. The gelding shook his head and stomped a front foot in aggravation. "Buck, you used to be more fun to run with back in the old days. We ain't got big drunk and busted up no saloons together in many a moon. Just plumb pains me, seein' you so all-fired serious all the time."

"Tomcatting and hell-raising has lost a lot of its appeal, Dobie." Hawkins stared toward the northeast for a moment, wondering where Marylou Kowalski was at this particular time, what she was doing. He sighed. "You'll understand someday, when the right woman comes along."

Garrett snorted. "Ain't no such thing as one right woman when it comes to talkin' about the rest of a man's life, Buck. They's too many fillies out in the pasture to cut just one outta the remuda."

"Well, Dobie," Hawkins said, "there's some things we never agreed on to begin with. This is just another one of them."

"Never seen a gal with such a tight rein on a man, and her not even around. Heard from her lately?"

Hawkins's spirits sank. "Not a word."

*   *   *

"Seems peaceful enough," Garrett said as the two men rode toward the livery stable at the northeast edge of town.

Hawkins didn't reply. His gaze raked the side streets and alleys, noting possible ambush shots, checking the roofs of buildings. Being the target of a bushwhacker made a man lean toward the cautious side. It also made a nervous way to live.

Dobie didn't seem overly worried, Hawkins thought. The stocky marshal rode relaxed in the saddle, whistled an off-key saloon ballad that wasn't to be found in any hymnal, and nodded cordial greetings to a couple of the Palace's girls on their way to work. But then, Dobie hadn't been shot at lately—

Hawkins barked a curse and slammed heels to the buckskin.

"What—" Garrett hesitated for only a second, then put the spurs to the bay.

Hawkins yanked Cornbread to a sliding stop and was over the top rail of the livery corral before Garrett caught up. Against a door of a box stall, a stocky cowboy hammered a fist into Trace Willis's bloodied face; a second man had the burly youth's arms pinned to his side in a bear hug.

Hawkins covered the distance in three strides and launched himself into the hitter; the impact of his shoulder sent the cowboy sprawling. The second man squawked and heaved Willis aside.

"Uh-uh! Bad idea!" Garrett yelled.

The second man froze, his hand on the butt of a six-gun at his hip. His eyes went wide at the sight of the sawed-off smoothbore leveled straight at his belly.

"Try it and there'll be guts splattered from here to Fort Worth," Garrett said. "Need some help, partner?"

The man Hawkins had tackled struggled to his knees, shaking his head, still stunned. Rage boiled through Hawkins's blood. He brought a fist up from almost boot level. The blow caught the cowboy square on the bridge of the nose. Hawkins felt cartilage crumple beneath his knuckles, then a sharp stab of pain through his hand. The cowboy went down on his back in a pile of horse droppings, twitched once, and lay still.

"Reckon you don't," Garrett said.

Hawkins plucked the handgun from the downed man's holster, tossed it over the corral fence, and strode to Willis's side. Trace's knees buckled. Hawkins slipped a supporting hand around the youth's waist. Tears traced pale tracks down the blood and dirt on Willis's cheeks.

"Are you all right, Trace? Are you hurt bad?"

Willis shook his head, still dazed. Pain showed through the shocked confusion on his bruised and torn face. "They—come at me," he said, his words cracking between sobs. "Took my—pocket knife—wouldn't—give it back." He pointed a quavery finger toward the unconscious man. "Then that one—hit me—while the other one—held my arms."

"It's all right now, Trace," Hawkins said. "They won't hurt you any more." He pulled the bandanna from around his neck and handed it to the youth. "Can you stand on your own?"

Willis nodded. Hawkins turned, pulled the second man's handgun from his holster, and tossed it aside. He grabbed the second man's shirt, high against the throat, and slammed him against the wall. he shoved his face to within inches of the cowboy's.

"All right, damn your soul," Hawkins said, his words tight with fury, "you want to fight, let's get it on!"

The cowboy's swarthy face paled. He raised a hand.

"Wait a minute, Marshal—we didn't mean nothin'. We was just funnin' the half-wit some, that's all."

"I'm not laughing."

"Wasn't my idea. Jody, there, he started it. We was just playin' a little game of keepaway, that's all—tossin' the dummy's knife back and forth. The halfwit got to cryin' and tried to fight—"

Hawkins yanked the man away from the wall and slammed him into it again. The cowboy's eyes went out of focus as his skull cracked against wood.

"It's lucky for you I'm a patient man, fellow," Hawkins said, "or I'd beat the ever-loving hell out of you just so you'd know what it feels like." He cracked the man's head against the wall again. "You're lucky that a law enforcement officer doesn't abuse prisoners" —he rammed a knee into the man's groin—"and you're also lucky that you didn't make me *really* mad." He released his grip on the man's shirt and let him fall, hands between his knees, moaning and writhing.

Hawkins became aware of the growing pain in his right hand. Blood seeped from torn knuckles. He tried to make a fist; the fingers wouldn't close. "Damn, Dobie," he said, "I think I broke my hand."

"Should've used my club. Or maybe a six-gun." Dobie clucked his tongue. "I swear, partner, I never seen you fly off the handle quite that wild. Don't reckon I'll be pickin' no fistfights with you."

Hawkins strode to Willis's side. The youth's finger raked the dirt, blood still flowing down his face. "My knife—I can't find my knife."

Hawkins crouched beside him. "It's all right, Trace. I'll come back in a bit and help you find it." He got the boy to his feet, led him to the water trough, and started cleaning the blood and dirt from Willis's face. "Are you going to be all right, son?"

Willis nodded. "It hurts some, Mr. Buck." He glanced toward the two men lying in the corral. "What are you gonna do with them?"

"A few days in jail and a hefty fine should teach them a lesson. You know these men, Trace?"

"Seen 'em around some."

Dobie sheathed his sawed-off shotgun, opened the gate, rode the bay into the corral, and studied the downed men. "I know 'em, Buck. Part of the Rockin' R bunch I locked up a few days back."

"So we'll lock them up again."

Willis touched a cut over his cheekbone. "What makes some folks mean, Buck? Like them? How come people just can't be nice to each other, like Jesus said we was supposed to be?"

A muscle twitched in Hawkins's jaw. "Some men are just like that, son. Just plain mean. Are you sure you're all right?'

"I . . . I'm okay, now. What if they come back at me?"

Hawkins patted Willis reassuringly on a thick shoulder. "Don't you worry about that, Trace. Dobie and I will have a little talk with them, after they've had a couple of days to think things over. I expect they'll decide to be nice."

The man Hawkins had slugged was still out cold. The one he had kneed in the crotch was on hands and knees, gasping for air between spasms of retching. Buck strode to the heaving man, grabbed the back of his shirt collar, yanked him to his feet, and twisted an arm none too gently behind his back.

"What do we do with that one?" Garrett said with a nod toward the unconscious cowboy.

"Toss a rope around his feet and drag him to the jail," Hawkins said. "Wouldn't hurt my feelings if you did it at a fast trot, Dobie." He turned back to Willis. "Do you feel up to taking care of Cornbread for me, Trace?"

Willis's nose was still bleeding. "Yes, sir. I'll take good care of him." He glanced at two saddled horses standing at the far side of the corral. "And them, too. It wasn't the horses' fault that mean men was ridin' them. But I got to find my knife." His last statement held a distinct note of panic; his gaze flicked around the corral.

Hawkins nodded in understanding. To a twelve-year-old, a worn pocketknife was the most important thing in the world. More important than pain or a bloody nose or the bewilderment of being attacked by grown men. And despite his man's body, Trace Willis was only twelve. Always would be. Hawkins remember his first pocketknife. It had been a gift from his grandfather. And it had been his most prized possession at age nine. He could still recall his own pain when he lost that knife.

Hawkins watched as Dobie reined Duckbutt toward the jail, the Rocking R cowboy bouncing along behind, Garrett's loop around his ankles and the other end dallied around the saddle horn.

"I know, Trace. Let me take this other fellow to the lockup and I'll help you look for it."

"Would you, Mr. Buck?" Hope flared in the boy's eyes.

"Sure I will, son. That's what friends are for. I'll be back in a few minutes." He yanked up on the prisoner's wrist and heard the satisfying yelp of pain. "Let's go, fellow. You know the way to the jail. Be nice and I won't break your arm."

"You can't get away with this, Hawkins. Clell Reynolds won't like it, you jailin' two of his top hands just for hoorawin' a halfwit—" The protest ended in an agonized yelp as Hawkins jerked on the arm.

"I do not," Hawkins said, his lips close to the prisoner's ear, "give one single solitary damn what Clell Reynolds thinks. If he gives me any trouble, he'll be in the lockup with you. Now, shut your mouth and move your butt—and don't try anything cute, mister, because I'm not in a real good mood right now."

9

"THAT'S ABOUT IT, Mr. McLocklin," Buck Hawkins said. He leaned back in the unpadded chair of the Texas and New Mexico Cattleman's Association office. "I wish I could report more progress, but I've hit a dead end."

Fess McLocklin frowned at the Mexican cigar clutched between gnarled fingers. A blood vessel throbbed in his temple.

"What makes you so sure Reynolds isn't behind all this, Hawkins? The man's been nothing but a trouble-maker for years."

Hawkins sighed. "I'm not sure of anything yet, sir. And I'm not ruling out any possibilities. But I honestly don't believe Clell Reynolds has had anything to do with the rustling. Or any killings."

McLocklin snorted. "I'm not so damned sure about that. Every member of the association's lost livestock over the last year. The J-Bar. The Slash-Y. Four C. My Keylock outfit. Somebody's behind it, and it wasn't the Miller brothers. It's too big an operation, and they're not smart enough or hosses enough to pull it off." He puffed at the cigar. "But now that I think on it, no association members have had cattle stolen since you two caught the Miller boys."

Hawkins nodded. "That's true, Mr. McLocklin, and I

agree with you on one point. I don't believe the Millers are capable of putting together a large-scale rustling operation. But I can't buy the idea that Reynolds is responsible. The Rocking R has lost stock in the past, too."

McLocklin's eyes narrowed to mere slits. "Suppose he has. Can you think of a better way to make it look like you're not at fault than to lose a few head from your own range?"

"No, sir," Hawkins said. "I can't. But the same could be said for any of the association ranchers, too."

"Including me?"

Hawkins wondered if he were about to step over a line in the dirt. "Yes, sir. Including you."

The mantel clock nestled between stacks of books on the shelf ticked several times before McLocklin finally shrugged and tapped the ashes from his cigar.

"All right, I'll grant you that. At least you've got the *cojones* to say what you think, Marshal. I like that in a man. Even if I don't agree with him."

Hawkins allowed himself an inward sigh of relief. At least he still had a job. An unfinished job. And one that might get him killed.

"I'm hoping Dobie and I can get to the bottom of this soon, Mr. McLocklin. A lot of it hinges on what the Miller brothers know. And how soon they decide to talk."

"Two-bit cow thieves," McLocklin said in disgust. "You should have let Joyner or Reynolds hang the both of them."

"We couldn't do that, sir," Hawkins said. "Any man is entitled to a trial. Even a small-time cow thief."

McLocklin stubbed out his cigar in the stone grinder ashtray. "I suppose you're right, Hawkins." The withered old man sighed. "Keep on digging. As far as I'm concerned, though, Reynolds is the man we're after. The other association members think the same."

"If he is, and if we can prove it, Dobie and I will arrest him just like we would any other lawbreaker, Mr. McLocklin. All I need is some time."

"Your time's expensive, Marshal. How much time?"

"I can't say, sir. But if you think Dobie and I aren't earning our pay, you hired us. You can fire us."

McLocklin's thin shoulders sagged. "That wasn't a threat, Marshal. I didn't intend it to sound like that. But there's a meeting of the association coming up here in Necesario in two weeks. I had hoped we could have some answers for them by then."

"We'll give it our best effort, Mr. McLocklin. Is there anything else?"

"One thing." Some of the anger drained from the old man's eyes. "I understand you jailed a couple of Rocking R hands the other day for picking on Trace Willis. Roughed them up some, I hear. I want you to know I appreciate that."

Hawkins said in all sincerity, "It was my pleasure."

"What happened to them?"

"We kept them locked up for two nights, fined them $40 each, and turned them loose. After they apologized to Trace. Reynolds sent them packing when he found out what they had done. He fired them on the spot."

"Well, maybe the cantankerous old badger has a decent moment every few years. Even Reynolds looks out for Trace. By the way, did you find Trace's knife?"

"Yes, sir. It took us until dark, but we found it."

McLocklin nodded. "Good. I gave the boy that knife four years ago. I was going to replace it, if need be. Keep me posted, Hawkins. Good news or bad, I want to hear it."

Hawkins reached for his hat. "You will, Mr. McLock-lin. By the way, I haven't seen your nephew around the last few days. Is he still out at the ranch?"

"No. Marty left for Fort Worth to tend to some business. Personal stuff, he said. I think it was the day after you caught the Miller brothers that he left. Why?"

"Just curious, Mr. McLocklin. Dobie and I try to keep track of what's going on around Necesario." He reached for the doorknob. "Anything you need, sir?"

"I'd like to have about four decades of my misspent youth back, if you happen to run across it," McLocklin said. He winced and shifted his weight. "It's hell to get old, Hawkins. The only thing that keeps me going is that there's only one other option."

Hawkins heard the spang of Garrett's tobacco juice against the syrup-can spittoon before he stepped into the office.

"Buck, son, come in here. You gotta hear this."

Hawkins hadn't heard Garrett sound this excited since the day he found out the Texas and New Mexico Cattleman's Association would be paying for his liquor and women in Necesario.

"Hear what, Dobie?"

"Archie done got a bunch of pages done on our book, and it's a surefire humdinger."

Hawkins pegged his hat and nodded to Wescott. The young man sat on the cot, papers in his lap and lying on the wrinkled blanket beside him. His nose was peeling. Folks with fair skin didn't handle the sun and wind well, Hawkins knew. But Wescott still wore a wool three-piece suit and cravat despite the heat.

"Start her over, Arch," Garrett said. "Let Buck hear it

from the front. I'd sort of admire to give it another listen myself."

Hawkins helped himself to the coffeepot and sat on a chair across the desk from Dobie as Wescott gathered and organized the sheets of paper.

Dobie said, "Okay, son. Let 'er rip."

Wescott cleared his throat. "To set the stage for you here, Marshal Hawkins, I decided to start the story with the gunfight with the Barker gang. Kick it off with some real action, so to speak. Readers like that. Ready?"

Hawkins nodded.

"Here we go. And I'm quoting from the manuscript here." Wescott cleared his throat again and began to read:

"The avengers charged through the pale gray dawn, the wind whipping the manes and tales of their fiery steeds, their reins held between their teeth, hot lead and death spitting from a blazing six-gun in each fist—"

Hawkins almost spewed a mouthful of coffee over the desk.

"—ignoring the buzz of bullets about their ears as they raced through the murderous outlaw stronghold, while from the hilltop five hundred yards away, a beautiful young woman with auburn hair calmly sighed down her rifle barrel, sending to his final judgment before the Almighty any desperado who dared show himself as a target."

Hawkins coughed and gasped for air, half strangled on the coffee.

"The best part's comin' up right here, partner," Garrett said. "Pay attention, now."

"They were the dealers of frontier justice, the two dauntless horsemen and the courageous young woman, and they left in their wake the broken remnants of a desperate, dangerous, deadly band of hooligans who had wreaked their last death, destruction, and thievery upon the citizens of the Southwest. The avengers in that rugged, desolate place known as the Valley of Tears were the fearless gunmen Dobie Garrett and Buck Hawkins and their beautiful and courageous companion, Miss Marylou Kowalksi—names that will live forever in the lore and legend of the Wild West."

"Damn, partner, ain't that somethin'?" Garrett's grin spread from ear to ear. "That's us, Buck . . . What's the matter, amigo? Swaller your tongue?"

"Just—poured some coffee—down the wrong pipe," Hawkins croaked.

Wescott said, "What do you think, Marshal Hawkins?" The young man leaned forward, brows arched in hopeful anticipation.

Hawkins lifted a hand. "Give me—a minute to—get my wind back." His voice was still croaky, but he was really stalling for time; he didn't want to hurt the kid's feelings, so he couldn't really ask the question he wanted to ask: *Who the hell were you writing about?*

After a moment, he cleared his throat. "Well, Archie, you know your craft, of course. But I don't seem to recall it happening exactly that way."

Wescott sighed. "Marshal, I know it's embellished a

bit and possibly somewhat overly dramatic, but it's what my editors and our readers want."

"Partner," Garrett said, delighted, "we're gonna be more famous than ever. Whooee—can this boy write, or what?"

"Yes, he can, Dobie. I'd say he's an excellent fiction writer."

Wescott beamed. Hawkins was relieved that the sarcasm implied in his comment had escaped Wescott's notice. Archie might not be the world's most accurate historian, but he was a decent enough young man. And he *had* gotten Marylou's hair color right.

Hawkins put the coffee cup he had hardly touched on the desk and stood. "If you gentlemen will excuse me, I'd better make the rounds and make sure it's really as quiet as it seems in town. I just dropped by to make sure everything was all right here."

"No problem, partner," Garrett said. "Them two boys in the lockup back there's sleepin' it off. I'll fine 'em a few bucks and cut 'em loose in a couple hours."

Hawkins reached for his hat. "Good. I'll see you both later."

As he went out the door, he heard Garrett say, "Come on, son—read her again to me. From the front. That's some piece of writin'."

It sure is, Hawkins thought. He wondered if it was too late to change his name before Wescott's book came out.

Hawkins leaned against a support post of the Santa Fe Hotel veranda, worried a sliver of dinner steak from between his back teeth, and surveyed his town.

The relative peace and quiet of the last three days had given way to the bustle of horses, buggies, and expensive surrey rigs pulled by matched teams. An air of ex-

citement and anticipation built over Necesario. Hotels
and boarding houses were already filled up, sometimes
four men to the room. The overflow crowd paid out
some hefty fees to individual families for a bed in a back
room or a cot in a corner somewhere.

Necesario's most noted industry was about to kick
into high gear. Once a month, the nickel-and-dime cowboy poker games were forced to move to the back
streets or the dingy cantinas on the south side. It was
high-dollar gambling time in Necesario. Men in business suits, silver beaver hats, and diamond-studded cra-
vats now outnumbered the rough-clad teamsters,
cowboys, and husky laborers in the crowded streets and
fancier saloons.

Hawkins knew some of the players by sight, a few by
name, and recognized other names he had seen listed in
hotel registers. Bankers, lawyers, merchants, physicians,
ministers, church deacons, politicians, mine owners—a
list of professions that went on and on. The list covered
three states and two territories. Buck idly wondered if
anyone was minding the store between Tombstone and
Dallas.

"Looks like ever' herd bull in the country's come
callin', Buck," Garrett said as he stepped from the hotel
café. "Be some big money changin' hands next couple
days."

"Winners and losers," Hawkins said. "Can't tell who's
which right now. They're all smiling and laughing."

Garrett fished his plug from his pocket, gnawed off a
chew, and settled it into his cheek. "At least the big-
money boys behave. Nobody pullin'knives and guns
over a five-dollar pot."

"They have to behave, Dobie. It wouldn't look good
to the voters, stockholders, wives, and parishioners back

home to have their names wind up in the paper for
brawling over a poker game or a woman. Speaking of
which, how's Miss Lucy?"

Garrett flashed a big grin. "Better all the time. Reckon
it must be the company she's been keepin'. You know,
that gal's even a passin' fair cook."

Hawkins lifted an eyebrow. "If I didn't know you better, Dobie, I'd say you're turning into a one-woman
man."

"Ain't never met a woman quite like her." Garrett
squinted into the early morning sunlight. "Stage comin'.
Right on time for a change."

The big coach pulled by a sweaty six-horse hitch
rocked to a dusty stop in front of the Santa Fe. The
coach looked to be full, and two men in range garb rode
atop the rig. Hawkins doubted they were up top by
choice. He stepped from the veranda, strode to the front
wheel, and greeted the driver.

"Any problems, Pete?"

"Not a hitch, Buck. 'Cept for havin' a full load. Hard
on the ponies, pullin' them long grades. Got a mail sack
in the boot." The driver set the wheel brake, dallied the
double handful of reins around the iron lever, and
climbed down, a wooden step in hand. "Let me get these
folks unpacked and sorted out, and I'll dig out the mail."

Hawkins studied the passengers as they stepped from
the coach. Five men and two women emerged, flexing
stiffness from legs and shoulders. Buck knew now why
the twice-weekly coach had actually arrived on time.
The two stage line owners were on board.

The two cowboys started handing baggage down from
the coach top. They looked ordinary enough, Hawkins
thought; cowhands either hunting work or on the way to
a job already landed. One of the women could have been

a new addition to the Palace's stable. Or she could have been the wife, or girlfriend, of one of the wealthy visitors. Hawkins thought it best not to ask. The second woman was different.

She wore a tailored, dark blue gown, a bit dusted from the long ride with the coach windows open, full petticoats, her waist cinched, and high-top button shoes. Impressive cleavage showed above the low cut of her gown. She was a knockout from the neck down. And except for the button-type nose that drew attention to protruding front teeth and the thumb-size cigar clamped between her lips, she was rather nice-looking from the cleavage up, Buck had to admit. She hadn't changed a bit.

Hawkins started to offer her a hand down, but two other men beat him to it. Hawkins tipped his hat. "Morning, Miss Catherine. Welcome to Necesario. Have a nice trip?"

"Not bad, Marshal, considering." She peered into Hawkins's face. Her eyes were blue-gray, with small crow's-foot lines that deepened when she smiled. She had a pleasant grin. "Have we met? I think I've seen you somewhere before."

"We have, Miss Catherine. I'm Buck Hawkins. We met briefly four or five years ago, in Mobeetie. You emptied the pockets of the Panhandle's top poker players."

"You weren't in the game. I never forget a man's face or name once I've seen him over a five-card-draw hand."

"Cowboys didn't have the money to sit in on your style of game, ma'am," Hawkins said. "I just nursed a beer or two and watched you play."

"You gonna make the howdys, Buck, or you gonna

hog the lady for yourself?" Garrett groused at Hawkins's elbow.

"Oh. Sorry. Miss Catherine Timberlake, Dobie Garrett."

Garrett's face brightened. "Kate Timberlake?" He grabbed her hand and pumped it. "I sure been wantin' to meet you, ma'am. Why, ever' serious poker player from Cheyenne to El Paso's got a story about Squirrel Tooth Kate—" Garrett's face flushed; he released her hand as if it had been a snake. "Sorry, ma'am, I—"

Catherine Timberlake chuckled, a musical, low-in-the-throat sound. "Don't be embarrassed, Mr. Garrett. All my friends call me that. Are you a player?"

Garrett regained his composure. "Not in your class, ma'am. Don't spend more'n a few dollars a month gamblin'. But I'd be pleasured to sit in sometime when the stakes ain't too big, when maybe you're just bored or needin' practice or somethin'."

"I'll keep that in mind, Mr. Garrett." She turned to Buck. "You don't have any objection to my being in town, do you, Marshal Hawkins?"

"Not at all, ma'am. We have no rules in Necesario about professional gamblers. At least as long as they don't cheat. Cardsharps are another matter."

Squirrel Tooth Kate flashed the grin again. "Then there's no problem. I've never had to cheat." She turned the cigar in her fingers. "Could I trouble you for a light?"

Hawkins patted his shirt pocket. "Sorry. I don't smoke, and I don't have any matches on me at the moment."

Garrett had a match fired before Buck finished his apology.

The stage driver tossed a dispatch case to Hawkins.

"Mail call. Sort out your stuff and I'll turn the rest over to the hotel clerk."

Hawkins thumbed through the pouch. Most of the mail with his or Dobie's name on it was routine stuff. Wanted notices, copies of a couple of newspapers, a letter from the sheriff at Santa Fe, three or four envelopes from people he had never heard of before, and a crude catalog of weapons and equipment "For The Professional Law Enforcement Officer" from an outfit in Boston.

His heartbeat picked up as he reached the bottom of the stack. There were two letters addressed in Marylou's smooth, flowery script, one from Cincinnati and one posted in Chicago, mailed only a couple of days apart, and neither of them a month old. They were addressed to him in care of the Marshal's Office, Necesario, Texas.

Hawkins fought back the urge to rip Marylou's letters open on the spot. Another envelope in a cramped, squiggly handwriting had been posted in Mobeetie.

"I'll take the rest in to the clerk, Pete," Hawkins said. "Much obliged."

Archie Wescott came down the stairs from his room, taking the steps two at a time, a bundle of papers in his hand, as Hawkins placed the mail pouch on the desk behind the harried clerk's registration counter. Excitement glittered in Wescott's blue eyes. Hawkins noted that Wescott's sunburned nose had stopped shedding skin.

"I have almost half the book finished, Marshal Hawkins," Wescott said. "I was up all night reworking the first two chapters. I think they're really good. I'd like you and Marshal Garrett to look them over and tell me what—"

"Later, Archie," Hawkins interrupted, a bit more sharply than he had intended; the glitter dimmed from Wescott's eyes. Buck deliberately softened his tone.

"Give me a couple of hours to catch up on my official reading first. By the way, you have some mail." The young man's face brightened again. "It's in the pouch behind the desk. Have yourself a cup of tea, look your mail over, then come to the office. Bring Dobie, if you can find him by then."

He left Wescott shuffling and squirming, impatient for the clerk to finish registering guests and sort the mail, and weaved through the wagon and buggy traffic to his office. He tossed the official stuff and the newspapers on the desk and sat, his heart thumping against his ribs. He didn't even take time to remove his hat. He pulled his pocketknife and carefully slit open the letters from Marylou and W. C. Milhouse.

He forced himself to read Milhouse's letter first.

It didn't take long:

Cattle and horses fat. Good rain last week both ranches. Grass green. May show profit sooner than thought. Money you sent got here. Keep your powder dry and don't get shot.

                                    WC

Hawkins smiled and tucked the one-page note back into the envelope. W. C. Milhouse didn't waste many words running the ranch. He wasted even fewer on letters.

Buck's fingers trembled as he lifted several sheets of paper from the letter of Marylou's with the earliest postmark. He scanned the letter rapidly; he would savor each word later, when there was more time.

She had finally received a half dozen of his letters on the same day, forwarded to her at the Cincinnati Fairgrounds, and, as she wrote, "almost fainted from sheer delight at receiving them after such a long time with no word from you."

She had known before the letters arrived that the two men were in Necesario.

All the big newspapers in the country told of the capture and killing of the Nueces Kid, but the stories do seem somewhat exaggerated. Shooting around a corner *and hitting a man on horseback? I'm sorry, dearest, but I had to laugh. For, you see, I know how well you shoot . . .*

The rest of the first letter was similar to the last Hawkins had received from her: accounts of the places the Wild West Show had visited, people she had met, a reaffirmation of her love and her worry about the danger he and Dobie faced as law enforcement officers. It ended with the request that he next write to her in care of the show at the St. Louis fairgrounds, where they would be within a few weeks. It was enough.

Her second, posted in Chicago, sent Hawkins's spirits soaring:

My dearest, I cannot express how delighted and absolutely jubilant I felt when your last letter arrived with the news that you and Dobie had bought the Quarter Circle Ranch! I know how much you have long wanted a place of your own. It sounds like a beautiful ranch.

There was more. Four pages more. But the paragraph that leapt off the page and sent Buck's heart racing read:

*While I do not for a minute regret taking my tour of
the bright lights, dearest Buck, I must admit that,
now that the glamour and excitement has dulled
with the passing of performances and towns and
states, I am beginning to tire of the constant travel
and being the "darling" of all those faces in the
crowd. Perhaps it is time I admitted to myself, and
to you, that in my heart and soul I really* want *to
settle down, to be with you forever. If that seems a
proposal of marriage, so be it; I always have been a
brazen, outspoken hussy, as you well know.*

Hawkins wanted to whoop aloud. To run shouting the
word along the crowded street. To turn in the star, grab a
seat on the outbound stage, and track down Marylou if
he had to search every fairgrounds east of the Missis-
sippi. The urge grew as he read the rest of the passage.

*If you agree that we belong together, let me know in
your letter to St. Louis, and I shall quit the Colonel's
circus. If you have found a woman more to your lik-
ing, or if I have lost you while indulging my selfish
whim by running away, I shall be on the boat to Europe . . .*

Hawkins's chest ached with the need to go to her. And
because he couldn't.

Not yet.

He had made more money in a few short weeks than
he had earned in years, but it wasn't enough to pay off a
ranch and take a wife. He had to ride this bronc that was
Necesario to the end and collect his bonus, or face a future of forty a month and grub as a cowboy. Marylou deserved more than that. Beneath the pang of regret the

realization brought, Buck Hawkins knew it went deeper than just money.

He had hired on to do a job. It wasn't finished. He couldn't just ride away. Not and be able to face himself every morning. Changing jobs was second nature to a simple cowboy. Saddle up and ride on to the next outfit. They all offered the same wages, which were few, and the same future, which was none.

But Buck Hawkins wasn't a simple cowboy any longer. He was a landowner, a rancher, a man ready to take a wife. Hawkins leaned back in his chair and sighed heavily. A man's life, he thought, got a lot more complicated when he found that one, special woman—

His train of thought shattered as Wescott barged into the room, his pale face drawn into an agitated frown.

"Now now, Archie," Hawkins said, irritatated. "I don't have time to read what you've written—"

"It's not that, Marshal Hawkins," Wescott waved a copy of a newspaper. "Have you read the latest copy of the *New Mexican*?"

"Not yet. Why?"

"It's the Miller brothers. They're dead. Shot. At long range."

10

BUCK HAWKINS STARED at Archie Wescott in stunned disbelief for a moment.

"What?"

"It's right here. Left column, page one." Wescott tapped a finger against the newspaper. "A deputy was taking the Miller brothers from the jail to the railroad station for transport to the federal penitentiary. Somebody shot the Millers with a long-range gun. The brothers were both down before the deputy even heard the first shot."

Hawkins grabbed the newspaper from Wescott's hand. His fingers chilled as he read the story. Wescott had told it right. Somebody had gotten to the Miller brothers. In the most secure jail in two hundred miles.

He handed the paper back and tore open the letter from the Santa Fe sheriff. The letter was an official report of what happened to the prisoners—with one small, but significant, addition. The sheriff had found the spot from where the shots had been fired: the top of a three-story adobe hotel almost three hundred yards from the spot where the Millers fell. He had also found more than twenty cigarette butts in the shooter's nest. And two spent cartridge hulls, both .50–95 caliber.

Hawkins dropped the report onto the desk and muttered a curse. The gunman had watched and waited, maybe for days, before he got the chance. And the damn .50–95 had turned up again—

"What do you make of it?" Wescott said, his brow furrowed.

"That somebody wanted the Millers out of the way bad enough to risk a long wait. That the shooter may be the same one who tried to bushwhack me. And that whoever the rifleman is, he is one damn fine shot."

Wescott slumped in a chair and toyed with his pencil. "Any idea who could be behind it, Marshal?"

A muscle twitched in Hawkins's jaw. "We've got plenty of suspects to go around, Archie. Clell Reynolds, for one. Ed Joyner, for another. Both men were ready to lynch them the day Dobie and I caught them. And it could be anyone who has ever lost stock to the Millers or other rustlers."

"Maybe the question isn't who," Wescott said thoughtfully. "Maybe the question is why."

Hawkins glanced up, surprised. "That's exactly what I was thinking, Archie. The question of who has the most to gain if they didn't testify before a judge or in open court."

"And who would risk a multiple murder charge over a few head of cattle." Wescott doodled on his notepad for a moment. "In addition, who would try to kill you. Or have you killed. I'm no lawman, but it seems to me the key to the whole thing is that unusual rifle caliber. If we can find out who owns the gun, maybe this would make more sense."

Hawkins stood. "Not 'we,' Archie. That's my job, not yours. Mine and Dobie's. And that's only half the puzzle. The other half is, did someone hire the shooter, and why?"

"You think someone hired him? An assassin, so to speak?"

Hawkins nodded. "I would lay odds on it. Whoever the man is, he's a professional. A hired killer. A man who wouldn't work cheap." He strode to the window and stared down the busy street, still numb from the news.

After a moment, Wescott cleared his throat. "If you don't mind my asking, sir, what makes you think someone would go to the trouble and expense of hiring a professional killer when every cowboy around here carries a rifle?"

The question jolted Hawkins a bit; he realized for the first time that he had been thinking like a lawman instead of a simple cowboy the last few weeks. "I can't really say, Archie. A gut feeling, as much as anything."

"Like a hunch?"

"Like that, I suppose." Hawkins's gaze raked the teeming main street. The crowd seemed to grow by the hour. And the man with the big rifle could be walking along fifty feet away. It was a chilling thought.

"I could ask around."

Hawkins turned to the newsman. "No, Archie. There's no sense in your taking the risk. If you start asking questions about this killer, you could be the next target. I'd as soon not see that."

"I meant asking around about who might profit from all this," Wescott said. "I have the feeling there's a big story in this. I do have some experience in digging up information. Maybe I could turn up something that would help."

Hawkins strode to Wescott's side and placed a hand on the youth's shoulder. "Thanks for the offer, Archie. But I don't want you involved. I've got my hands full now, without having to worry about whether somebody might be after a New York reporter. The biggest favor you could do me is to see if you can find Dobie."

Wescott's shoulders sagged in disappointment, but he nodded. "I know where he is. Playing poker with Miss Timberlake."

"All the more reason to fetch him, then. Before he loses every dime we have." Hawkins forced a smile and dropped his hand away. "If you can drag him away from Squirrel Tooth Kate, tell him what's happened. Ask him to keep an eye on things for a while. I've got to go talk to some folks."

Dobie Garrett leaned back in his chair in a back room of the Palace, thumbed up his hole card, and took a peek. Spade eight.

"Aw, come on, Garrett," the drummer in the suit across the table said with a snort, "you don't expect us to believe you played poker with Doc Holliday and Wyatt Earp. You're pulling our legs."

"Not even a little bitty tug," Garrett said. He caught a queen of hearts on the first up-card deal of the five-card-stud hand. "Was down in Fort Davis. The old one, on the Brazos. John Larn and John Selman set in on that one, too."

"How'd you do? Queen's high."

"Bet a quarter." Dobie turned his head, spat, and grunted at the ping from the brass spittoon. "They cleaned me out. Lost twenty bucks. Them boys could flat play poker, I tell you."

"See your quarter and raise you a quarter, Mr. Garrett," Squirrel Tooth Kate said. She had the deal and a diamond nine up. Dobie hadn't noticed how long her fingers were until now. He wouldn't doubt that she could load up a deck with the best of them if she was of a mind to do some cheating. He was sure she wasn't, though. The stakes weren't high enough in this game.

"What were they like? Holliday and Earp, I mean?"

"Doc was mighty sickly. All humped over, most of the time." Garrett became aware he was being watched. Lucy Ledbetter stood in the doorway, staring at him. Her eyes were hard. A muscle twitched high up on her jaw-line. Garrett nodded a greeting. She didn't answer. He wondered what had got Miss Lucy's bloomers in a wad all of a sudden; she sure didn't look happy about something.

"Dollar to you, Mr. Garrett," Kate said. "How was Wyatt?"

"Seemed fit and happy. Course, he should've been. Had a wad of cash. Call." He tossed a dollar into the pot. "Seems he'd just got through sellin' some gold-painted bricks up in the Panhandle. Met some folks who'd bought 'em, later on. They wasn't grinnin' real big whenever his name come up."

"Thought that was Pat Garrett who sold those bricks," the drummer said. "You any relation to Pat?"

Dobie caught a heart five up. "Nope. He come from a different herd of Garretts. Tell you, ol' Pat had the longest legs I ever seen on a man. Stuck plumb out from under his soogans when we bedded down in them buffalo camps—"

"You're not going to tell us you hunted with Pat Garrett, are you?" the drummer said.

Dobie winked at Squirrel Tooth Kate. "We put a few shaggies down." She winked back. Dobie's blood warmed a bit under the glow of her smile. She had a nice grin. The kind that gave a man the tingles in places. He forced back a grin and leveled a steady glare at the drummer. "Now, feller, you ain't callin' me a liar, are you?"

The drummer, whose line was ladies' undergarments—a job Dobie thought would be a fine way to make a living—blanched. "No, sir—not at all. I certainly wouldn't want to insult a man of your reputation, Mr. Garrett."

"Ace bets," Kate said to the man at her right. The burly teamster tossed a quarter in the pot. Twenty-five-cent bets weren't a table rule. The players had just gotten used to it for a casual game. "Mr. Garrett, are you really as fast with a gun as the stories I hear?"

"Bump a quarter," the player at Dobie's right said.

Garrett shrugged. "I get by." He studied his cards, saw little of promise, but was about to toss in fifty cents just for the sake of company when he felt a tap on his shoulder. He glanced up and lifted an eyebrow. "What is it, Arch?"

"Something important's come up, Marshal—"

"Important enough to bust up a good poker game? Just when I was gettin' on a roll?"

"That you were, Mr. Garrett," Kate said, a twinkle in her eyes. "You haven't won a pot yet."

"Marshal, please," Wescott said urgently. "I have to talk to you. Now." He leaned down and whispered into Garrett's ear.

"I'll be double damned for a scalded possum," Garrett muttered. He pulled the sawed-off double shotgun from its holster, broke the action, and checked the loads.

The corset-seller's eyes went wide. "What the blazes is that thing for?"

"Killin' folks. What else would it be for?" Garrett holstered the weapon, raked in his few remaining coins, and stood. "Deal me out, folks. Little speck of trouble come up." He tipped his hat to Squirrel Tooth Kate. "Been a true pleasure playin' cards with you, ma'am."

"And you, Marshal Garrett. Will you rejoin us later?"

"Doubt it. This here little problem might take a spell. You all have a good time in Necesario, hear?"

Garrett nodded, shook hands, and turned down drink offers as he ambled through the crowd to the door; it was early in the day, even for Dobie, but the liquor was already flowing.

"What was that for?" Wescott said as they stepped onto the veranda. "Checking the shotgun, I mean."

Garrett shifted his chew, spat, and flashed a grin. "Just raggin' that drummer a bit. Give him a chance to yarn his grandkids someday about how he played poker with the fastest gun in the West just before his good friend Dobie Garrett went out to kill somebody." The grin faded as fast as it had formed. "What's this about them Millers gettin' bushwhacked? Just gimme the short end of the yarn, son."

Wescott kept it brief. He had finished the story by the time they had threaded their way through the crush of humanity to the office. Garrett tossed his hat toward the cot, missed, and let it lay.

"Where's Buck at?"

"He said he had to go talk to some people," Wescott said. "I think we should be here when he returns."

Garrett spat his chew into the syrup-can spittoon beside the door and poured himself a cup of coffee. "Reckon you're right, Arch. Sure wish I knowed what the hell's goin' on around here and where that buffalo gun's at right now. Kinda gives a man the crawlies."

"Yes, sir. It does that." Wescott wandered to the window and stared into the street. "That man with the big rifle could be out there right now, watching us."

Garrett winced. "Son, you could've talked all day and not said that."

"Tell me the truth, Marshal," Wescott said over his shoulder, "and I promise I won't use it in the book. Aren't you a bit worried? Maybe even scared?"

"Worried? Hell, no, I ain't worried. Ain't nothin' Buck and me can't handle." He sniffed aloud. "You the one been writin' what fast guns and dead shots me and him are, son. How come you ask?"

"No offense. Just curious, I suppose. I'm trying to imagine what it's like to be a lawman. A gunman. Someone facing death at any moment—Uh-oh."

Garrett's heart skipped a beat. "What is it?"

"Ed Joyner's coming. He's in a wagon. He has a couple of others with him."

"Prob'ly just comin' in for a little poker, son," Garrett said with an inner sigh of relief.

"I doubt that, Marshal. Most people don't ride into town for a poker game with their rifles drawn."

Garrett came to his feet, hurried to the window, and barked a curse. Joyner and his crew were headed straight toward the office. Even from this distance, Dobie could tell Joyner was not a happy man.

"See if you can find Buck, Arch," Garrett said. "Appears we got trouble on the way."

Hawkins stood beside the spring wagon, his gut churning. The sound of someone retching against the alley wall a few feet away did nothing to calm the yelps in his own stomach.

Buck halfway expected it to be Archie Wescott tossing his breakfast biscuits in the alley. It wasn't. Wescott stood beside Garrett, his face showing no expression as he studied the body.

The man in the back of the wagon didn't have much chest left. Shattered rib fragments protruded pinkish-white from the clotted goo that had been the man's left lung, heart, and chest muscles. His deep brown eyes were wide open, but they didn't see the mare's tail clouds in the sky overhead. Big Chihuahua rowels on the ornate spurs, still strapped to his dusty boots, glittered in the sunlight. The J-Bar brand was carved into the spur straps.

The dead man was Juan Montoya. He was—or had been—the *segundo,* the strawboss, of the J-Bar.

The crowd of onlookers jammed five deep around the wagon said little. The few words that were spoken were soft, little more than mutters.

"Jesus," one of the voices said in awe, "it looks like he got hit with a damn cannonball."

Wescott glanced up. "Large-caliber rifle. Most likely at fairly close range. Soft lead bullet, probably whittled or grooved for maximum expansion."

Hawkins cut a surprised glance at Wescott. The young man's voice had been matter-of-fact, almost casual. Wescott had his head down now, scribbling in his note-book, his face shadowed by the brim of the derby hat. Buck let his gaze drift around the crowd for a moment, then swallowed against the acrid taste of bile on his tongue.

"You folks go on about your business now," Hawkins said. He hoped his own voice didn't sound as shaky as it felt. Nobody seemed in a big hurry to move. Dead men always drew a crowd, Buck thought. "Go on. Break it up."

A few of the bystanders began to drift away. Most ignored the order and stayed clustered around the wagon.

"Nothin' here but a dead Messkin," a swarthy man

standing by the rear wheel muttered. "No big loss—"
The color faded from his face. The barrels of Garrett's
sawed-off shotgun were an inch from the man's nostrils;
the clunk of heavy hammers drawn to full cock were
loud in the sudden silence.

"Feller," Garrett said, his tone icy, "if you don't shut
your damned mouth and git—right now—your nose
holes is gonna be a helluva lot bigger than they was.
Savvy?"

The swarthy man savvied. He took a couple of hesi-
tant steps back, then turned and hurried away. The man
had done him a favor, Hawkins thought as he watched
him go. He had stirred up a glimmer of anger that
calmed the yelps in Buck's belly. He turned to one of the
men standing beside the wagon.

"Mr. Doolin, fetch Fess McLocklin, please. There'll
have to be a coroner's inquest. Mr. McLocklin's a judge.
He can handle the details." He turned to Joyner. "What
happened?"

"What the hell does it look like happened? Jesus, I
have to draw you a picture? Somebody bushwhacked my
segundo, that's what happened!"

Hawkins leveled a steady gaze at the J-Bar boss. The
man was about ready to explode, Buck thought. "All
right, Mr. Joyner, calm down. Just tell me what happened."

Joyner drew in a deep breath. The sarcastic rage in his
tone eased. "We found him five miles north of J-Bar
range, on Reynolds's land. Shot in the back. Juan had a
wife and two young kids. What are you going to do
about it, Hawkins? Or do we have to handle it ourselves?"

"We'll investigate, Mr. Joyner," Hawkins said. "Go
on."

Joyner's shoulders seemed to sag. "As near as we could tell from the tracks, Juan was trailing about a hundred head of cows. J-Bar cows. Prime Hereford stock."

"Stolen?"

"Hell, yes, they were stolen! Herefords don't drift fifteen miles from good water and grass. You ought to know that."

Hawkins nodded. "I know. Go ahead with the story."

"We knew something was wrong when Juan's horse came back with the saddle empty. We found him in the bottom of a shallow wash. The slug hit him between the backbone and left shoulder blade and came out his chest." Joyner shook his head. "My God, I've never seen a man blown open like that . . ." His voice trailed away.

"Did you search the place where it happened? Find any tracks?"

Joyner seemed to collect himself with an effort. "We didn't find any sign of the bushwhacker. A couple of other hands followed the stolen cows for several miles. Said it looked like there were five riders moving them. They were headed for the badlands country on the west side of the Rocking R." A blood vessel throbbed in Joyner's temple. "I never thought Clell Reynolds would stoop this damn low—shooting a man in the back."

Hawkins and Joyner stepped aside as a grim J-Bar rider pulled a canvas tarp over what had been Juan Montoya.

"Maybe Reynolds didn't do it," Hawkins said.

"Who the hell else would? That scrawny little chicken-neck bastard's been nothing but trouble. Stealing my stock. Hogging the water. And now, Juan." Pure rage flashed in the black eyes. "By God, he's not getting away with this, Hawkins! I'll put every man in my crew in the saddle and shoot Reynolds and his hired guns to pieces—"

"No, you won't, Mr. Joyner." Hawkins held the lean man's stare. "Dobie and I will check it out, talk to Reynolds. If there's proof, or even the hint of it, that he's behind this, we'll bring him in. But nobody is going to go shooting up anybody unless they go through Dobie and me first. Is that understood?"

"You standing up for that back-shooter, Hawkins? Are you on Reynolds's payroll too? Like the Miller brothers?"

"Watch your mouth, Ed," Garrett said, his tone sharp. "Nobody owns Buck and me. Nobody."

"Dammit, you're association men," Joyner protested. "I'm helping pay your wages—"

"Maybe. That don't mean you own these badges."

"I helped get you hired. I can get you fired."

"Could be we ain't that easy to get rid of, Ed."

Buck lifted a hand. "Settle down, Dobie. We don't have the time to get into a pissing contest right now. Mr. Joyner, how do you know the Millers were taking money from Reynolds?"

"Everybody in the county knows that. If you'd been doing your job around here, you'd know it, too." The hard, cold fury surged back into Joyner's face.

"I suppose you have proof of that?" Hawkins said, making it a question more than a comment.

"Don't need proof. There's got to be something behind all that talk."

"Talk doesn't carry much weight in a courtroom, Mr. Joyner."

Joyner tapped a hand against his holstered revolver. "This is my courtroom, Hawkins. Judge and jury. And I won't shy away from calling Colonel Colt's court into session."

"You do," Hawkins said, "and I'll have to lock you up. For murder. Don't make me do that."

For a tense moment, Joyner stared into Hawkins's eyes and his weight shifted onto the balls of his feet. The blood vessel in his temple pulsed. Then he seemed to relax; his hand dropped away from the weapon.

"All right, Hawkins. I've got a good man and a good friend to bury. And after that, figure out how to keep his widow and two little kids from starving." Joyner's black eyes softened, but didn't lose their spark. "I'll give you this much slack. One week. Find out who did this, or it's war. Between the J-Bar and the Rocking R."

Hawkins nodded. "We'll find out, Mr. Joyner. But I warn you, there will be no range war here as long as I'm wearing a badge."

"Judge's comin'," Garrett said.

Hawkins glanced across the street. Fess McLocklin shuffled toward the wagon. Dust puffs kicked up from the tip of the ornate cane that carried most of the wizened old man's weight.

Buck turned to Garrett. "Dobie, put together four or five days' worth of trail supplies. We'll use Buttermilk for pack. Ask Trace Willis to saddle Cornbread for me. Bring the mounts back here. As soon as the judge is finished, we'll ride out. Mr. Joyner can point us to where it happened."

Wescott flipped his notebook closed and tucked it into the inside breast pocket of his suit. "I'll help." He followed Dobie.

The inquest didn't take long. Killed by person or persons unknown. The same preliminary finding handed down for the Miller brothers. A common ruling on the frontier, Hawkins thought.

"Better get Juan home and buried, Ed, or this heat . . ." McLocklin shook his head. "Damn shame. Juan was a good man."

"Go ahead, Mr. Joyner," Hawkins said. "We'll catch up with you on the way."

McLocklin blinked against the glare of sunlight. "How long was Juan with you, Ed?"

"Ten years. We rode many a long, hard trail together."

"Express my sympathies to Triciana. Tell her not to worry about the future. The association will take care of her."

"Thanks, Fess," Joyner said, "but the J-Bar takes care of its own." He pinned a quick, pointed glare on Hawkins, then climbed into the wagon seat and picked up the reins.

The association leader leaned on his cane at Hawkins's side and watched as the wagon and the J-Bar riders reached the bend of the main street and disappeared from sight.

McLocklin finally broke the silence. "So, Marshal. What do you plan to do now?"

"Find out who did it."

"And if you can't?"

Hawkins sighed. "Then, Mr. McLocklin, we could be in a mess of trouble. Headed for a range war between the J-Bar and the Rocking R unless Dobie and I can stop it."

McLocklin hawked and spat. "Reynolds." He spoke the name as though it were a curse word. "Mark my words, Hawkins. There's going to be a lot of blood spilled over that man. Ed Joyner and Juan Montoya have a lot of friends around Necesario."

"What makes you so sure Reynolds is behind it?"

"Who else could be?"

"That's what I intend to find out, sir," Hawkins said.

McLocklin's cane thumped the boardwalk. "If he is—and I have no reason to believe he's not—most of the blood spilled will be Rocking R blood. The association won't roll over to get its belly scratched like a hound. We'll fight, if that's what Clell Reynolds wants."

Hawkins didn't reply. He stood and watched the old man shuffle back across the street, then turned and went into the marshal's office. He took his rifle and Garrett's long-barreled shotgun from the rack, and a couple of extra boxes of ammunition for each from a desk drawer. Marylou's letters still lay atop the desk. Hawkins's blood chilled. For the first time, he fully realized just how much he stood to lose.

He folded the letters with care and placed them into a tin box in the bottom desk drawer. There wouldn't be much time for reading over the next few days, and he would know they were there when he got back. If he did. A man with a big gun was still out there someplace.

Saddle leather creaked outside. Hawkins picked up the weapons and ammunition, strode through the door, and abruptly stopped. Archie Wescott sat in a flat English-style saddle atop a mule.

"What's this?" Hawkins said.

"I'm going with you this time, Marshal Hawkins," Wescott said, his tone firm. "Either I ride with you or I follow you, but you're not making me stay behind. I'm going along—"

"The hell you are," Hawkins snapped. "Son, we're in for a long, hard ride that could just wind up in a shooting. It's going to be tricky enough without having a raw greenhorn underfoot all the way."

"I can hold my own." Wescott's jaw was set, the look

in his eyes determined, his shoulders squared. "Marshal, you've been telling me to go away and be quiet ever since I got here. By God, I'm tired of being left out. I won't be this time."

Hawkins glanced at Garrett. Dobie shrugged. "Boy's done got his neck bowed up on us this time, Buck. Tried to argue him out of it. Might as well be fussin' with a stump. We got to take him along, knock him in the head, or lock him up. Reckon it's up to you, partner."

Hawkins sighed. "Must be the heat."

"What?"

"Seems like everybody wants to pick a fight today, Archie." Hawkins glared at the young man. "I haven't got the time or inclination to argue. Can you ride?"

"Some."

"Can you shoot?"

"Some."

"Well, hell," Hawking snorted in disgust, "I suppose that puts you one up on Dobie, anyway. Are you armed?"

Wescott lifted the lapel of his coat. The grips of a revolver showed from a shoulder holster under his left arm.

Hawkins sighed. "All right, son, you can go. But here's the rules. Watch the landmarks while we ride, because if you can't keep up, you're on your own to get back. If there's shooting, get the hell out of the way. You don't ride across any hot trails, and you pull your share of camp chores. Agreed?"

"Yes, sir, but—"

"No buts. Enough talk for one day." Hawkins handed Garrett the long-barrel shotgun and 12-gauge shell box, stuffed his own Winchester into the saddle scabbard and the .44–40 cartridges in his cantle bags, and mounted Cornbread. "Let's go."

"Son," Garrett said with an amused glance at the young man on the mule, "I thought you said you could ride. You look like you got a corncob stuck up your backside."

Wescott's face flushed. At least Hawkins thought it did; the New Yorker's fair skin had already started to sunburn again. Apparently, Buck thought, the sun never shone on the East Coast.

"I beg your pardon?" Wescott said. He sounded a bit miffed. "I am maintaining the proper seat on his animal."

"You're stiff as a board, son. And that mule's gettin' a bit put out with you. He's likely to buck your skinny butt off any minute now if you don't relax and work with him."

Wescott's flush deepened. "I'll have you know, Marshal Garrett, that I had several lessons less than a year ago with the finest equestrian instructor in Central Park."

"Eck-what?"

"Equestrian. It means horsemanship."

Garrett shook his head in dismay. "Arch, horsemanship ain't prancin' around no big corral on some shiny, high-steppin' pony and wearin' one of them fancy swallowtail coats. Brushin' the frost off a green bronc's back on a February mornin' before saddlin' up and steppin' onto the hurricane deck's horsemanship. Buck there, he's passin' fair at ridin' the rough string. Not as good as me, but fair."

Hawkins twisted in the saddle to study the young man riding beside Dobie. Wescott's back was ramrod straight, his legs stiff in the leathers of the flat, hornless saddle, the toes of his dress shoes turned up in the stirrups, the reins in both hands, like a farmer driving a team. Sweat rings already darkened the armpits of Wescott's three-piece suit. His narrow-brimmed felt derby was covered in a fine layer of dust; the red cravat at his neck, held in place by a pearl stickpin, was soaked at the neck. Wescott looked like the raw greenhorn he was, Hawkins thought.

"Dobie has a point, Archie," Hawkins said. "The English riding style has its place, but not out here. Relax. Let your body move with the animal. Work with the mule, not against him, or you'll both be worn out in two hours."

Garrett chuckled aloud. "Besides which, son, that mule's been gettin' madder by the mile. He's about ready to either buck or sull up. Mules is like that. How come you're ridin' a long-ear, anyway?"

"The livery owner said this was the only saddle animal he had for rent."

"He was puttin' you on, Arch. Prob'ly thought it'd be quite a show, puttin' a greenhorn on a mule. Reckon he was right at that. You're some sight." Garrett nodded toward the flat saddle. "Guess you rented that rig, too?"

"Yes, sir. I was most fortunate that he actually had an equestrian saddle available. Those Western saddles look terribly uncomfortable. And heavy."

"They don't leak."

"Pardon?"

Hawkins said, "What Dobie means, Archie, is that it's easier to ride a bucking horse in a stock saddle than in one of those English numbers. At least with these, we've got a horn to grab if a horse blows up with us."

Garrett shook his head. "That little piece of leather ain't big enough to strop a razor on."

Hawkins reined in at the top of a low rise. "We're here. This is the place Joyner described. Time to go to work, Dobie."

The rocky ridge overlooked a shallow valley about half a mile wide. Scrub brush, Spanish dagger plants, and a smattering of mesquites battled with the sparse bunchgrass for any sip of moisture. A dry creek bed ambled its way down the sun-baked valley. Hawkins figured the creek had been dry for weeks. On the edge of the badlands and sand hills in this part of New Mexico, water was scarce the year around. It was even more scarce in summer.

"This is where Mr. Montoya was shot?" Wescott stared toward the valley floor.

Garrett worked his chew for a moment and spat. The bay ducked the tobacco spit glob. "That's what Ed Joyner said. Found him down layin' just past that little cedar bush down there."

"It seems such a—I don't know. A lonely place to die in," Wescott said, his voice soft.

"Son, there ain't no good place to die," Garrett said. "'Cept maybe in a pretty gal's bed with a bottle of good whiskey on the nightstand and a big grin on your face." He glanced at Hawkins. "What's your pleasure, partner?"

"Scout around and see what we can find, if the J-Bar riders haven't tracked the place up too bad." He turned to Wescott. "Archie, remember what I said. Watch where you're going. Don't ride over any hot trails and stay out of the way. Dobie, it's time we earned our keep."

11

BUCK HAWKINS SHOOK his head in disgust as he knelt on the sandy floor of the valley twenty feet beyond the lengthening shadow of the twisted cedar tree.

The J-Bar cowboys who found Montoya's body had managed to track up the ground worse than a buffalo stampede. The only signs recognizable for yards around were a blackish stain where Montoya's blood had soaked into the sand and the tracks of the wagon that had picked up his body.

Hawkins sighed and looked around. Dobie Garrett was thirty yards away, on foot, leading his bay horse as he peered at the ground. Garrett glanced up, caught Hawkins's gaze, and shook his head. Archie Wescott was still in the saddle almost a hundred yards off. The mule he rode appeared to be asleep, ears flopped and hipshot, one hind hoof cocked onto the toe.

"Waste of time, Buck," Garrett called. "There's more tracks around here than the Fort Worth stockyards. No way we can sort 'em out as to who's who."

Hawkins stood, glanced at the lowering sun, and motioned to Garrett to come in. "I was afraid that's what we'd fine, Dobie," he said as Garrett mounted and rode up. Dobie never walked more than ten feet when he could ride a horse. "We'll have to do it the hard way now. We're losing light fast. We'll camp here tonight and start hunting tomorrow."

"Mind if I take a look?" Wescott's call carried well as the wind died to a soft breeze.

"Might as well let the kid take a gander," Garrett said. "Ain't nothin' here he could mess up."

Hawkins waved Wescott to come ahead. The young New Yorker woke the mule up long enough to ride to within a few feet of the cedar. Wescott stood in the narrow iron stirrups, looked around for a moment, then dismounted. He flexed his legs, rubbed his knees, and then stared silently at the blackish blood smudge for a moment. A frown creased his sunburned brow.

"Is this where the body was?"

Hawkins nodded.

"That would be a bloodstain, then. Mr. Montoya's blood."

"That's the way Dobie and I see it," Hawkins said. "It's about the only sign the J-Bar riders didn't wipe out with all their milling around. We'll never find the shooter's tracks now."

"Maybe the men who found him didn't stop to think things through—to figure out where to look."

Garrett sniffed aloud. "And I reckon you can?"

"Perhaps. If you would hold my mule for a moment, Marshal Garrett?"

"Prop the jackass up is more like it," Garrett groused. "Damn long-ear's asleep again." But he took the reins.

Wescott squatted beside the dark stain for a moment, then duckwalked a step and brushed his fingertips on the sand. He moved a yard to his right, then to his left.

"Prospectin', son?" Garrett said, a hint of amusement in his tone.

"In a manner of speaking, yes, sir." Wescott stared at

the ground. He studied the ground a bit longer, shook his head, and stood. He strode to the south side of the stunted cedar and touched a finger to a thin leaf. "I may have found it."

"Found what, Archie?"

"The blood pattern, Marshal Hawkins."

"Blood pattern?"

"Yes, sir. Mr. Montoya didn't fall from the saddle immediately when he was shot. His horse probably bolted and carried him a couple of strides past the cedar before he fell."

"Yeah," Garrett said, disgusted, "and I'm probably richer'n the Pope—"

"Wait a minute, Dobie," Hawkins interrupted. "It could be he's on to something. We've both seen deer shot through the heart and lungs and still run a hundred yards before they went down. Go ahead, Archie."

Wescott rubbed another cedar branch and peered at something between his fingers. "Lung tissue." He squinted into the cedar, then grunted. "Here's a limb clipped. Probably by the slug, after it went through Mr. Montoya." He stepped back a couple of feet and stopped. "I'd guess he was about here when the bullet hit him."

"Damned if we ain't got a wet-behind-the-ears greenhorn actin' like he was Tom Horn on us," Garrett said with a snort.

"Shut up, Dobie," Hawkins said. "Quit talking and listen. We might learn something here."

Wescott didn't speak for a moment. He stood and stared at the cedar, then toward the bloodstain in the sand. Finally, he turned and started walking. Hawkins and Garrett followed, leading the horses.

Fifty yards to the south and west of the cedar tree, a

twisted mesquite with a thick, gnarled trunk drooped against the heat, its thin leaves dry and brown. Wescott stopped beside the tree.

"The shot was fired from here," he said. He knelt beside the mesquite. "See the scuff mark on this limb? Where it grows from the trunk?"

Hawkins peered at the fork in the tree. He would have missed the faint scrape if he hadn't been looking down at Wescott's finger. He would also have missed the marks in the soil three feet behind the tree. The marks were the imprint of a knee and the toe of a boot.

"The rifleman used the fork for a rest, I think," Wescott said. "I would guess that whoever it was knelt here on one knee, propped the rifle barrel against the fork to steady his aim, and waited for just the right shot he wanted. Judging from the distance between the toe mark and the knee, he'd be a heavy man. Medium height."

Garrett frowned at the young Easterner. "I suppose you've got his name in your back pocket, too—well, I'll be damned."

"What is it, Dobie?"

Garrett crouched, reached into a prickly pear clump, cursed as one of the spines bit him, and then held up a brass cartridge case. "The kid just might of been right, Buck. This here brass come from a .50–95 Express. Like another one we've eyeballed here lately." He tossed the case to Hawkins.

Hawkins studied the head stamp on the brass for a moment, then pulled from his pocket the spent cartridge that had been fired at him.

Wescott held out a palm. "Mind if I take a look?"

Hawkins handed over the cartridge brass. Wescott turned them between his thumbs and forefingers, tilted

the cases to catch the angle of sunlight just so, then nodded. "They're from the same rifle," he said.

"What?"

"Take a close look here, Marshal. The firing pin strike
is slightly off center on both cartridges. Examine it
closely and you can see that both primers were struck by
a firing pin that is somewhat flat on one side, not completely round, yet not quite triangular. More of a three-
quarter moon shape. The odds of two rifles having such
strange-shaped firing pins are rather long. The odds
against two such rifles being in the same general geo-
graphical area at the same time are astronomical."

Hawkins studied the case markings intently for a moment. His heartbeat increased. "Archie's right, Dobie.
I'd bet a good horse and a year's wages these came from
the same rifle. Here, take a look for yourself."

The scorn in Garrett's expression faded as he examined the casings. "Son," he said, "it 'pears to me you got
something between them jug ears after all." He handed
the brass back to Hawkins. "Reckon I owe you one of
them sorry-I-said-thats, Arch. How come you know so
much about this man-shootin' business, anyway? Ever
done it?"

"No. But I learned a few things from my father."
Wescott's words were soft. "He was a detective with the
New York police department when I was working the
police beat for the *Times*. He was the chief homicide in-
vestigator."

"Oh," Garrett said. "I reckon that's how come you
didn't toss your breakfast biscuits when they brung pore
ol' Juan in lookin' like he'd caught a cannonball through
the gizzard. Like to have urped myself, but it didn't
seem to bother you none. And you sorta surprised me

with that talk about shavin' off and cuttin' bullets to make big holes like that one in Juan."

Wescott's shoulders sagged. "I've seen similar wounds before, Marshal Garrett. In my father. Two years ago."

"Jesus," Dobie said.

"I was the one who found him, in the alley behind our house. They never caught the man who killed him. Or even figured out why." He sighed and stared toward the east. "I guess that was one reason I jumped at the chance to do the novel on you two. To get away from the big city for a time. And for the money, of course. Dad never made much money, so it's up to me to provide for Mom, to make sure she doesn't lose the house and all."

Hawkins dropped the spent casings into his pocket and put a hand on Wescott's shoulder. "I'm sorry, Archie. We didn't know."

"I never mentioned it, and I doubt that the assassination of a New York policeman made it to the cowboy campfire news. Don't concern yourselves with my problems. It looks like we have enough to worry about right here." The young man squared his shoulders. "So, what do we do now?"

Hawkins glanced at the sun. It was within a handspan of the western horizon. "Light will be gone soon. We can't do much except camp for the night. By the way, I noticed you limping a bit."

Wescott grimaced. "My ankles. They are a bit raw."

"Should have got yourself a pair of boots, son," Dobie said.

A faint smile twitched Wescott's chapped lips. "Another lesson learned by the greenhorn about life in the West. I've already picked up one valuable tip."

"What's that, Arch?"

"That a man on the trail should take a leak whenever he gets the chance, Marshal Garrett. I've been about to pee in my pants for the last hour. So, if you'll excuse me?" Wescott strode a few yards back of the mesquite, relieved himself, and started back to the camp Garrett and Hawkins had set up.

Wescott stopped in mid-stride and peered at the ground. "Marshal Hawkins," he called.

Buck strode to his side. "What is it, Archie?"

Wescott squatted beside a prickly pear patch. "A hoof-print. It could be one left by the rifleman's horse."

Hawkins knelt beside Wescott, studied the single print, and a chill went up his spine. The print was identical to the one he had found after the bushwhacking attempt on the way back from San Jon. A triangle-shaped piece the size of Hawkins's little fingernail was missing from the right front quarter side of the shoe.

"Think it could be something, Marshal?"

"No doubt about it, Archie." Hawkins called to Garrett. "Ever notice a track like this during our scouts, Dobie? Or around town?" he asked as Garrett stopped alongside.

Garrett studied the print for a moment, frowning, then shook his head. "Can't say as I have, partner. Reckon it was left by the shooter's hoss?"

"I'd bet on it. I found the same track after somebody took a few shots at me. Archie, do you have your notebook and pencil with you?"

"I never go anywhere without it, sir."

"Can you sketch that for us? All Dobie and I can draw is flies."

"Sure." Wescott pulled his notepad from an inside coat pocket, flipped to a blank page, and went to work. Moments later he had a remarkably detailed sketch,

down to the number of nails, a scale that showed the size
of the print and the triangular chip, and notations that included the date, time, and location of the find. He had to
ask Hawkins the location. Buck took a guess; he wasn't
exactly familiar with the stretch of country.

"Good job, Archie," Hawkins said. "If that track was
left by the shooter's horse, it just might lead us to him. If
we can find the animal, we can find him."

"I'll get on the trail first thing in the mornin'," Garrett
said. "I'm the tracker in the outfit. Buck here couldn't
follow a three-legged, gut-shot buffalo through belly-
deep snow."

"If the man riding that horse has a bottle of whiskey
with him," Hawkins said to Wescott, "Dobie can find
him. If he doesn't, it's a lost cause. Let's get some grub
and a little rest. We'll be on the move at first light."

Garrett had skillet duty, which meant overcooked
bacon, cold biscuits from the possibles sack, and coffee.
Hawkins tended the mounts. The bacon had started to
sizzle when he walked back the few yards to camp.

Wescott stood with his back to the campfire, staring at
the western horizon. The sun had set. In its wake was a
red-gold wash that lifted from the black of jagged, distant hills, and filled a quarter of the sky before fading to
shades of ever deepening blue to purple. A wisp of
mare's tail clouds above the skyline blazed crimson
slashes through the gold. On impulse, Hawkins strode to
Wescott's side and stood, silent, for a moment.

"My God," Wescott finally said, his words tinged with
awe and hushed in reverence, "I've never seen such a
spectacular sunset."

"Pretty showy at that, even for New Mexico,"
Hawkins said. He didn't add that he had seen many such
sunsets before. And never got tired of looking at them.

"That's one of the things about this country that grabs hold of a man and won't let go, Archie. Sort of the Creator's payback for filling the place with thorns, rattlers, scorpions, and cactus, I suppose."

Wescott didn't speak for a long time. The colors began to fade as the sky darkened. Finally, he sighed. "We never see things quite like this in New York City. Too many buildings, too much smoke, too many ground lights in the way."

"Chuck's ready," Garrett called.

"I think I understand now why this country can set its hooks in a man," Wescott said. "But it's a shame."

"What's a shame?"

"That man can destroy something like this. Just by being here."

"You got that right, Archie. Let's get some grub. Don't expect Dobie's cooking to compare with those fine French restaurants back East, though."

Wescott reluctantly turned away from the last splash of color. "Right now," he said, "I don't care how fancy it is. I could eat anything that didn't eat me first." He glanced at the revolver on Hawkins's left hip. "Marshal, weren't you carrying your gun on the right side before?"

Garrett glanced up and grinned. "Ol' Buck's a two-gun man for sure, Arch. Greased lightin' with either hand. Found out he was faster on the draw with the left biscuit hook."

"Yeah," Hawkins said. "I can pull that weapon in less than a half hour from that side. I'm a lot faster than Dobie."

"Sorry, Arch, no tea," Garrett said. "Have to make do with coffee."

Wescott pulled a tin cup from his pack, which was a simple burlap bag tied with sturdy cord. "Coffee's fine.

If I'm going to write about the West, I might as well pick up the relevant habits."

"Won't get much of a coffee habit on this trip, son. It's twenty miles to water, and that water might not be no good," Garrett said. "We'll have one last pot in the mornin'. Got to save what drinkin' water we got. And no washin' or shavin' or any other such tomfoolery till we get back to town, Arch. You gonna be a Western man, you gotta learn grubby."

"That," Hawkins said with a wry grin and a scrape of his thumb across a stubbled chin, "is something we can definitely teach you. Fork and pour, Dobie. It's hungry out tonight."

Archie Wescott was learning, Hawkins thought.

The young New Yorker was beginning to catch on to riding *with* the mule instead of just *on* him. He still sat a bit too stiff in the saddle, but he had relaxed some.

As much as anyone could relax under the circumstances.

Hawkins had a fair case of the yips himself. Dobie Garrett hadn't helped much when he sort of offhandedly mentioned that until they cut sign on the shooter with the buffalo gun and knew for sure where he was, the man could be drawing the sights down on them right now.

So far, there had been no sign.

Four hours into daylight, they still rode ever-widening circles from the spot where Montoya had died. And still no hoofprint with a chip missing from the upper right quarter. It was enough, Hawkins granted, to spook any thinking man.

Garrett didn't seem to be worried. He was out of sight now, riding the outside loop, but Hawkins could still swear he heard Dobie's off-key whistling, as if the stocky cowboy didn't have a care in the world.

Hawkins rode the middle loop, with Wescott trailing fifty yards or so behind. Hawkins had to force himself to study the ground, when every nerve in his body yelped at him to pay attention to the surrounding countryside. They had no trouble cutting sign on the stolen cattle. Over a hundred head of cows left a wide track. The herd trailed north by northwest, toward the ragged, broken, and almost waterless badlands on the west side of Clell Reynolds's Rocking R outfit.

That didn't make sense either, Hawkins thought. Rustlers didn't trail stolen stock to a place where there was little grass and even less water. A thief could lose money on stolen stock that way.

Hawkins fretted, too, about the wind. It had started just after sunrise and gained strength throughout the morning. Already, it threatened to rip the hat from his head, and it showed no signs of easing. Swirls of blown sand and red dirt soon would wipe out any sign left by a single horseman. If they didn't cut the shooter's tracks soon, they might never find them.

A shrill whistle jerked Hawkins's head up.

Garrett sat the saddle on a ridge a hundred yards away, waving his hat. Hawkins motioned to Wescott to follow and kneed the buckskin into a trot.

Dobie had dismounted at the bottom of the ridge and was whittling off a fresh chew as Hawkins reined in, Wescott close behind.

"Cut sign, Dobie?"

Garrett popped the chew in his mouth and nodded. He pointed to the ground in front of his boot with the tip of his pocketknife blade.

"Got the jasper, partner," Garrett said. "Sign's old.

Drifted over some. Looks to me the shooter followed the herd a ways, mixed his tracks up with them others, then dropped off. Near as I can tell, he headed thataway." He pointed toward the northeast with the knife blade. "Toward Rockin' R headquarters, if he kept movin' on a sort of straight line." Garrett folded his pocketknife and tucked it back into the special pocket sewed into his shotgun-style leather chaps.

Hawkins swung down and studied the hoofprints. "How long do you figure since he came by here, Dobie?"

Garrett shrugged. "Hard to say. I was to guess, I'd guess not all that long after ol' Juan got blasted." He worked the chew and spat. "Cold trail, Buck. Way this wind's blowin', we can maybe cut sign on him again and maybe not. We can try trackin' him, or we could see can we get them J-Bar cows back. What's your pleasure?"

Hawkins's brow furrowed. After a moment, he sighed and stood. "We have to try to find him, Dobie. Before he finds us first."

"You think he would try to kill us, Marshal?"

"Hell, yes, he would, son," Garrett said with a glance at the wide-eyed and sunburned Wescott. "He's done took a pop at Buck and shot the Miller boys, ain't he? No reason to think he'll stop here. 'Specially if that jasper knows we're trackin' him." He worked the chew a moment and spat. "Killin' men's like eatin' chicken legs, Arch. Man gets a taste of it, he can't hardly stop."

Dobie stood. "Mount up, gents. Could be a long day ahead. Arch, Buck, and me's gonna be some busy lookin' at the ground. Might be best if you was to sorta keep your head up. You see anything move or somethin' don't look right, holler. And don't waste no time before yelpin'."

The sun had slid halfway down the western sky by the time Garrett, kneeling in the windswept sand, looked up and shook his head.

"No use fightin' this bronc any longer, partner," he said to Hawkins. "Wind's done whupped us, far as trackin' goes. Been two hours since we last cut sign on that jasper. Trail's still a day old, and we ain't four good miles from where we started."

Wescott took his nervous gaze from a cedar-studded ridge up ahead long enough to glance at Garrett. "Are you sure, Marshal Garrett? You don't think he could be waiting for us up ahead?"

Garrett tongued his chew and spat. "Didn't say that, son. Just sayin' we lost the trail."

"I never thought following a trail could be such hard, slow work." Wescott said. "In all our books, a bent blade of grass or an overturned stone is all a Western man needs."

"Better quit readin' them books, Arch. Why, Tom Horn hisself couldn't foller this feller, and Horn weren't no slouch at trackin'. I remember one time back in 'Pache country, ol' Tom and me was after this bronco bunch—"

"Save the wild yarns for hot stove time, Dobie," Hawkins interrupted, his tone a bit sharper than he'd intended. "At least we have an idea where he might have been headed. The Rocking R's still quite a ride off. We're going to call on Reynolds. He has some questions to answer."

Garrett shrugged. "Fine by me."

"Wait a minute," Wescott said, his face pale beneath the sun- and windburn, "you're planning to ride into a nest of men, all armed, whom you've already humiliated and put into jail once? And *ask* them if they killed a man and stole cattle?"

"Reckon so, son. You got a better idea?"

"Yes. Go home before we get shot."

Garrett cast a sly wink at Hawkins. "Boy's got the makin's of a real Western man after all. Reckon some of the shine's gone off the manhuntin' business." He turned to Wescott. "Arch, you got a reason to fret. But do you really reckon Reynolds'd take a chance throwin' down on two mean-eyed, fast-draw, dead-shot gunslingers like us?"

Wescott swallowed. "It isn't out of the realm of possibility, from what I've seen of Mr. Reynolds. He doesn't strike me as the type who would be afraid of anybody."

"And we ain't afraid of him, neither. Are we, partner?"

"As a matter of fact, no, we're not afraid," Hawkins said. "Don't ask about terrified. Let's ride."

Garrett swung into the saddle. "Well, son," he said to Wescott, "as the Injuns say, it ain't that bad a day to die. A tad windier'n I'd like, but not bad."

Hawkins said, "Archie, there's no need for you to take a chance. Can you find your way back to Necesario?"

"I could, but I won't," Wescott said. "I can't write the story if I don't see what happens. I'm going along."

Garrett shrugged. "Your funeral, son. Let's ride."

Hawkins tried to ignore the sudden, insistent yelp from his bladder as he reined in before the Rocking R headquarters, Garrett at his right and Wescott to his left.

The main house was stone and adobe, with a porch running the full length. And with five men standing on the porch. Two held rifles. The other two had their hands near holstered six-guns. Clell Reynolds stood in the middle.

"What the hell are you doing on my place?" Reynolds growled by way of greeting.

"Hunting a killer, Mr. Reynolds," Hawkins said. He kept his hand on the saddle horn as much to hide the tremble of his fingers as to reassure the Rocking R owner he didn't intend to pull a weapon.

"What killer?"

"Somebody bushwhacked a J-Bar rider yesterday. We trailed the killer from the spot toward your ranch."

Reynolds lifted a bushy gray eyebrow. "That a fact? And you ride in here like Christ Almighty, saying one of my men did it? Marshal, you're walking on quicksand. One word from me, and my boys here will cut you to pieces."

Hawkins's bladder yelped again. His gaze swept the men on the porch. A wiry little man called Jackknife was next to Reynolds, a big revolver strapped around his narrow hips. Two men Hawkins didn't know were on Reynolds's right.

Garrett leaned to the side and spat; the bay ducked, but this time the horse's ears hadn't been in the line of fire.

"Be a shame was it to come to that, Clell," Garrett said, his tone calm. "Hate to see you and your boys get dead."

Reynolds's eyes went cold and narrow. "You think you two are hosses enough to take five of us?"

"They's three, in case you ain't noticed," Garrett said. "Archie, somebody here tries to pull iron, you kill them two on the left. I'll drop the others. Way I count, that'd leave just you for Buck, Clell."

"Easy, Dobie," Hawkins said, hoping his voice didn't crack. "It doesn't have to come to that."

For a couple of heartbeats, Hawkins was afraid Reynolds was about to start the dance. Buck tensed, half expecting to feel the wallop of a lead slug within seconds. Then Reynolds snorted and shook his head.

"Damned if you boys don't have bigger balls than a Kiowa war chief," he said. He glanced at the men on the porch. "Back off, men. We'll parley some first. Shoot them later if we have to."

Hawkins breathed a silent sigh of relief as the men on the porch lowered their rifles or dropped hands away from holstered revolvers.

"Who got killed?"

"Juan Montoya."

Reynolds winced. "Damn shame. Juan was a good man, even if he did ride for that son of a bitch Joyner. What happened?"

"He was shot in the back while trailing some stolen J-Bar cattle," Hawkins said. "It happened on your range—"

"*My* range?"

"Yes, sir." Hawkins chanced a glance around. "Where are the rest of your hands?"

"Doing what cowboys do. Punching cows. All right, Hawkins, lay it out for me. The whole blanket."

A muscle twitched in Reynolds's jaw as Hawkins wound down the story.

"Hawkins," Reynolds said, "I can't say there's any love lost between you and me, but I think you're telling it straight. And I'll tell it to you the same way. None of my men had a damned thing to do with it." He pulled a battered pipe from his pocket. "In the first place, if I wanted somebody shot, I'd do it myself. In the second place, if I was going to shoot anybody, it'd be Joyner."

"Why?"

Reynolds pulled a pouch from his pocket and tamped tobacco into his pipe. "Because Ed Joyner's been after my place since who laid the chunk. He tried to buy it from me back ten, fifteen years ago."

"And you said no?"

Reynolds flicked out the match. "I told him I wouldn't sell him a bucket of horse piss if his britches were on fire. That's the last time we had a civil word between us."

Hawkins crossed his forearms over the saddle horn. "Why does he want the Rocking R?"

"Water. Pure and simple. I got here first by a couple years. Except for that stretch of badlands where you say the J-Bar cattle were headed, I have the best water in this country. Joyner's hurting for water. We've been droughty the last three, four years. His springs are drying up. You've been on his range. You're cowboy enough to see he's short of grass, too."

Hawkins nodded. He had noticed the condition of the J-Bar range. So had Garrett. Dobie had said on one of their long scouts over Joyner's outfit that a jackrabbit couldn't live on most of the J-Bar. But that applied to a lot of range around here.

"Mr. Reynolds, I don't doubt your word, but I have to ask a question. Do any of your men own .50–95 caliber rifles?"

"No. I supply all weapons and ammunition except sidearms. We use nothing but .44–40s. Buy cartridges by the case. Cheaper that way." He dragged at the pipe and waved the stem. "Look around if you want. If you find a damn buffalo gun here, I'll personally shoot the man who owns it. Like I said, I liked Juan Montoya."

Hawkins shrugged. "I'll take your word for it, Mr. Reynolds. But we still have the question left. If you or your men didn't shoot Montoya, who did?"

Reynolds scratched another match into life. His pipe had gone out. "Wouldn't surprise me one damn bit," he said between puffs, "if Ed Joyner wouldn't have shot his own man and stole his own stock just to make folks think I did it."

"I don't know," Hawkins said solemnly. "Maybe it's possible, but Joyner doesn't seem the type."

"Then maybe you better check out some of the other association men, Marshal. Because if Joyner isn't behind it, somebody is who wants us to kill each other off." He puffed hard on the pipe, his eyes narrowed and glittery. "And that could damn well happen. You said Joyner threatened me back in town. You tell him that, by God, anytime he thinks he wants a chunk of the Rocking R, we'll be happy to oblige him."

Hawkins took a long, slow breath. "Mr. Reynolds, I'll tell you the same thing I told Mr. Joyner. There won't be a range war. I'll come after any man who starts one. And he'll go on trial for murder."

Reynolds shrugged. "That's plain enough. It won't be me who starts it. But if it happens, by God, I'll finish it, and you can take that to the bank." The Rocking R owner glanced at the lowering sun. "Day's getting long in the tooth, boys. Stay for supper if you've a notion."

Hawkins finally managed a weak grin for the first time. "That's a better invitation than one to a gunfight, Mr. Reynolds, but we'll pass. We've still got some stolen cattle to find, if we're not too late."

"Suit yourself. If you need some help, I'll send a couple of boys with you to the badlands. Rough country. Even folks who know it could ride within a half mile of a thousand head and never know the herd was there."

Hawkins tipped his hat to the wiry little rancher. "Much obliged for the offer, but we'll handle it as best we can. We'd better be moving on now. We can still make five or six miles before dark."

"One thing," the man called Jackknife said, the only Rocking R hand to speak a word except for the boss. He stared at Archie Wescott. "The greenhorn kid, there. He was going to take down two men? And he's not even packing iron?"

Wescott's expression didn't change. He slowly lifted the left lapel of his sweat-stained suit coat to expose the handgun in the shoulder holster.

Jackknife nodded. "Just wanted to make sure. See you boys around."

Hawkins reined away toward the northwest, relieved; he didn't even worry about getting shot in the back. Clell Reynolds wouldn't let that happen. He didn't know why he knew that. He just knew.

The three had covered a bit over a mile, Garrett whistling off-key again, before Wescott cleared his throat. "What we did back there—I mean, the threat to gun down all five of those men. Was that what you Westerners call running a bluff?"

Garrett spat and nailed the unsuspecting bay square on the left ear. He turned to Wescott and grinned.

"The biggest damn bluff you'll ever see, son," Dobie said. "Even gunhawks like Buck and me couldn't likely take down five men. When it comes to gunfightin' and poker playin', if you can't beat 'em, bullshit 'em." He chuckled aloud. "And speakin' of poker, I'm flat chompin' at the bit to match hands with Squirrel Tooth Kate when we get back to Necesario."

Hawkins said, "Don't get too comfortable just yet, Dobie. We've got a lot of rough ground to cover. And there's still a man out there somewhere with a big-bore rifle."

The grin faded from Garrett's face. "Partner, you sure got a way of cloudin' up on a man's sunshine. You could've gone all night and not said that."

12

"I TELL YOU, boys," Dobie Garrett said as the grayish-brown buildings of Necesario shimmered through the late afternoon heat waves a mile away, "I'm so tuckered out I can't make a decide as to which one of two things I want to do first."

"I have the same problem," Archie Wescott said, slouched in the saddle, his ramrod posture crumpled by the passage of miles. "I don't know whether to get a big steak first, or a bath."

Buck Hawkins, riding between the two, managed a gritty wink at Wescott. "Somehow, Arch, I don't think Dobie has bathwater and beefsteak in mind."

"You got that right, partner." Garrett tongued the last of his chewing tobacco and spat. The bay gelding was too tired to even duck. He just took the glob on the right ear, shook his head, snorted, and clomped on. He didn't even bother to stomp a front foot. "I was tryin' to figger whether I ought to call on Miss Lucy Ledbetter or Squirrel Tooth Kate first."

Hawkins wrinkled his nose. "I'd recommend you try a bath before calling on either of them, Dobie. You're a touch ripe. Riding downwind of you makes a body's eyes water."

"You ain't exactly smellin' like rose water yourself, Buck."

"Four days on the trail does that to a man." Hawkins turned to Wescott. "Well, Archie? What do you think of the glamorous and exciting life of a frontier lawman now?"

Wescott ran a finger across his sunburned cheek. Hawkins heard the faint whisper of almost invisible blond stubble. "I never thought it would be this much work. Or so boring and nervous all at the same time."

"Yep," Dobie said, "over two hunnerd miles in the saddle and nothin' to show for it 'cept a sore butt from saddle leather and a stiff neck from tryin' to look nine ways at once. It ain't all whiskey drinkin' and shoot-outs, son. Gonna put that in your book?"

"A bit of it, perhaps. About how hard we looked for those cows in some of the wildest, meanest country I've ever seen in my life." Wescott lifted up on the reins as his mule stumbled. "The editors will probably take it out, though. Not enough action to keep the readers' interest, they'll say. Is this animal asleep, or just exhausted?"

Hawkins glanced at the mule. The long ears flopped like a courthouse flag at half-mast when a president or someone else important died. "Hard to tell with a mule, Archie. Sort of like with Dobie, here. Tough, stubborn, and just a tad lazy."

"I need a drink," Wescott said.

"Get behind on your tea-sippin'?" Garrett said.

"I mean a real drink. A beer—"

"Beer ain't a real drink, Arch."

"—followed by a double shot of the best whiskey in town."

Garrett lifted an eyebrow at Hawkins. "Boy's learnin',

partner. Be a sure 'nuff Western man, he lives long
enough. I'll even buy the first round. On the association's nickel." Garrett glanced around as they rode down
Santa Fe Street. "Looks mighty quiet. Reckon the high-
stakes gamblers done left town. Hope Kate's still
around."

The three reined up at the livery. Trace Willis was
waiting at the gate. "Seen you ride in," Willis said. "Any
luck?"

"We didn't get shot. I'd consider that lucky enough,
Trace," Hawkins said.

"Luckier than poor Juan," Willis said. "He was nice to
me. It's not right, somebody shooting him like that. And
him with babies and all. Folks around town's mighty
upset about it. There's talk Mr. Reynolds done it."

"He didn't, Trace. At least as far as I'm concerned he
didn't." Hawkins pulled his rifle from the saddle scabbard and dismounted. His knees almost buckled when
his boots hit the ground.

Willis reached for the reins. "I'll take care of the animals for you." He ran a hand over the buckskin's
sweaty neck. "Poor Cornbread's mighty tired. I'll see
they're all rubbed down, watered, and fed good." He
gathered up the reins of Garrett's bay and Wescott's
rented mule. "You all right, Archie?" he asked as
Wescott dismounted stiffly and sagged for a moment
against the mule's side.

"I'm fine. Just a few raw spots and wobbly knees. I
only thought I knew how to ride. Twice around Central
Park a couple of times a week is a bit different from
this." He rubbed his rump and winced. "Speaking of
which, Trace, do you know anyone who has a *real* saddle for sale? One like Marshal Hawkins rides?"

"By God, Buck," Garrett said with a grin, "this here

greenhorn learns quicker'n I thought." He clapped Wescott on the shoulder. A cloud of dust flew. "Come on, boys. First round's on me."

Hawkins sagged against the corral fence, waiting to get his ground legs back under him. "You two go on. I've got to stop by the office, write up a report for Fess McLocklin, and get some letters ready to go out."

"Buck does the readin' and cipherin'," Dobie said to Wescott. "It ain't that I can't. He just does it better and quicker. We'll be at the Palace most likely, Buck, should you change your mind on that drink."

"When I'm through pushing paper, I'm heading straight for a hot bath and a night's sleep in a real bed."

"Arch," Dobie said with a nod toward Hawkins, "there is one mighty tired feller. When a man's too wore down to drink good whiskey and chouse women, us Texans say he's had too many wet saddle blankets pulled off him."

"Wet saddle blankets? What does that mean?"

Garrett draped an arm over the New Yorker's narrow shoulders. "Come along, son. I'll tell you about it over that first beer." He licked his lips, chapped and cracked from wind and sun. "Sure is gonna slide down good. Sure you don't wanna come along, Buck?"

Hawkins shook his head. "Maybe next time, Dobie. I still have a lot to do."

"Arch," Garrett said, "I'm sure 'nuff gettin' the frets over ol' Buck right now. Bad enough he turns into a one-woman man and don't hardly drink no more. What tickles my worry bone most is it looks like he's started thinkin' he's a real star packer." He sighed heavily. "Sure hope we can still save him, 'fore it's too late. Hate to lose a good partner. See you in the mornin', Buck. But not too early. Ol' Lady Smither's damn rooster squawks me up at daylight again and we're gonna have chicken and dumplin's for dinner."

Hawkins watched the two men, the bowlegged, weathered, beat-up cowboy and the dusty, skinny, sun-burned New Yorker, walk away, both still a bit unsteady on feet that had spent too many long hours in the stir-rups. "Dobie," he muttered, "I don't think you've lost a partner. I think you've picked up a second one."

He heaved himself away from the fence and slogged toward the marshal's office.

Fess McLocklin looked even smaller and more humped over than usual behind the big desk, Hawkins thought. The old man's right hand was folded into something as near a fist as his arthritic joints allowed. The body may have turned frail on him, but the passage of years hadn't dimmed the fire in his eyes.

"Are you still thinking Reynolds isn't behind all this, Hawkins?" McLocklin said. "The words came out more as a snarl than as a question.

"I can't be absolutely positive about anything just yet, Mr. McLocklin," Hawkins said, "but in my own mind, I don't think Reynolds or any of his Rocking R hands had anything to do with the Montoya killing or the theft of the J-Bar stock."

McLocklin sniffed. "I'm not sure about that, Hawkins. It looks to me that you've got enough on him to haul Reynolds in. Montoya was shot on Rocking R land. Joyner's cows were trailed onto Reynolds's range."

"True enough. What's bothering me is, by who?"

"What are you driving at, Hawkins?"

"First of all, Reynolds may be a tough, stubborn man, and he may be hotheaded. But he's not dumb. He wouldn't back-shoot a J-Bar strawboss, and he sure wouldn't drift stolen cattle wearing a neighboring out-fit's brand onto his own range."

"Why not?"

"Because that would be an open invitation to a shoot-ing war. One in which he has the most to lose."

McLocklin flexed his arthritic fingers. "So who would win?"

"Ed Joyner. Slash-Y. Four C. And you."

The old man stiffened; the look in his eyes went even colder. "What the hell are you insinuating, Hawkins? That you think I could be causing the trouble?"

Hawkins shrugged. He tried to make the motion ca-sual. "You asked the question. I answered it. Joyner's place is short of water and long on livestock. I've ridden over your ranch several times in the last few weeks, Mr. McLocklin—and your ranch is in the same shape as the J-Bar. Maybe even worse."

"Damn you, Hawkins, I won't stand for that sort of talk!" The old man's face flushed; the rush of angry blood made the liver spots on his skin more notice-able. "If I could get out of this chair, I'd climb your tree—"

Hawkins lifted a hand. "I didn't say you were behind it, sir. I just said that at this point, I can't rule out any-one, association member or not. Even you. Or Ed Joyner." He lowered the hand. "I'm now convinced that someone—maybe somebody inside the association, maybe an outsider—is going to an awful lot of trouble to start a war none of us want. Or need."

Some of the anger faded from McLocklin's eyes. "All right, maybe you do have a point, Hawkins. If we set aside the fact that Joyner and Reynolds have hated each other since the buffalo patties were still flopping out here, and ignore the idea that this could be just another play in a long feud. But Reynolds has been making talk against Joyner and the association."

"Talk didn't kill Juan Montoya," Hawkins said. He almost added, *or the Miller brothers, or try to kill me.* He checked the impulse. He couldn't really believe Fess McLocklin had anything to do with the troubles, but he wasn't ready to rule anybody out. Even the man who paid him. "The talk's been going both ways, Mr. McLocklin. If making talk is against the law, I'd have to bring in Joyner, too. Along with three-quarters of the population of Necesario."

The old man's brow furrowed. He rubbed swollen knuckles against his jawbone. "So who *is* behind it?"

Hawkins held McLocklin's stare. "That's what I intend to find out, Mr. McLocklin. And I don't have that much time to do it." He nodded toward the three sheets of paper he had placed on McLocklin's desk. "The details are in my report. Now, if you'll excuse me, I still have some letters to write before the westbound mail stage comes through in the morning."

"Letters?"

Hawkins stood. "Yes, sir. To every law enforcement officer I can find names for between here and the Union Pacific railroad line. A hundred head of prime Herefords should draw someone's attention. I'd like to know where those J-Bar cattle wind up."

"So would I, Hawkins. I wish I could talk the telegraph people into stringing a wire through Necesario. It would save everybody a lot of time."

Hawkins had to light a lantern against the dusty gloom of the marshal's office. Sundown came quick to Necesario. He stowed his rifle, thought about going to get something to eat, and decided his belly could wait a bit longer. The inkwell atop the desk was still open.

He reached for a blank piece of paper and went to work.

The lantern had burned through most of the oil in its glass base by the time Hawkins sealed the last of the letters. Maybe a waste of time, he thought, but then you never knew. He flexed the writer's cramp from his forearm, stretched his shoulders, and glanced at the eight-day clock on the wall. It said midnight. The taste in his mouth and the grit under his eyelids felt more more like four in the morning.

On impulse, he pulled the tin box from the bottom drawer of the desk, opened it, and took out Marylou's last letters. A pang of guilt hollowed his gut for a moment; it had been a week since he had written to her. But maybe she would understand—

The door swung open.

Garrett stood in the doorway, Archie Wescott slung over his shoulder like a sack of oats, the stained gray derby in Dobie's free hand.

"Good Lord, Dobie," Hawkins said, "what happened?"

Garrett's grin was a bit crooked. "Arch plumb made us proud, partner. At least till he hit the end of his whiskey rope." He carried Wescott to the cot and dumped the young man onto his back. Wescott's eyes were closed, his breathing deep and regular, a bit of spittle bubbling at the corner of his slack lips. A reddish-purple bruise was already forming on Wescott's left cheek. Blood beaded on a scratch over his left eye and seeped from torn knuckles. A pocket of his gray suit hung from a few remaining threads. The once-red cravat sagged askew around his neck, the pearl stickpin bent.

Hawkins sighed. "All right, Dobie, give me the short version of the story."

"Real short rope?"

"Real short rope. I'm too tired for the long loop."

Garrett loosened Wescott's cravat, stuck the pearl stickpin in the derby brim, and dampened the soiled red cloth with the last dribbles from the water pitcher. He dabbed at the scratch over the youth's eye, clucking like an old hen.

"Well, Dobie?" Hawkins prompted.

"Couple Rafter L punchers decided it'd be fun to hooraw Arch a little, him bein' a greenhorn and a Yankee and all."

"And?"

"Arch took it good-natured like for a spell, but they just kept at him. 'Bout an hour later they was still pickin' when the rye whiskey kicked in. Arch took 'em both on. Damn near whupped 'em both by hisself, too."

"And you just stood there and let them beat up on him?"

Garrett shrugged. "As long as he was holdin' his own and learnin', didn't see no reason to butt in. The kid's a scrapper, partner. He don't fight fair. Just like a born Texan." He squinted at the scratch he'd been working on and grunted. "Had the big one down on his back, Arch did. Worked that feller over pretty good."

"Looks like Archie caught his share of punches."

Garrett flashed a quick grin. "That big feller Arch was thumpin' on looked a hell of a lot worse. Or at least he did when I threw 'em both out the back door."

"Both? Archie whipped them both?"

"Had to help him just a bit. While he was whappin' on the big guy, the other puncher tried to pull a knife. That didn't hardly seem fair in a fistfight, so I whopped him upside the head with this here hickory stick." He tapped the club in his belt rig. "Dropped him like a poleaxed steer."

"Then why did Archie get knocked out, if he was holding his own?"

"He didn't. He was still thumpin' on this feller—the one he had down on the floor—when Arch sort of set straight up, went all glassy-eyed, and fell over. Passed out. Tried to tell the boy it warn't good drinkin' style to put five shots of rye whiskey on top of four beers."

"I didn't know you'd ever learned that lesson yourself, Dobie," Hawkins said.

"Takes practice, partner. Arch can't learn to swim whiskey rivers right without he does some wadin' first." He lifted an eyebrow at Hawkins. "You ain't worried that I can't teach him, are you? After all, I learnt you pretty good."

Hawkins leaned forward to study Wescott's slack face. He was impressed with the colors. In addition to the pinkish tint of sunburn, Archie's skin boasted splotches of purplish red bruises with blue-green marks in the middle. Lighter streaks marked the trickle of sweat droplets through layers of dust and dirt and a light sprinkle of blond whisker stubble.

Wescott was going to have some colorful bruises and maybe a black eye, but there didn't seem to be any major damage. The biggest hurt would come when he woke up in the morning. If Hawkins was any judge of potential hangovers, Archie would have a hellacious one come daylight. An eyeball-bulging hangover would teach him the rye whiskey and beer rules a lot more emphatically than Dobie Garrett could.

"Let him sleep it off here," Hawkins said. "I'd hate to be looking at the world through his side of his skull come morning. Boy's had a few hard lessons over the last couple of weeks."

Garrett chuckled. "Yes, sir, we done busted Archie's maidenhead several ways here lately. Taught him about ridin' and drinkin' and cantinas and all sorts of stuff. We'll get around to the woman-chousin' part soon as Arch feels better. Reckon he'll thank us for it? The teachin', I mean?"

Hawkins took the soiled cravat from Garrett and tossed it into the washbasin. "I doubt it, Dobie. I seriously doubt it."

"Ain't that just like youngsters these days?" Garrett shook his head. "Don't even get the gratefuls when their elders goes to a bunch of trouble to learn 'em somethin'." He stood and flexed his shoulders. "Reckon I'll bunk out here tonight myself, in case Arch wakes up and needs somethin'. I'll sleep on one of the cell cots."

"You have had a bit of practice at spending nights on jail cots, Dobie," Hawkins said.

"This ain't a bad jail. Not like some I've bunked out in before," Garrett said. "At least that damn rooster won't be screechin' in my ear come daylight."

Hawkins scooped up Marylou's letters, his hat and rifle. "You'll need to fetch some fresh water, Dobie. I drank up the last of the coffee an hour ago. I'm going to the hotel for what's left of the night. I'll see you boys tomorrow."

"Good morning, Marshal Garrett."

Dobie groaned aloud, cracked one eye open a sliver, and immediately regretted it. A drunk Comanche medicine man thumped a drum—a big drum—hard in his temple every time his heart beat, and his belly was doing a full, rolling boil. Even his whiskers hurt.

"Son," he muttered at the hazy figure of Archie Wescott standing at the side of the bunk, "one thing I can't stand is somebody so damn cheerful before daylight. How come you ain't at death's door like I am?"

"Death's door?" Wescott sounded puzzled.

"Hungover. You drunk more'n I did last night."

"Oh, that. I never have hangovers, Marshal Garrett. Well, once. But that was after I mixed gin and red wine. I think it was the wine that caused the problem. It was Italian."

Garrett groaned aloud. His stomach flipped again. "Damn, Arch. All this time I thought you was human. Never seen anybody didn't get waylaid by the rye whiskey sidewinder's bite."

"Coffee's ready. Breakfast will be here in a few minutes. I asked the restaurant man to fix some sunny-side-up eggs, ham steaks, biscuits, and gravy. I'll go get it in a few minutes."

Garrett groaned again. "Arch, there ain't no way I can face eggs when I'm hungover. It's like a couple weepy, yellery eyes was starin' up at me."

"Oh. Well, I guess I should have checked with you first, but I didn't want to wake you before six o'clock—"

"Six o'clock! Jesus! Son, you're worse'n that damn rooster, and I done threatened to make dumplin's outta that noisy pullet-chaser." He swung his feet over the edge of the bunk, sat up, and wondered if that had been another mistake. The Comanche drummer picked up the beat inside his skull. He managed to open the second eye and stare at Wescott.

The kid had a shiner on his right eye, a big, purple

bruise on his left cheekbone, and a big grin on his face. It was the grin that grated most on Garrett. The green-horn ought to have been hurtin' at least some, he thought.

"Would you like me to order something else for you?"

"Lord, no," Garrett groaned. "Just pour coffee until I know for sure I ain't gonna die. Wouldn't hurt to sweeten it a bit with some hair of the wolf."

"What wolf?"

"Whiskey, son. The wolf that bit a chunk out of my butt last night."

"Oh. Is that what you meant when you said we were going to 'howl the wolf,' Marshal Garrett?"

Garrett nodded. The Comanche dropped the drum and whapped the inside of Dobie's skull. "That's what I meant, Arch. There's a pint of Old Overholt in the bot-tom drawer of that desk. Pour a cup about a quarter full of that and fill the rest with coffee. At least I'll be awake when I die."

Wescott was back in less than two minutes, a mug in each hand. He handed one to Garrett. Dobie sipped at the brew and sighed; his belly quivered again, then set-tled down a bit as the warmth spread. "Mother's milk. Ought to ease my passin' into ol' Satan's range." He raised a sore eyebrow at Wescott. "You sure you ain't hurtin'? Just a little bit?"

The New Yorker fingered his bruised cheek. "A little touchy here and there. And my knuckles sting a bit." The grin came back. "That was the most fun I've had in years. Want to go howl the wolf again tonight, Marshal Garrett?"

Dobie groaned aloud. "No way, son. The buzzards are done gnawin' on the carcass of this old man's wolf. And you might as well call me Dobie. Like you was last night."

"Sure thing, Mar—Dobie. Our breakfast should be ready now. I'll go fetch it."

"Don't bother with mine. I ain't up to it."

"That's no problem. I'll eat yours, too. I'm absolutely famished." Wescott took a swig from his coffee, turned, and strode away, his steps light and bouncy.

Garrett leaned back against the cell wall and tried to hate the kid. It wasn't fair, a greenhorn like Archie Wescott downing that much whiskey and not even hurting the next morning. He took a couple more swigs of the curative mixture and decided he might live another hour or so after all. A rank odor tickled his nostrils. Dobie spent a moment wondering what crawled under the bunk and died, then realized where the smell came from. Hungover or not, he was going to have to take a bath.

"Well, look what the cat dragged in," Hawkins said from the doorway, a cup of coffee in his hand. He was grinning, too.

"Oh, Christ. Just when I was startin' to get used to some peace and quiet," Garrett groused. "How come everbody around here's so damn pup-perky and talkified this mornin', anyway?"

"Met Archie crossing the street," Hawkins said. "He looks more pup-perky than you do, partner. Losing your touch?"

"No need to lay insults on top of headhurts, partner," Garrett said. "That boy ain't human, Buck. Lays on a load of liquor that'd stop a six-horse hitch, gets in a fight, and wakes up actin' like some kid with his first pony." Garrett took another hit from the wolf-hair cup. "Didn't expect you up and around this early."

Hawkins sipped at his coffee. "Wanted to make sure I didn't miss the mail stage, and I have another letter to write before then. I'll be in the office if you need somebody to administer the last rites, Dobie."

Garrett had almost recovered by mid-morning. The rest of the pint of Old Overholt, half a gallon of coffee, a bath, shave, and change of clothes left him reasonably sure he wouldn't be needing Buck's last rites.

Wescott's face looked like he had tangled with a grizzly, but he was still damned irritatingly chipper.

He had found a new suit somewhere. A light blue one with a bright red vest and a gaudy green cravat. Garrett didn't even know Necesario stores stocked town clothes. But that was something Dobie never looked for, anyway. At least the kid had shown some sense. He'd bought a pair of boots. He still walked a bit unsteady on the high riding heels, but he was getting the hang of it. Archie's new suit did a better job of hiding the shoulder holster than the gray one had. Garrett wondered idly if the youngster had ever drawn his handgun. Or if he could use it. With luck, he'd never have to find out.

The dust kicked up by the mail coach, which had been on time—meaning only a couple of hours late—had hardly settled. Hawkins sat at the desk and sorted through a stack of letters, newspapers, and dispatches. He put most of them aside, but passed a few to Wescott, seated across from him.

As usual, Garrett didn't have any personal mail. It didn't worry him much. He didn't know that many people who could write anyway, outside of Hawkins and the kid. Dobie rose from the cot where he'd rested and gathered his strength for the last couple of hours.

"You boys don't need any help with that readin' stuff, I think I'll wander over to the Palace. Heard Squirrel Tooth Kate's still in town. Might be fun to bump heads with her on a couple hands of draw poker."

"Don't lose all your money too quick, Dobie," Hawkins said without looking up. "We'll send for you if anything happens."

"Don't let it," Garrett said. "I still ain't up to handlin' too much excitement. Least not till sundown."

Wescott glanced up. "What's special about sundown?"

"That's when my hair starts gettin' curly, Arch."

"Pardon?"

"Dobie means that's when he gets the urge to turn the wolf loose," Hawkins said. "Time for whiskey, women, and song."

"Not tonight, partner," Garrett said with a wince. "That wolf done got caught in a stout trap last night. He ain't gonna have to gnaw off a leg to get loose. He sure won't be doin' no prowlin' this day."

Wescott watched as Garrett strode through the door and headed up the street. "Marshal Hawkins, I'm a little worried about Dobie," Wescott said. "He doesn't look too good today."

Hawkins finally looked up. A wry grin touched his lips. "That's just Dobie's way of coping with a hangover. Seems to be taking him longer to get over them here lately, though. Could be he's getting a little long in the tooth for carousing."

"Long in the tooth?"

"Cowboy expression, Archie. Just means getting old."

"Must be tough on a man. Getting old, I mean."

"As Fess McLocklin pointed out the other day, not nearly as tough as the alternative." Hawkins handed another envelope to Wescott. "This one came all the way from New York."

Wescott dropped the other envelopes on the floor beside his chair and ripped open the New York letter. A wide grin spread across his sunburned and bruise-colored face.

"It's from my editor at Haskell and Grant. They loved the first four chapters of the book. They're already getting orders in from all over the world." His tone went up a notch in excitement. "This could make you and Dobie really and truly famous, Marshal Hawkins."

Buck winced. "In this line of work, famous isn't always good. It tends to draw lead a man's way. But congratulations, anyway. There's only one thing that bothers me."

"What's that?"

"We don't know how it's going to end yet."

"Oh. I see what you mean." Wescott tucked the letter into the breast pocket of his new coat and opened a half dozen other letters.

"More good news?"

Wescott shrugged. "More bank vouchers from newspapers. Payment for stories I've filed so far. It's nothing important. Just money."

"Just money, the man says." Hawkins shook his head. "Nothing important, he says—Well, I'll be. What's this?" He picked up a small package wrapped in plain brown butcher's paper. It was addressed to him, in Marylou's boldly feminine script. It had been postmarked in Chicago.

"One way to find out, Marshal. Open it."

Hawkins clipped the twine from the package and unwrapped it with care. Inside was an expensive brown leather box. Buck fumbled with it for a moment, found the latch, and flipped up the lid. A heavy, gold-cased trainman's pocket watch nestled in the linen packing. The case was engraved with a scene of a man on horse-back, a herd of cattle in the background, the Quarter Circle brand beneath the horse's hooves, and a single engraved word: "Ours."

Buck opened the watch. A lump formed in his throat. The inscription engraved in the cover read, "To Buck Hawkins, the Man I'll Always Love. Marylou."

"What is it, Marshal?" Wescott asked, a note of concern in his tone. "Something wrong? You look a bit—well, strange."

Hawkins swallowed hard and shook his head. "Nothing wrong, Archie. Nothing at all." He fondled the watch for a moment, then tucked it into his shirt pocket. Its weight against his left breast was solid and reassuring. He checked the rest of his mail.

There were two letters from Marylou. They said the same thing the watch said; it just took them a couple of pages each to say it again. Hawkins ignored the official mail, the flyers, and the newspapers as he read Mary-lou's letters twice more.

Wescott opened one of the papers, scanned the front page, and said, "Uh-oh."

"What?"

"Two of the men you and Dobie captured at Quitaque Valley, after the Albany bank robbery—Silas Barker and Harve Turcotte."

Hawkins's blood chilled. "What about them?"

"They broke out of prison. Killed two guards. About a week ago, it says here." Wescott's gaze raked the rest of the article. "The prison authorities found a newspaper clipping in Barker's cell. One of the stories I wrote about you and Dobie, datelined Necesario." Wescott looked

up. "Your names were underlined, Marshal. Yours and
Dobie's. The word Necesario was circled. What do you
think that means?

Hawkins didn't speak. It was hard to talk when a mule
had just kicked him in the gut.

13

BUCK HAWKINS KNELT beside the body that lay half in, half out of the spring-fed pool, his gut churning.

Nace Keller's speed with a handgun hadn't helped him this time. The big slug had taken the Rocking R rider in the back of the head. It hadn't left much of Keller's face when it came out between his eyes.

Six days. Two killings. The J-Bar's Juan Montoya, the Rocking R's Nace Keller. Both shot from the back, ambushed. With a large-caliber rifle.

"Well, Hawkins?"

Buck turned to face Clell Reynolds. The Rocking R owner sat in the saddle, flanked on each side by three grim-faced riders. The calm, quiet expression on Reynolds's weathered face chilled Hawkins. It seemed more menacing than if the slightly built rancher had been in a towering, full-blown rage. Reynolds's pale blue eyes pinned Hawkins with an unblinking gaze.

"Nace Keller was more than just my foreman. He was like the son I never had. Somebody's going to pay for this, and pay hard." Reynolds's tone was soft and deadly. "What are you going to do about it?"

Hawkins squared his shoulders and held Reynolds's gaze. "I'm going to try to find out who did it, and why, Mr. Reynolds."

"We know who did it. Ed Joyner."

"Maybe he did and maybe he didn't," Hawkins said. "Right now, I don't know either way. There's no proof—"

"I've got all the proof I need, Hawkins." Reynolds's baritone dropped another octave. "If you won't do anything about it, by God, I will." He turned to the rider at his left. "Bert, gather up every man riding for the brand. We're going to take care of that damn Joyner and his boys once and for all."

The rider nodded and started to rein away.

"Hold it!" Hawkins called. The man checked his mount. "I can't let you do that, Mr. Reynolds."

"I suppose you think you can stop me?"

"Probably not," Hawkins said. He was surprised at how calm and level his words were despite the churn of his gut and the yelps from his bladder. "But I'll have to try. I can't allow a range war. There's been too much killing already. I won't stand by and see more men die without reason."

Reynolds's eyes narrowed; his hand dropped to the revolver at his side. "You're about half a second away from getting yourself dead, Hawkins."

"And you're about to make a big mistake, Mr. Reynolds."

"Buck ain't whistlin', amigo." Reynolds's head swiveled toward the voice that came from behind him. Dobie Garrett stood beside a cottonwood tree. The sawed-off shotgun in his hand was trained on Reynolds. "Don't reckon it'd be real smart to pull that there handgun."

Reynolds stared at Garrett for a moment. "Where the hell did you come from?"

"Back yonder. Not that it matters much."

"Garrett, you won't live ten seconds if you pull the trigger of that thing."

"That'd be nine seconds longer'n you would, Clell." Garrett shifted the chew in his cheek. "And longer'n a passel of your boys there. Get your hand off that six-gun and call off them wolves with you."

"And if I don't?"

Garrett's gaze never wavered. "These here cards been dealt, Reynolds. Reckon it's your call."

"You're bluffing again, Garrett."

"I'm holdin' the high card. Twelve-bore makes a gawdawful mess of a man at this range."

The air all but cracked with tension for several heartbeats, the silence broken only by the rustle of wind through the cottonwood leaves and the jangle of a bridle as a horse tossed its head. Hawkins thought the thud of his own heart against his rib cage was audible for a quarter mile.

Finally, Reynolds shook his head. "Got to hand it to you, Garrett. Like I said, you got *cojones*. And the high card to go with it. Put that thing away."

"I'll do that after you call in the dogs there and give Buck a listen."

Reynolds lifted his hand from the six-gun grips and gestured to the Rocking R riders. "All right, sit easy, boys. We aren't killing anybody who isn't J-Bar today." He turned his back on Garrett. "So now what, Hawkins?"

"Give me time to find out who's behind this, Mr. Reynolds."

Reynolds stared at Hawkins for several heartbeats. A muscle twitched at his jawline. Finally, he nodded. "All right, you want time, I'll give you time. Three days."

"That might not be enough."

"Make it enough." The hard edge was back on Reynolds's words. "I didn't start this, Hawkins. If you don't finish it, I damn well will." He turned to the man he'd called Bert. "Go fetch a wagon to haul Nace home in. Turk, go with him. Both of you keep your eyes open. There's a back-shooter out there somewhere."

Hawkins breathed a silent sigh of relief as the two men rode away. Garrett lowered the hammers and cradled the shotgun-pistol in the crook of an elbow.

"Give me the man who did this, Hawkins," Reynolds said, "or the war starts. And I know where to find Joyner. Right outside your front door. Find the bushwhacker or get out of the way."

Hawkins's blood chilled again. Every association rancher and many of their riders would be in Necesario in three days. Of all the damn times for an association meeting, Buck thought, why now? He nodded, toed the stirrup, and swung about his palomino.

Garrett disappeared behind the cottonwood and emerged a moment later, mounted on his big bay. He still hadn't sheathed the smoothbore.

Hawkins kneed Buttermilk toward Necesario. Garrett rode alongside, outwardly relaxed. Neither man looked back.

"Now what, partner?" Garrett said after they had ridden a half mile.

"Now I'd like for you to put that scattergun up, Dobie," Hawkins said. "I'm spooked enough without that thing pointed in my direction."

Garrett sheathed the weapon and spat off the side. The bay ducked anyway. "You ain't the only one got the yips, Buck. Reckon Reynolds'll keep his word?"

"I believe he will. We have three days until all hell

breaks loose." Hawkins sighed. "You pulled me out of a bog back there, Dobie."

"That there's what makes a team, partner. Come at a rattler's den from different sides, ain't near as likely both of us gets bit."

"Find anything out there?"

Garrett nodded, fumbled in a shirt pocket, and brought out a shiny brass cartridge case. "Same shooter. 50–95. Same hoss track, too. Chip out of the shoe, just like them others. Shot was from about fifty yards out."

"I was afraid of that." Hawkins rode in silence for a moment. "We've got to find the shooter, and fast. Or we're going to be up to our butts in blood."

Archie Wescott was waiting in the office when Hawkins and Garrett reined in. The young New Yorker didn't look pleased.

"Why did you two sneak off without me, Marshal?" he snapped at Hawkins.

A spark of irritation flared in Hawkins's belly. "I didn't know we had to check with you when something came up, Archie."

Wescott flushed. "Sorry. I didn't mean it to sound like that. I just got back into town a few hours ago. What happened?"

Hawkins stored his rifle and briefed Wescott on the shooting of Nace Keller. "Another foreman dead. Same rifle, same hoofprint," he concluded, "and Dobie couldn't track the shooter more than a mile before the trail petered out."

"Whoever that jasper is, he can sure hide his tracks," Garrett said in grudging admiration. "Top hand with that fifty-caliber, too. Got to be a hired gun, a professional shooter."

Wescott pursed his lips in thought for a moment. "Maybe he isn't a professional."

"How do you figure that, Archie?" Hawkins asked.

"It seems to me that a professional killer wouldn't be apt to leave spent brass lying around after a shooting. Especially an unusual caliber like a .50–95. Coffee's fresh, by the way." Wescott poured three cups.

Hawkins took the mug, nodded his thanks, and lifted an eyebrow at the young newsman. "I get the feeling you're onto something, Archie."

"Could be. I just need a little more time to find a missing piece of the puzzle."

"Time's somethin' we ain't got a lot of, Arch," Garrett said. "You got somethin' on your mind, spit her out."

Wescott sipped at his coffee, sighed, and peered into the cup. "I do believe I'm developing a taste for this stuff. Haven't had a cup of tea in two weeks—"

"Archie," Hawkins said, "spit. Like Dobie said."

"All right. We know Ed Joyner isn't behind it. We know Clell Reynolds isn't. They don't like each other, but they aren't the sort of men who would shoot someone in the back. Or hire it done. Which brings up the question we've been trying to answer. Who is behind it."

Garrett snorted. "What the Sam Houston hell do you think we been studyin' on so hard, son?"

"I have an idea"—Wescott lifted a hand to ward off Hawkins's question—"but I have no proof yet. I sent off some telegrams at the stage station stopover in San Jon today. The replies should be back tomorrow."

Garrett's brows bunched. "Who hung a badge on you, Arch?"

"Nobody." Wescott sipped at his coffee. "I don't intend to tread on your turf, gentlemen, but I am a reporter.

I've had some experience uncovering paper trails, even if you still think I'm just a wet-behind-the-ears kid."

Garrett sniffed in disdain. "Paper trails? What the hell's paper got to do with it?"

"Everything, Dobie. Motive. Opportunity. Finding out who stands to gain from a range war besides the undertaker." He drained the last of his coffee. "Like you said, it's not all fast guns and whiskey and wild women. Now, if you'll excuse me, I have some land records to check—"

"Archie, we need a name," Hawkins said.

"I can't give you one yet, Marshal. In a day or two, when we have more information, perhaps." He tugged his derby snug against the gusty mid-afternoon wind, then paused at the door. "By the way, those two fellows who escaped from prison, Barker and Turcotte? The ones who threatened to get revenge on you?"

"What about 'em?"

"According to the sheriff at San Jon, a deputy caught up with them three days ago near a little town called Tomasco, down near the Rio Grande."

Hawkins breathed a sigh of relief. "It's about time we had some good news around here."

"I'm afraid it isn't good news, Marshal," Wescott said. "They killed the deputy. They're still on the loose."

Garrett scratched his ear as the door closed behind Wescott. "Tomasco. Looks like Silas and Harve are doin' the smart thing for once. Headin' into Mexico." He sighed. "I got to tell you, partner, that's a load off my worry wagon, bein' shut of them two. So what's your druthers?"

"About what?"

"What we do now. Town's gonna be full of mighty mad men with big guns pretty quick."

"What do you think we should do?"

Dobie launched a glob of tobacco spit into the syrup can. "Anybody with any smarts would be in the saddle and skedaddlin' for the tall timber by sundown."

The hollow spot in Hawkins's belly got bigger. He shook his head. "We can't, Dobie. Not while there's still a chance we can head off a shooting war. We haven't finished the job here."

Garrett sighed. "You could've talked all day and not said that, Buck. Oh, well. Nobody ever said we was loaded up on smarts, anyway. How the hell can a couple simple cowboys round up so damn much trouble, anyhow?"

"Just raw talent, Dobie. Raw talent."

Garrett strode to the window and watched Wescott cross the nearly deserted street toward the one-room land office a hundred yards away. "Reckon that young feller knows what he's doin'?"

"I have no idea," Hawkins said, "but right now I'd welcome any help we can get. And either way this turns out, he'll have the last chapter for his book." He reached for his hat. "Take the horses down to the livery, will you? I'm going to pay a call on Ned Dawson. Maybe he's got an idea how we can head off this war."

Garrett shrugged. "Suit yourself, partner. You don't need me for a spell, I'd admire to go see Squirrel Tooth Kate. She's got ten dollars of my money I'd sure 'nuff like to get back."

"Go ahead, Dobie. But stay sober."

"Partner," Garrett said solemnly, "this is one time you can count on it, and that's a sure 'nuff fact."

* * *

Hawkins paced the boardwalk on Necesario's main street, too jumpy even to feel his exhaustion or the heat from the late morning sun.

It was the third day.

And he had nothing. Two days of talking to nearly everyone in town, and he'd come up empty. Two days of sleepless nights, two days he had been running on coffee and raw nerves. Already, horses wearing the J-Bar brand stood at hitchrails along the north side of the street. By noon, the Slash-Y and Four C crews would be here. And sooner or later, the Rocking R.

The men in the saloons or in the Palace café were armed to the teeth. And surly. A few of the younger faces were pale but determined. Hawkins knew he sat on a powderkeg and the fuse was lit. There was going to be one hell of an explosion in Necesario this afternoon. And only two men, Buck Hawkins and Dobie Garrett, to try to stop it.

By nightfall, both of them could well be in a pine box. The tick of the heavy pocket watch against his breast was a painful reminder of just how much Hawkins stood to lose. He had already written a letter to Marylou, another to the folks he had not seen in years, on the farm over in East Texas—he didn't even know if his parents were still alive or not—and a last will and testament addressed to W. C. Milhouse. He had left the letters in the tin box and asked Archie Wescott to mail them if one Buck Hawkins wound up shot so full of lead it would take a six-horse hitch to drag the coffin.

Dobie Garrett prowled the other side of the street, the sawed-off shotgun propped against his shoulder. Garrett hadn't had any family to write to, but he had Hawkins scribble out a short note to Miss Lucy Ledbetter. Miss Lucy could have what was left. As of now, that amounted

to a ten-dollar IOU payable to Squirrel Tooth Kate Timberlake, a worn-out saddle, a bay horse with a permanent
tobacco-spit stain on his ears, and not much else. That
note was in the tin box, too.

Dust swirled over and around the horse droppings in
the street. Several stores were closed, windows boarded
up, as if a quarter-inch chunk of wood could stop a slug.
There were no townsfolk on the streets. It was as if they
had crawled into a hole somewhere and pulled the hole
in after them. The tension in the air seemed heavy
enough to cut with a knife.

Buck Hawkins had never felt quite so alone.

He told himself there was still time to saddle this
horse and leave. He also knew he couldn't. He and
Dobie were too deep into the game to fold their hands
and leave. The badge on his chest weighed more than the
Winchester in the crook of his arm.

He stiffened as Garrett waved a hand from across the
street and pointed to the east.

"Rider coming fast," Garrett called. "Could be
Archie."

Hawkins all but ran toward the stables a hundred
yards away. He reached the corral gate just as Wescott
reined his lathered, heaving mule to a stop.

"I've got it, Marshal," Wescott said as he jumped off
the mule, "all we need except one last thing—one thing
that will nail down the name we've been looking for."

"We're out of time, Archie," Hawkins said, his words
heavy. "Reynolds will be here soon. Go lock yourself in
your room. I don't want you catching a stray slug."

Wescott grinned through the trail grime on his sunburned face. "I've been a fool, Marshal—"

"We all have, son. Now get out of here."

"The key to the whole thing's been right under our

noses all the time. Five minutes and you'll have the name."

"What are you talking about, Archie?"

"The hoofprint. With the chip out. Find that horse and we've got our man." The words tumbled over one another in Wescott's excitement. He fumbled in his pocket for his notepad. "Who's the one person in town who knows every horse in and around Necesario?"

Hawkins's jaw dropped. "Trace. Trace Willis."

As he said the name, the door of a box stall swung open. Trace Willis hurried to open the gate. His gaze whipped from the lathered mule to Wescott. "You like to have killed this poor mule, Archie. You ought to know better—"

"I know, Trace. But this is important. It might save many lives." He flipped open the notepad to the sketch he had drawn of the hoofprint found at the ambush sites. "Do you recognize this, Trace? Have you seen a horseshoe chipped like this?"

Willis studied the sketch for a heartbeat, then wiped a hand over the moisture at the corner of his mouth and nodded. "Sure do. I told Mr. Beecham that shoe was gonna crack—"

"Beecham?" Hawkins almost squawked the name. "Couldn't have been! He's been out of town since a couple of days after we got here."

"No, he hasn't, Marshal," Wescott said. "He never caught the stage to Fort Worth. Gave his ticket to a cowboy. He could have been around here the whole time."

Hawkins flicked a glance at Willis. "Trace, think hard. When was the last time you saw Marty Beecham?"

"This morning." Willis ran a hand over the mule's shoulder. "Poor mule's maybe crippled—"

"What time this morning?"

"Huh?"

Hawkins tried to check his impatience. "What time this morning did you see Mr. Beecham, Trace?"

Willis frowned, thinking. "Little before the sun come up. Woke me up when he rode in. Time I got dressed, he was gone. That shoe's done cracked plumb across, Marshal. He don't get it fixed, he's gonna cripple that horse for sure. He's a good one, too. The black in the box stall down on the far end. I fed him on account of Mr. Beecham didn't. Just put him in the stall and left, and the horse all lathered up and gaunt. Sure hate to see a good horse like that treated so bad—"

Hawkins drew a deep breath to settle his jangling nerves. "Trace, did he have a rifle with him?"

Willis's brow furrowed again. "Didn't see it this morning. But he's got one, Marshal. A big one. At least it had this big hole in the end—"

Hawkins started as the heavy *thump* of a shotgun jarred the air. He barked a curse, vaulted the corral fence, and sprinted toward the sound of the shot.

"I said that's far enough, dammit!" Garrett's voice boomed above the gusty wind. "Back off! Everybody!"

A crowd in the center of the street blocked Hawkins's way. It grew by the moment as armed men poured from buildings along the street. Hawkins shouldered one young cowboy aside, staggered two others as he plowed between them, and skidded to a stop, winded, alongside Garrett.

Dobie stood in the middle of the street, the muzzle of his sawed-off shotgun pointed at the sky. A dozen or more Rocking R riders fanned out in their saddles behind Clell Reynolds. Rifle and shotgun muzzles bristled from among the mounted men; others held cocked revolvers.

Hawkins chanced a quick glance around. Behind him and spread across the street were more then twenty men. Ed Joyner stood in front of the crowd, knees flexed, black eyes gleaming in hate, a six-gun in his hand. Hawkins recognized others in the crowd behind Joyner. Association men. J-Bar, Slash-Y, Four C riders. All with weapons drawn or their hands on six-gun grips.

Hawkins's gut turned to ice. He and Garrett stood alone, in an open strip of street less than ten yards wide, between two groups of grim, heavily armed men. Hawkins knew they were a heartbeat away from a blood-bath—and two marshals would likely be the ones whose blood spilled first.

"Step aside, Garrett," Reynolds said, his gaze still locked on Joyner, "or you'll be dead before you can break wind. The association hired you, by God, they can bury you."

"Come ahead, Reynolds," Joyner yelled. "Let's settle this now!'

"Hold it!" Hawkins shouted. "There won't be any killing in this town!" He was surprised at the ring of authority in his voice; he could only hope he didn't wet his pants and spoil the whole thing.

"Hawkins," Joyner snapped, "I don't give a good god-damn how waspy you two *pistoleros* are, you can't stop it now—"

"And I don't give a good goddamn what started this feud, Joyner," Hawkins interrupted with more confidence than he felt, "but there won't be any shooting in Necesario. Not today."

"Enough of this yammering," Reynolds barked. "Let's get it on, Joyner! Garrett, Hawkins—step aside now, or you'll be the first ones down!"

"I doubt that, Clell!" The call from nearby jerked
Reynolds's head around.

Hawkins chanced a quick glance off to his right. Ned
Dawson stood fifty feet away on the veranda of the
Santa Fe. The big buffalo rifle in his gnarled hands
rested against a post, the sights trained on Reynolds.

"Ned, what the hell? This isn't your fight."

"It's nobody's fight, Clell. Because there won't be
one. Unless you want a 500-grain slug through the head
to start it off with."

"Ned, why—"

"I've never had much patience with stupid folks,
Clell. And you and Joyner haven't been real long on
smarts here lately."

Joyner glared at the old buffalo hunter. "Deal yourself
out before it's too late, Ned. We've been friends a long
time. I'd hate to have to kill you."

"I don't recommend you even try, sir."

Joyner started at the voice in his ear. Archie Wescott
stood behind Joyner. The muzzle of Wescott's short-bar-
rel six-gun was an inch from his neck.

"You have the guts to use that, greenhorn?" Joyner
half snarled.

"There's one way to find out, sir. I sincerely recommend that you listen to what Marshal Hawkins has to
say. Then, if you still want to fight, well . . ." His voice
trailed away.

"I'll give you boys one thing," Joyner said. "You got
nerve. Four men against thirty guns?"

"Five."

Hawkins turned toward the voice. On the other side of
the street, Miss Lucy Ledbetter leaned casually against a
wall, a double shotgun in her hands. "Well, four men and
a woman," she said.

"Lucy, what the hell are you—"

"Hush up, Dobie Garrett. I have a personal stake in keeping your skin whole." The muzzles of the smooth-bore drifted back and forth over the association crowd. "Gentlemen, I don't know how many of you would be willing to shoot a woman. But I do know there's one woman here who won't hesitate to pull a trigger." Several of the men near Lucy began to edge away.

"Well, Mr. Joyner? Mr. Reynolds?" Lucy said.

An undercurrent of indecisive muttering spread among the gathering of gunmen. For a tense moment, Hawkins feared someone was going to make a wrong move, a mistake—and all hell would break loose.

"Gentlemen," Wescott said, raising his voice, "it appears we have a standoff here. A shooting war would be rather expensive to both sides under the circumstances, don't you think?"

"Ed," one of the J-Bar riders at the edge of the crowd said nervously, "I signed on to ride for the brand. I didn't sign on to shoot women. Or get shot."

A mutter of agreement rose from both sides. Hawkins grabbed the opening.

"Mr. Reynolds, I believe you're a man of his word. You said if I found out who the man who killed Keller and Montoya was, you'd let it go—" Hawkins broke off as the crowd of association men parted.

Fess McLocklin stumped through the opening, his cane in his hand, Marty Beecham at his side. McLocklin stopped six feet from Hawkins, blinking in the sun and wind.

"Well, Hawkins?" McLocklin said. "Is it true? That you know who the killer is?"

"Yes, sir, I do." Hawkins nailed Beecham with a hard glare. Beecham tried to sneer. It didn't work. His face was the color of the gray suit he wore, and his Adam's apple bobbed nervously.

McLocklin turned to the association riders. "Stow the guns, boys. Let's hear what the marshal has to say."

"Mr. Reynolds?" Hawkins prompted.

Reynolds's eyes narrowed, but he nodded. "Put 'em up, boys. Won't cost a dime to listen."

Hawkins sighed in relief at the soft whispers as iron and steel slid back into leather.

"Go on, Hawkins," McLocklin said.

"You aren't going to like what I have to say, sir."

"Whether I like it or not is beside the point. Lay it out straight."

Hawkins took a deep breath to calm his yapping nerves. "The man who killed Montoya and Keller—and the Miller brothers—is standing right beside you, Mr. McLocklin. Your nephew. Marty Beecham."

A mutter of disbelief went up from both factions.

McLocklin's expression didn't change. "I suppose you have proof of that, Hawkins?"

"Enough. Where's the rifle, Beecham?"

Beecham's gaze flicked about, touched everything but Hawkins's eyes. "What rifle? I don't know what you're talking about. This is the most absurd—"

"The .50–95 Express, Mr. Beecham. The weapon that's killed at least four men. Maybe more. Spent cartridge hulls were found at the arroyo where Montoya died, at the spring where Keller was shot, at the place in Santa Fe where the Miller brothers were killed." Hawkins paused for a couple of heartbeats. "And at the place where someone tried to bushwhack me on the way back from San Jon." He shook his head. "Not bright, Marty. That particular rifle caliber is mighty scarce. I'd lay odds there isn't more than one in five hundred miles of here."

Droplets of sweat formed on Beecham's upper lip. Hawkins didn't think it was all from heat. "This is totally absurd," Beecham sputtered. "You've got to be out of your mind, Marshal! Even if I had a rifle like that, I wasn't even here when this all happened. I was in Fort Worth—"

"No, you weren't, Beecham. You never caught that stage in San Jon. We have proof of that. And we found the tracks of your horse where Montoya and Keller were shot. And where you tried to shoot me."

"That's the most ridiculous thing I've ever heard," Beecham said. He turned to McLocklin. "Uncle Fess, you can't believe this—"

"Shut up, Marty. Go on, Marshal. How do you know it was my nephew's horse?"

"Trace Willis identified the horse's shoe from a sketch Archie Wescott made," Hawkins said. "It leaves a distinctive mark."

"Trace Willis!" Beecham squawked. "A halfwit! Who'd take the word of the town idiot?"

"I would, Beecham," Hawkins said, "and I think a jury will, too. Because Trace Willis knows every horse in the county. And he has no reason to lie. You should have had that shoe fixed when Trace first pointed out that nick in the right forequarter, Marty. Now, where's the rifle?"

Beecham squared his shoulders and turned to McLocklin. "Uncle Fess, you've got to help me! I swear I had nothing to do with any of this."

"You'd by God better not have, Marty," McLocklin said. "Now, shut up." The old man seemed smaller, more twisted, as he turned a misty gaze back to Hawkins. "Without the rifle, Marshal, a good defense lawyer could tear your case up in court."

Hawkins nodded. "There is that possibility. But we have enough to hold Beecham for investigation of murder—"

"Marshal! Marshal Hawkins!" Trace Willis pushed through the crowd, a long leather case in his hands. "I found it! Mr. Beecham's rifle! It was hid way back in a corner of the loft, under some old hay. It took a long time to find it, but I knew you wanted to see it, 'cause you asked."

Hawkins took the sheath from Willis's hands, untied the flaps, and slid the weapon free. It was a Winchester Model 76, caliber .50–95. The initials *MB* were engraved on the receiver behind the loading port. He elevated the muzzle, worked the action, and kicked a cartridge into his hand. The soft lead slug had been scored deep, twice across, and a nail-size hole drilled into the tip. He handed the cartridge to McLocklin.

"Mr. McLocklin, you saw Montoya's body. Only a slug carved and hollowed like that would tear a man half apart the way Montoya was." Hawkins turned a hard glare on Beecham. "Well, Marty?"

"That—that isn't mine—"

"Rare caliber rifles, especially engraved ones, are easy to trace, Beecham. You're under arrest."

"I want a lawyer."

"Lawyer, hell," some in the crowd shouted, "get him a rope!"

"No!" Hawkins's voice boomed over the sudden murmur. "No man gets lynched! He's entitled to a trial—"

A strangled cry tore from Beecham's throat; he made a wild grab for the six-gun in Ed Joyner's holster. He never made it. He went down hard at the solid pop of wood against bone.

Fess McLocklin lowered the cane he had decked his

nephew with, toed the still form, and turned back to
Hawkins. "He's all yours, Marshal. Get this pile of crap
out of my sight."

"I'm sorry, Mr. McLocklin. For your sake."

"Don't apologize for doing your job, Marshal,"
McLocklin said. "What I don't understand is, why?"

"Water, Mr. McLocklin," Archie Wescott said. "I did
some checking—at the marshal's request. Mr.
Beecham's geology studies at college focused on a rela-
tively new science. Hydrology."

"Hydrology?"

"Yes, sir. The study of probable water-bearing forma-
tions. I checked the land records and maps of the J-Bar,
the Four C ranch, the Slash-Y. Your Keylock. Every one
of the maps shows a strong probability of underground
water supplies, less than forty feet below the surface.
With a few good windmills in the proper location, not
one of those ranches would ever hurt for water again."

McLocklin shook his head. "I still don't understand.
The Keylock would have been Marty's as soon as I'm
dead and buried. Why would he . . ."

"He wanted more, Mr. McLocklin," Hawkins said, his
words soft. "He wanted it all. The J-Bar and the Rocking
R in particular, the Slash-Y and the Four C if he could
force them to sell. That would have made him the
biggest rancher in four states. And the best way to get all
that land was to cause a shooting war, a blood feud."

Hawkins paused for a breath. He saw hurt and comprehension flicker in the old rancher's eyes. "He thought
it was worth the gamble if he could pick up the other
land for pennies on the dollar. So he shot Montoya and
Keller. And the Miller boys."

"Why them? Why shoot two small-time rustlers?"

"I can't prove it yet, Mr. McLocklin, but I think I

know why. Because they worked for him." Hawkins sighed. "Maybe I'm wrong. But I'm convinced now that on top of everything else, your nephew was the brains behind the rustling from association ranchers. And others, including the Rocking R, around Necesario."

"That doesn't make sense, Hawkins. My former nephew had all the money he would ever need. And why would he steal from the ranch he was going to inherit?"

"To make anyone checking into the rustling look elsewhere, Mr. McLocklin. A man doesn't steal his own stock. He used you, the association, and your own ranch to stir up hard feelings, to try to make Reynolds and Joyner each think the other was behind it."

Joyner stepped alongside McLocklin. "What Hawkins says makes sense, Fess. But two men couldn't steal as much stock as we—all of us—have lost in the last six months."

Beecham stirred and moaned at McLocklin's feet.

"Could be he had more than the Millers working for him," Reynolds said, his cold blue eyes fixed on the twitching Beecham. "Maybe we ought to just ask him. Right now."

Hawkins shook his head. "Not 'we,' Mr. Reynolds. Dobie and I will handle it. I won't risk having things get out of hand now. Maybe we'll never know. But Beecham will stand trial for murder. I can promise you that."

Beecham tried to push himself up on his elbows, groaned aloud, and sagged back onto the street. Hawkins helped Garrett drag Beecham to his feet. Dobie locked a fist behind Beecham's collar and all but dragged the half-conscious man toward the jail.

Hawkins turned to McLocklin. "Maybe a good lawyer could help him, sir. Maybe negotiate a life sentence instead of the gallows."

McLocklin seemed to wilt even more, to sink deeper into the suit that was too large for his time-ravaged frame. But fire flickered deep in the still sharp eyes. "Marshal Hawkins," he said after a moment, "Marty Beecham is no longer a relative of mine. He has brought dishonor to the family, to the memory of my dear dead sister, and to the cattleman's association. I would hang the little bastard myself if I had the strength."

The old man managed to square his slumped shoulders a bit. He stared around the silent gathering of ranch hands. "Go on home, boys," he said. "It's over."

14

BUCK HAWKINS AND Dobie Garrett stood by the door of the marshal's office and watched as the eastbound stage grew small in the distance, a dark dot under a lead-gray sky. The smell of rain lay heavy beneath the cloud cover that had moved in at daybreak, dropping the temperature and raising stockmen's hopes.

The stage had been on time as usual—two hours late—but Marty Beecham, shackled at the ankles and wrists, was out of the Necesario jail and out of their hair, headed for the Fort Worth lockup in the custody of two large, tough U.S. marshals.

The federal marshals also carried a thick packet of papers. Beecham's full confession, in which he named names, dates, times, and buyers of stolen livestock, and detailed the plan to trigger the range war. It had been a bigger operation than even Hawkins had suspected.

The marshals carried warrants for the arrests of more than two dozen men on Beecham's list. One of them was the tall, lean man who had made a quick exit when Hawkins and Garrett walked into the Crazy Woman Saloon for the first time. The man had been Beecham's contact with a dozen organized rustling gangs that operated over four states.

A lot of ranchers would be able to rest easier soon, Hawkins thought.

The stage also carried a lengthy letter addressed to Marylou Kowalski, in care of the Bar C Wild West Extravaganza, Fairgrounds, St. Louis, Mo. Hawkins only wished he could be on that stage instead of the letter. It would have put the finishing touches on a fine day.

"Well, partner," Garrett finally said, "I reckon we done worked ourselves out of a job now."

Hawkins let his gaze drift over the streets of Necesario. The town was quiet and peaceful, almost deserted. The town even smelled clean under the cool air. Best of all, Hawkins thought, there were no bloodstains on the sandy streets.

"I can't say I'm especially sorry about that, Dobie," Hawkins said. "Nothing against Necesario, but it's sure going to be good to ride away from here and get back home."

Garrett shifted his chew and spat. "That's a sure 'nuff fact. Cows don't pack guns." He glanced at the cloud cover overhead. "Gonna be one of them slow soakers, not a quick thunderpopper like we usual get around here. Mighty nice day not to have nothin' much to do." He fell silent for a moment, then cocked an eyebrow at Hawkins. "When's McLocklin gonna pay us that bonus, Buck?"

"Day after tomorrow."

"Two thousand dollars," Garrett's words were soft, as if he were breathing a prayer. "That's a mess of money for two saddle bums. How much we made here already, partner? With the rewards and bonus money and our share of fines and all?"

Hawkins shrugged. "I haven't thought much about it, Dobie. But it's going to add up to a bundle."

"Reckon it's enough I might draw twenty in advance?"

"Why? The association's still paying all our expenses."

Garrett scratched a stubby finger against his chin. He didn't look much like Dobie today, Hawkins thought: new clothes, whiskers shaved, a nick on his chin still raw from the razor, trail dirt left behind in a tub of water and soap. The scent of bay rum replaced Garrett's normal aroma of sweat, dust, and horse. If he had met Dobie in a dark alley, Hawkins wouldn't have recognized him today.

"Thought I might see could I get even with Squirrel Tooth Kate," Garrett said with a grin. "That gal can flat play poker. But I got me a lucky streak comin' today, Buck. I can feel it brewin'. About that twenty?"

Hawkins fished in his pocket and handed over a couple of crumpled bills. "I'd say you've earned it, Dobie. I'll bet you another dollar you're back in an hour, broke as ever."

Garrett chuckled and fondled the coins. "Call that bet, partner. Lady Luck's ridin' sidesaddle with ol' Dobie today."

Hawkins watched the bowlegged Garrett stride away with the limp and drooped shoulder that marked him as a cowboy and rough string rider. Buck freely admitted that Garrett was the best hand he'd ever seen with green broncs and wild cattle. As a poker player, though, he was out of his league in a cowboy camp nickel-ante game, let alone going head-to-head with a pro like Kate Timberlake. Dobie probably would be back in less than the hour they'd put the wager on.

Hawkins sighed, relaxed for the first time in weeks, and patted the engraved watch in his shirt pocket. The

timepiece seemed to thump against his heart with each
tick. It was a reassuring feeling.

He took in a deep breath of the cool, clear air, and
headed for the marshal's office. Reassured or not, he still
had reports to fill out and two Slash-Y cowboys in the
lockup. They should be over the miseries of too much
panther juice the night before. He decided he wouldn't
fine them. It hadn't been much of a fight. Hawkins gave
working cowboys some slack whenever he could, even if
it did cost the two lawmen a dollar or two in fine shares.
He'd worked many a month for thirty-five and found
himself. Besides, it was a week since payday. The Slash-
Y hands probably couldn't scrape up five dollars between them.

No blood spilled, no harm done.

He shared a fresh pot of coffee and a touch of been-
there sympathy with the two Slash-Y hands, both young
and both still suffering the torments of cheap whiskey,
and turned them loose. He flipped through the new stack
of wanted notices, saw nothing of interest, and opened
the latest letter from W. C. Milhouse.

It was as lengthy and wordy as usual:

*Livestock fine and fat. Got more rain. Grass good
both outfits. Meier died last week. He didn't hurt.
Buried him on Quarter Circle. Figured you
wouldn't mind. Keep your powder dry. W.C.*

He reread Marylou's last letter for probably the twen-
tieth time. He lingered over the passage that said she had
already told the colonel she would be leaving the Wild
West show at the end of the St. Louis fair and catching
the nearest train headed in the general direction of the
Texas Panhandle, then the stage to Mobeetie. If Haw-

kins's figuring was correct, that would be in six days. Six days that seemed forever.

He smiled again at the postscript below her signature. It said, "Three kids okay with you?"

Three, Hawkins thought, seemed like a nice, round number.

Dobie Garrett sat across the green felt-covered table from Kate Timberlake in the private back room of the Palace and watched her rake in the last of his twenty dollars. They were the only two players. No one else was in the small room.

Squirrel Tooth Kate grinned at him around the thick cigar in her mouth. "You're losing what little touch you had for the game, Dobie," she said in that husky, musical voice. "I thought your stake would last longer this time."

Garrett grinned back. "Just tossin' out some bait, honey," he said. His gaze drifted again to the impressive cleavage showing above her simple blue gown. "What would you say to real serious poker now?"

"Serious poker? I thought you were tapped out?"

"Hell, Kate, that's just money. I'm talkin' about a *real* eyeball-to-eyeball showdown. With more interestin' stakes. Ever play strip poker? Loser winds up buck nekkid?"

Kate chuckled deep in her throat. "A couple of times, just for fun. In the right company."

"Reckon as to how I might be right company?"

Kate's grin spread. "Five card draw, anything opens." Her eyes twinkled as she shoved the deck across the table. "Deal the cards."

For the first seven hands, Garrett was on a roll. And he had begun to salivate a bit. Kate's shoes, gown, and petticoats lay across a vacant chair. He had her down to camisole, pantaloons, a wry smile, and nothing else.

Dobie had lost only his bandanna, one boot, and a sizeable dollop of his concentration. At least on the cards. Squirrel Tooth Kate Timberlake was even finer looking now than she had been in the full gown rig. The cleavage was deeper. And obviously real. She didn't need a whalebone corset.

"I knowed Lady Luck was ridin' with me today," he said as he rubbed his hands together in anticipation. "Looks like I got you this time, Kate. Two more hands like I been catchin', you'll be down to your birthday suit. Deal 'em, honey."

Half a dozen hands later, Garrett was wishing he had bought new underdrawers to go along with the new shirt and pants. His old ones were ragged enough to bring a blush to even his cheeks as he peeled off his new Levi's. Sweat dotted his forehead.

Kate puffed casually on her cigar as Garrett dealt the cards. "Lady Luck's a fickle slut, Dobie," she said. "She'll turn on a man at the damnedest times."

Garrett fanned his cards and grinned in triumph. "Sometimes she comes back, Kate." He held four aces, cold. His heartbeat picked up. Kate was as good as naked from the waist up, he thought, and she wasn't any shy violet. She was a gambler, and gamblers backed their bets. He licked his lips in anticipation at the thought of watching her peel off that camisole—

The door creaked opened.

"Dobie, they said I'd find you here . . ." Lucy Ledbetter's voice trailed off into shocked silence. Her gaze flicked from Kate in camisole and pantaloons to Garrett in his underdrawers and back to Kate.

"Hi, Lucy," Garrett said. "Be with you in a minute."

Lucy Ledbetter never said a word. She strode up to Dobie, doubled a ladylike fist, and hammered the whey out of his left cheekbone. The blow was stout enough to lean Garrett half out of his chair; he'd been hit less hard by full-grown men.

"Lucy, what—"

The slam of the door behind Lucy cut off Garrett's comment.

He sat for a moment and stared, bewildered, at the closed door, then lifted a hand to his cheek. "Wonder what the hell that was all about?" he said.

Kate Timberlake chuckled. "I've seen worse round-house rights in the bare-knuckle fight ring," she said. "Miss Lucy swings a mean punch."

"But how come she done that?" Garrett asked through the ring in his ears.

"I would say," Kate all but purred, "that the lady who just stomped out of here was one very angry and extremely jealous woman." She leaned back in her chair and puffed a perfect smoke ring. It drifted straight toward Garrett's nose. "I'd lay eight-to-one odds you have a serious problem on your hands, Dobie," she said.

"But—but—"

Kate reached for her gown. "Buts are for billy goats, friend. I'm thinking I'll take a nice long walk. Maybe to the far end of town. Before Miss Lucy comes back with that derringer she packs. Or maybe the shotgun."

Garrett grabbed his pants.

An oil lamp on the corner of Hawkins's desk cast a yellow gold tint over the last page of his final report to the Texas and New Mexico Cattleman's Association.

Outside, the cloud cover had thickened until the streets of Necesario took on a deep gray wash. Hawkins had been forced to light the lamp three pages ago to see what he was writing. The door stood open to catch the soft breeze, heavy with the scent of rain. The thick adobe walls normally kept the heat at bay, but the cool air brought welcome relief from the stuffiness of the office.

Hawkins glanced up at a tap on the door frame and said, "Come in, Archie."

Wescott hesitated for a moment, brows raised, his sunburned face clearly visible in the lantern light. "Am I interrupting you, Marshal?"

"Not from anything I want to do. Come on in and have a seat. Leave the door open. We don't get fresh air in here often. Haven't seen you in a couple of days," Hawkins added as Wescott sank into a chair.

"I haven't been out of my hotel room much, trying to finish the book. It's supposed to be in New York by the end of the month." Wescott sighed. "It seems that every mail coach brings more letters from my editors, screaming for the manuscript."

Hawkins nodded. "That's the way the world is, Archie. Everything needs to be done by yesterday at the latest. How's the book coming along?"

"It's almost done." A frown put a slight crease between Wescott's eyes. "The problem is that it seems to be a little flat. I'm worried that my editors won't like it—at least the part about Necesario not having a shootout and a range war. Our readers like lots of riding and shooting and dead people in their books."

Hawkins half smiled. "I'm not the least bit sorry it didn't happen the way your editors wanted, Archie. But we had plenty of riding. The job of a lawman is to stop shooting and killing, not start it. Maybe it wouldn't hurt to have a little bit of truth show up in a dime novel."

Wescott shrugged. "I've written that part just the way it happened, except for leaving out what I did." He shook his head. "Lord, I can't believe I actually pulled a gun on Ed Joyner. I don't know what I was thinking. I could have gotten us all killed."

"And I never did really thank you for that, Archie," Hawkins said. "You did the right thing. In fact, you did more than any of us to prevent that main street shoot-out your readers like. You may have spoiled your book, but you saved some lives. Probably several. Mine included. We're all in your debt."

"Other people helped, too, Marshal." Wescott's frown faded. "Maybe I can rewrite that chapter, emphasize that angle—a town rallies behind its lawmen to stop a war. That good investigative work is more important, even in the Wild West, than gunsmoke. It might not sell as well, though. Readers like blood and gunplay."

"Unless there's a chance they might be the ones bleeding," Hawkins said. "Then the play part disappears from gunplay."

"I noticed that firsthand, out there in the street. I've never been so scared in my life, Marshal. I couldn't keep anything down all that night. Spent most of my time in the alley, retching my guts out." Wescott sighed. "I suppose I'm not too long in the courage department."

"No one but a fool would be anything but scared in a situation like that, son."

"You and Dobie and Miss Lucy and Ned Dawson weren't scared."

Hawkins chuckled. "I don't know about the others, but I nearly peed in my pants, and it won't shame me if you tell your readers I said that."

A slight grin lifted Wescott's lips. "I can't do that, Marshal. It wouldn't fit the image of a cold-eyed, competent gunhawk. Vicarious violence, my editors call it. Readers want to be gunfighters by proxy." Wescott's frown returned. "At any rate, I'm having trouble with the final chapter. I can't seem to come up with the right ending."

Hawkins put his pen down and leaned back in his chair. "How about ending it the way it's really going to happen? With your two heroes riding off into the sunrise to hang up their guns and go back to herding cattle and raising horses. And in my case, raising kids. Three of them, Marylou says. I don't know about Dobie—"

"What about Dobie?" Garrett said from the doorway.

"Archie and I were just talking about . . ." Hawkins's voice trailed off as he stared at Garrett. "What happened to you? Get kicked by a mule?"

"Sure felt like it," Garrett said. He touched a finger to the red splotch on his cheek, winced, and shook his head. "I swear, I don't know what got into that woman."

"What woman?"

"Lucy. Just walks in and whops me a good one upside the noggin." Dobie shook his head, bewildered. "There just ain't no figgerin' females. Man can get a pretty good handle on what a bronc's gonna do, or when a cow's fixin' to try and stick a horn in him. But there just ain't no way to tell when a woman's gonna go on the prod."

Hawkins tried and failed to hide his grin. He winked at Wescott. "Archie, there could be another fearless, cold-eyed, gunslinging marshal story in the works here. Coffee's hot, Dobie. Pour yourself a cup and tell us all about it."

"Reckon I could use a cup right now, at that." Garrett took a stride away from the door.

A slug cracked past Garrett's shoulder and thunked

into the wall. Adobe dust sprayed as the whipcrack of a rifle shot rattled the office.

"What the hell—"

"Get down, Dobie," Hawkins yelled. Glass exploded from the single front window; the slug sizzled past Buck's head and spanged off the cast iron stove. The rifle report came atop the splat as the deflected lead whacked into a far wall. Hawkins bolted from his chair and sprinted toward the gun rack beside the door. A third slug splintered the edge of the door frame. Buck winced as a sliver of wood stung his cheek.

Wescott sat as if frozen in his chair, eyes wide, glass from the shattered window sprinkled over his derby and lap. Hawkins grabbed Archie's shoulder, flung him to the floor, and whipped his rifle from the rack. He levered a round into the chamber and glanced over his shoulder. Garrett crouched in a corner, mouthing curses as he yanked the sawed-off shotgun from his holster and thumbed back the hammers.

Hawkins flattened himself against the wall as adobe chips flew from the ledge of the shattered window. The coffeepot bounced from the stove, spewed liquid, and clattered to the floor. The echoes of the gunshots rolled down Necesario's main street and faded into the distance.

"Hawkins! Garrett!" The yell from across the street seemed as loud as the gunshots.

The hairs on Hawkins's forearm prickled. He knew that voice.

"Son of a bitch!" Garrett barked. "Silas Barker. Dammit, he's supposed to be in Mexico!"

Barker's voice boomed again. "Answer me, Hawkins! I know you're in there!"

Buck chanced a quick glance through the shattered

window. He couldn't see the big man, only a pall of powder smoke from the mouth of an alley across the street.

"What do you want, Barker?" Hawkins yelled.

"Guess I got your attention after all, Hawkins!" Barker's words were thick with hate. "You know what I want! You and that beat-up old saddle bum you ride with! We got a score to settle, you and us!"

"Then come on, Barker! Let's get it settled now!"

"Not while you're hidin' behind adobe walls, Hawkins! We're playin' this hand my way! And I got aces back-to-back! We've got the halfwit and the whore—Garrett's gal Lucy!"

A cry of pain and rage tore from Garrett's throat. He came to his feet and charged toward the door. Hawkins grabbed him by the collar and jerked him aside. "Easy, Dobie!" Hawkins snapped. "It won't help anybody if you get yourself killed now!"

Hawkins waited a moment until Garrett got control of his wits, if not his red-faced fury, and nodded. Buck eased back to the window. "What's the game, Barker?" he called.

Barker's laugh rode the raw edge of madness. "It's time to find out how much guts you really got, Hawkins! Let's see if you two jalepeño-hot gunhawks got the balls to meet Harve and me straight up, man-to-man! You got fifteen minutes to get to the stable."

"And if we don't?"

"Harve shoots the halfwit! Ten minutes later, the whore! They worth it to you, Hawkins?"

"They're worth it, Barker!"

"All right! You got fifteen minutes or the halfwit gets a slug in the head!" Barker fell silent for a moment, then called, "I'm leavin' now! Try and back-shoot me, and Harve'll blow their heads off!"

Hawkins caught a glimpse of wild red beard and broad shoulders and heard the sound of heavy footfalls as the big man sprinted down the alley. Buck had a chance for a quick shot, but didn't take it; it wasn't worth the risk. Barker might have told the truth. And Harve Turcotte wouldn't hesitate to kill Lucy Ledbetter and Trace Willis.

Garrett stared at Hawkins for a moment, the sawed-off double in a white-knuckled fist. "You heard the man, Buck. Let's go." The deep weathered brown of his face had flushed an angry mahogany, his jaw set, eyes narrowed.

Wescott struggled to his feet and reached under his arm.

"No, Archie! Stay out of this!" Hawkins snapped.

"But—"

"Stay put, dammit! You've done enough." Hawkins grabbed a box of .44–40 cartridges, ripped it open, and dumped the ammunition into his shirt pocket. "This is our fight, Archie. Mine and Dobie's. It's personal. But there's one thing you can do." He handed a box of shot shells to Garrett. "Go get Ned Dawson. Tell him to bring that buffalo gun of his. If those bastards get past us, they'll probably kill Trace and Lucy. If they do, tell Dawson to drop them both. I don't want Barker and Turcotte to leave this town alive."

A muscle twitched in Garrett's jaw as he stuffed shotgun shells in his pockets. He double-checked the loads in the shotgun-pistol and chunked the action closed. "We gonna stand here yammerin' all day? Time's wastin'."

Hawkins shifted his rifle to the crook of his right arm, drew his Bisley Colt, and thumbed a sixth round into the chamber. "Dobie, we can't just walk up to that corral, or we'll wind up like Custer did. We're no match for two professional gunmen like Barker and Turcotte, and there are two innocent lives at stake."

"By God, I'm goin'—"

"Hold up a second, Dobie. We've got to give ourselves a fighting chance." Hawkins holstered the Bisley and realized his mouth had gone dry; he barely had enough spit left to speak. "We'll split up. I'll circle around, come up on the east side of the stable. You slip up on the south, by the corral. With luck, we can catch them by surprise. If we're really lucky, we can get them in a crossfire without getting Trace and Lucy killed in the process."

Garrett nodded impatiently. "Makes sense. Let's get movin'. The clock's tickin'."

"One more thing, Dobie—watch what you're doing with that nubbed-off scattergun. I'd hate to get shot by my own partner."

"You watch it too, partner. You're better'n you was, but you still ain't exactly Wild Bill Hickok when it comes to shootin'. You ready?"

"Ready as I'll ever be. Let's go."

Hawkins sprinted the last few yards from the scant cover of the mesquites on the north side of the stable building and skidded to a halt against the rough wood of the barn.

His lungs screamed for air and his heart banged against his ribs. The loudest sound he heard was the clock ticking in his head. The fifteen minutes were almost up.

The lead weight of raw fear sat heavy in his gut; the receiver of his rifle was slick from sweat despite the chill in his fingers. He wiped his hand against his pants leg, gasped in another lungful of air, and chanced a quick glance around the corner of the building.

He mouthed a silent curse.

The situation was worse than he had feared.

Trace Willis sagged against the ropes that bound him to a support post, a dirty rag stuffed into his mouth. Lucy Ledbetter was tied to the nearest post—directly between Hawkins and Harve Turcotte. Hawkins could see only enough of Turcotte to know that the slight gunman stood beside Trace, a six-gun in his left hand shoved against the boy's temple. Hawkins didn't have a clear shot at Turcotte without running the risk of hitting Lucy.

"Time yet, Silas?" Turcotte's voice was high-pitched, eager in anticipation.

Barker stood behind a thick corner post of the corral fifty feet away, staring down the street. "Not yet, Harve. They still got a couple minutes."

"Any sign of 'em?"

"Not a whisker," Barker said. "Guess we'll have to kill the halfwit after all."

Hawkins's heart skidded. There was no way he could get a slug into Turcotte from this angle.

"Wait a minute," Barker called. "One of 'em's comin'. The old man. Sneakin' along across the street. Don't see Hawkins." Barker whipped his rifle to his shoulder, fired, and cackled in glee as the powder smoke billowed around him. "Nailed Garrett. Sent him down hard—son of a bitch!"

"What?"

"He got up. Dammit, how—where—"

Turcotte's gun hand dropped. He took a step forward and peered past Barker. "You sure you hit him, Silas?"

Hawkins knew it was now or never. Turcotte wouldn't stay distracted forever. He hurled himself from the cor-

ner of the barn, rolled onto his belly, swung the rifle into
line, fired—and missed. The slug brushed Turcotte's
shirt and whacked into the box stall behind him. Turcotte
spun and fired. The slug kicked dirt and sand six inches
from Hawkins's right ear. Buck yanked at the lever of
the Winchester and knew he was going to be too late; he
could see the round hole in the muzzle of Turcotte's revolver lined on his head.

Hawkins flopped onto his side as fire flashed from
Turcotte's weapon. He felt a slight jar and a burn across
his shoulder. The Winchester action closed. Buck fired
by instinct, the rifle supported only by his trigger hand.
The muzzle blast came a split second before the flatter
crack of Turcotte's six-gun. Turcotte's left leg snapped
from beneath him; his slug sprayed dirt two feet from
Hawkins's face. Turcotte went down.

Hawkins twisted, half-blinded from the geyser of
sand, trapped on his left side, unable to work the action
of the rifle or reach the Bisley caught between his hip
and the ground. Through blurred vision he saw Silas
Barker's rifle swing into line, the bore trained squarely
on him. Hawkins braced himself for the wallop of
lead . . .

Garrett ignored the burn and numbness in his left hip,
dove beneath the lower rail of the corral, and loosed both
barrels at the only part of Barker's body he could see.
Barker's feet seemed to explode in a cloud of dust. His
rifle shot sailed skyward as the buckshot charge ripped
both feet from under him. Garrett glanced toward
Hawkins and saw Buck scramble to his knees. Hawkins
levered a round into the Winchester, aimed, and drove a
.44-40 slug through Barker's head.

Garrett broke the action of his nubbed shotgun,
ejected the spent hulls, fumbled fresh loads into the

chamber, and snapped the action shut. He scrambled beneath the corral pole and heaved himself to his feet, the smell of burned powder, dust, and horse manure sharp in his nostrils. He was halfway across the corral when he heard Hawkins's warning shout. Turcotte had managed to get to his knees, the revolver still in his hand, less than twenty feet from Garrett.

Dobie skidded to a stop, the shotgun trained on Turcotte's chest. The wiry little gunman's face twisted in pain and stunned disbelief.

"Howdy again, Harve," Garrett said, "you sorry little son of a bitch."

Turcotte opened his hand and let the six-gun fall. "I—give—up—Garrett. My—leg—"

"It won't be hurtin' long, Harve," Garrett said. He pulled both triggers.

The heavy shot charge hammered Turcotte onto his back. Garrett didn't bother to check on the gunman. A twin charge of double-ought buck from that range didn't leave anything much to check. He hurried as fast as he could, dragging his left leg, to the post where Lucy was tied. He dropped the shotgun, whipped out his pocketknife, and cut the gag free.

"You okay, honey?" he said as Lucy gasped in air. She could only nod, her face ash-white, as Garrett sawed through the ropes that bound her to the post. She collapsed against him.

"God—Dobie—I—I thought—I was afraid—"

"So was I, honey. But it's all right now," Garrett said. "It's done with. They hurt you?"

She shook her head. "I was afraid they'd—shoot you."

"Reckon they wasn't as good as they thought, Lucy." Garrett managed a slight grin for the first time. "Buck, you okay?" he said as Hawkins fumbled with the knots that bound Trace Willis. "You hit, partner?"

"Nothing serious as far as I can tell. You?"

"Feels like I caught one in the hip. Don't reckon it's too bad, on account I can still walk."

"We'll have a look in a bit," Hawkins said as he loosened the last knot of Trace's bindings and stripped the gag from his mouth. "Are you all right, son?"

Willis nodded, tears pooled in his lower lids. "It's my fault, Marshal Buck. Them men—they grabbed Miss Lucy when she was walkin' past—I couldn't stop 'em."

"Trace tried, Buck," Lucy said. "He fought them like a tiger until the big one hit him in the head with a rifle stock."

Hawkins patted the young man on the shoulder. "You did well, Trace. You tried. That's all a man can do."

"Marshal, you're bleedin'."

Buck glanced at his right shoulder. It had begun to sting; he hadn't noticed it before. "Just a shallow burn, Trace. Nothing serious. I would have been a lot worse off if Dobie hadn't pulled my bacon out of the skillet. Barker had me square in his sights."

"All right, you two," Lucy said, her tone firm now that she had recovered her composure, "let's take inventory and see what's left of the both of you."

15

"WELL, GENTLEMEN," FESS McLocklin said as he pushed a sizeable stack of bills across the desk, "the Texas and New Mexico Cattleman's Association thanks you for your work."

Buck Hawkins said, "I'm sorry it had to work out the way it did, Mr. McLocklin."

McLocklin sighed and seemed to sink deeper into his chair. The old man had aged another ten years in the past few days, Hawkins thought.

"It's best to find the snake in the family before it's too late," McLocklin said. "At least Marty Beecham won't be getting his hands on half the cow country in Texas and New Mexico. And good riddance. You men did your jobs well."

Hawkins somewhat reluctantly picked up the currency, folded it, and tucked it in his pocket.

"Aren't you going to count that, Marshal Hawkins?"

"No, sir. You counted it. That's good enough for us."

"What you reckon'll happen to your nephew, Mr. McLocklin?" Dobie Garrett asked.

McLocklin shrugged his bony shoulders. "I don't care. He is no longer my nephew. As far as I'm concerned, he no longer exists, and whatever happens, he earned it. Any man who wallows with hogs smells like a pigpen to me." The old man shook his head. "I still have trouble coping with the idea that my late, beloved sister's son could be responsible for so many deaths and so much thievery. She was such a sweet, loving person . . . But that story is history now. I suppose you two will be moving on soon?"

"Yes, sir," Hawkins said. "We're rather anxious to get back to our own place now. We plan to leave in the morning."

Garrett winked at Hawkins. "Buck here's gettin' mighty twitchy the last day or so. Has somethin' to do with the stage from Dodge City to Mobeetie, I reckon."

McLocklin struggled to his feet and extended an arthritic hand. "Well, good luck to you, gentlemen. May your future hold only green grass, fat cows, and good kids."

Hawkins took the hand, careful not to squeeze. "Thank you, sir."

"And nobody packin' guns," Garrett said as he shook McLocklin's hand. "I'm gettin' some tired of havin' the rep as a fast gun. Hell, a man could get hurt bein' shot at."

"Speaking of which, how's the hip?"

"It's fine," Hawkins said, answering for Garrett. "He, or rather both of us, had a fine nurse in Lucy Ledbetter. Of course, Dobie exaggerates the limp a bit in public. He enjoys sympathy, I think. Expecially from the ladies."

Garrett feigned a wince. "Now, partner, that ain't fair, pickin' on a man who's been shot and crippled up somethin' fierce."

"Shot up? You barely got a bullet nick on the left cheek of your butt. I wouldn't exactly call that a serious gunshot wound."

"Well, I seem to recall you was whinin' like a whipped

pup over gettin' a little hole in your butt up in Colorado. Don't see no difference." Garrett reached for his hat. "I reckon this means we ain't on no association expense account no more?"

A faint smile tugged at McLocklin's lips. "I'm afraid not, Garrett. The association members better hope for a good calf crop and a strong market this year, or we'll be borrowing money to pay the bills you've run up at the Palace, let alone your hotel. You have to pay your own way now. However, it was money well invested."

Hawkins and Garrett turned for the door, then paused as McLocklin said, "Oh, by the way—I almost forgot. You *do* have more money coming."

"How's that?"

"There was a reward out for Silas Barker and Harve Turcotte. A thousand dollars each, dead or alive. It's yours; you were still on the association contract when you killed them."

"I'll be double damned," Garrett said. "You know, it's kind of a shame we shot them fellers, I reckon."

"How do you figure that, Garrett?"

"Why, hell, Mr. McLocklin," Garrett said with a grin, "we was makin' big money on them boys. Collected two rewards on 'em already. Might be we could've cashed 'em in again."

McLockin smiled again. "I believe you'll find there's more money in good livestock. Going to wait around for the reward money?"

"No, sir," Hawkins said. "If you don't mind, just forward it to us in care of the Quarter Circle Ranch in Mobeetie."

"I'll do that. Good luck, gentlemen."

Hawkins and Garrett paused outside the association office. The slow, soaking rain that had started an hour after the livery gun battle had lasted all day, all night, and most of the next morning. But there was little mud and no standing water; the moisture had all soaked into the parched earth. The countryside around Necesario had burst into green. The air smelled fresh and clean now, with no scent of dust. Even the sun seemed less intense, as though the rain had appeased the spirits.

"Well, Dobie," Hawkins said, "what's your pleasure?"

Garrett licked his lips. "I could handle a drink or three. Even if I have to buy it myself. How about the Palace?"

"Sounds good. I might even join in hoisting a glass as a final toast to the fine city of Necesario."

Hawkins's cheeks were beginning to feel numb. He waved off an offered refill from one of the crowd packed four deep around the table in the Palace.

"Better quit now," Hawkins said. "I'm out of practice." Which was, he admitted to himself, the truth. It had been months since he'd had more than a couple of drinks at a time. He idly wondered if just the idea of becoming a family man took the fun out of carousing around at all hours.

Garrett didn't seem to be feeling the whiskey yet. He sat at Buck's right, Lucy Ledbetter perched on his knee, her arm around Dobie's neck. She had matched him shot for shot. She didn't look any the worse for riding the whiskey trail this far, either, Buck thought.

Young Archie Wescott, seated across from Hawkins, had rounded several bends in the liquor river. His face was even redder than usual, his cheeks flushed beneath the sunburn. His cravat was askew, his starched collar loosened, his derby pushed back on his head. He drank gin. The stuff smelled like juniper bushes to Hawkins.

But as Dobie had said, the kid was making progress. He'd gone from tea to coffee to hard liquor in a mighty short time. "Boy's gettin' to be a real Western man sure 'nuff," Garrett had said.

Hawkins granted Wescott cause to celebrate. The book was done, on its way to New York, complete with the rousing gunfight ending Wescott had needed. Hawkins hadn't even looked at the story, but he strongly suspected the shoot-out at the Necesario livery had grown past recognition in the retelling.

"Something to tell my kids about, I ever have any," Wescott said, his words a bit slurred and blue eyes less than fully focused. "Sharing a last drink with two sure-enough legends of the Old West. And getting paid to do it." He poured his glass full and lifted it. "Here's to the finest two men, tallest in the saddle ever, and the fastest, deadliest gunhawks on the frontier. Buck Hawkins and Dobie Garrett."

Cries of "hear, hear," went up from the crowd. Hawkins decided not to protest. He lifted his glass and took a final sip.

"Say," Garrett said, "anybody seen Squirrel Tooth Kate? Me and her got somethin' to finish—"

"Damn you, Dobie Garrett!" The outburst from Lucy Ledbetter caught Hawkins by surprise. Expecially when she jumped up from Garrrett's lap as she said it. "You are not dallying around with that . . . that *whore* any-more!"

Hawkins thought it a bit odd that a professional prostitute would call a professional gambler a whore. But as Dobie had said, there just wasn't any figuring women. Some women, anyway.

Garrett looked up at Lucy, brows raised, as if she'd

just told him his drawers were on fire. "What brung that on, Lucy?"

"You know damn well what brought that on! I saw you two sitting there in nothing but your underwear!"

"Lucy, what—"

"And there will be no more of that, Dobie Garrett! Not now, not ever!"

Garrett looked bewildered. "But, honey, we was just playin' a little strip poker, that's all."

"Don't you lie to me, Dobie, or I'll slug you again!" Lucy stomped her foot. Tears pooled in her lower lids. Buck couldn't tell if they were tears of hurt or tears of anger.

"Well, I'll be," Hawkins said. "Was that what happened? You never got around to telling us that story, Dobie."

"Stay out of this, Buck Hawkins! This is between my man and me!"

"My man—" Garrett was past bewilderment now, Hawkins though. He was thunderstruck.

Hawkins caught the bolt of understanding well before Garrett. It made sense now. The way Lucy looked at Dobie. The way she was never far from him whenever he was in the Palace. Why he had seen her turn down every would-be client since the first night she'd spent with Garrett. And, come to think of it, Dobie hadn't been with another woman since they'd hit town. That was most assuredly, absolutely definitely, un-Dobie-like.

"Partner," Hawkins said with a chuckle, "I think you're in a speck of trouble here."

Garrett glanced from Lucy to Hawkins and back, unaware of the chuckles and grins among the crowd around the table. "Girl, I swan, I don't know what's got into you. What you talkin' about, anyhow?"

"I'm talking about *us*, Dobie Garrett. You and me."
Lucy's voice had dropped a bit; she wasn't shouting
now. The tears still threatened to flow.

"You and me?"

"Damn you to hell, Dobie Garrett! Do I have to draw you
a picture? Are you going to marry me or not?"

"Marry?"

"And anytime you want to play strip poker, by God,
you'll play with *me*. And another thing—all this drinking
and carousing and hell-raising and woman chasing is
going to stop! Is that clear?"

"Marry?"

"Yes, dammit, marry! You could do worse! I've got
over a thousand dollars saved up, and I've been told I'm
not hard to look at, and I'm sick and damned tired of this
life, and I'm retired—have been since I met you. Well,
what's it going to be?"

Garrett turned a confused face to Hawkins. "Partner—"

"Don't 'partner' me, Dobie. You're on your own."
Hawkins was aware of the silly grin on his own face.
"You did say she was a passing fair cook."

"Damned right I am," Lucy said. "Well? I'm waiting
for an answer."

"Marry? You mean, like hitch up?"

"You thick-headed, chuckle-brained, slow-witted, bro-
ken-down saddle bum, what in the blue-eyed hell do you
think I mean? Of all the aggravating men I've ever seen
in my life, Dobie Garrett, you take the cake!"

"But—" Garrett's frown dissolved in a sudden rush of
comprehension. "Damn, girl. You're serious, ain't you?"

"She's serious, Dobie," Hawkins said. "Better give
her an answer."

"But I didn't—"

"Didn't what?" Lucy sniffled.

"Didn't know you cared none, girl." Garrett's face brightened. "Would've mentioned it myself, I thought there was a chance you'd take me up on it."

"Ask me. I'll take you up on it. But there's something you should know first. I can't have kids."

Garrett reached out and took her hand. "Honey, that ain't no problem. We'll just borrow one of Buck's and Marylou's once in a while."

"So ask."

"Ask what?"

"Propose, dammit! Do it right, or don't do it at all!"

A grin spread across Garrett's weathered face. "Miss Lucy Ledbetter, will you marry me?"

She jumped on Garrett with enough force to almost knock him out of the seat, buried her head in his shoulder, and started sobbing.

Garrett turned to Hawkins, a worried frown on his face. "What'd I do wrong, partner?"

"Nothing, Dobie. I think you did just fine."

"So what's this female bawlin' about now?"

"Oh, I'd say she's happy."

"Happy? Bawlin' like a weanin' calf, and she's happy?" Garrett shook his head and sighed. "I swear, there just ain't no figgerin' women."

"We can build another house next door to the Quarter Circle headquarters," Hawkins said. "No problem with water, either. We can share the windmill. The ranch is more than big enough to support two families. And Marylou and I will be glad to loan you one of the kids from time to time."

Garrett patted Lucy's shoulder. "See, honey?" he said. "There ain't nothin' to worry about. Reckon you can get packed by sunup tomorrow?"

Lucy raised her head. "I've been—packed for—two

days," she said between sobs. "Oh, Dobie! I've never been so happy."

Garrett sighed. "Buck, I ain't never gonna figure out women."

"Don't try, Dobie," Hawkins said. "It's the only way to live with them and stay sane at the same time." He pushed his chair back, shook hands all around, and paused for a moment with Wescott's hand in his. "What are you going to do now, Archie?"

"I'll go back East for a time. Make sure that Mom has everything she needs. Then I'll come back out here. To the West. I think I've found my calling as a chronicler of the life and times of this country. Who knows? Maybe I'll be a famous writer and get rich in the process."

"Well, good luck, Archie. If you ever get down Mobeetie way, drop by for a visit. Just ask anybody where the Quarter Circle outfit is."

"I'll do that. And I'll send you some copies of the book as soon as it comes off the presses."

Hawkins turned to Dobie and Lucy Ledbetter, who now had both arms around Garrett's neck.

"I'll see you two in the morning," he said. "Don't be late, or I'm riding off without you. There's a stage coming into Mobeetie I want to meet."